BREAKING POINT

Detective Laura Warburton Series

Book Two

JAY DARKMOORE

Copyright ©

Jay Darkmoore 2023

Also, by Jay Darkmoore –

Horror

The Space Between Heaven and Hell

The Space Between Heaven and Hell – The Shadow Man

Thrillers

Det Laura Warburton Series

Left for Dead

Breaking Point

Deadly Silence

Downward Spiral

The Reckoning

Stand Alone

I See You

Short Story Collections

Tales From the Inferno Volume One

Tales From the Inferno Volume Two

Compilations

Into the Nightmares

Novellas

Lorna – A Dark Romance

The Night Shift

Dark Fantasy

The Everlife Chronicles – Hunted

The Everlife Chronicles – Conquest

Nonfiction

The Jobs F****d – Secret Diary of a Police Officer

Inside each of us, there is the seed of both good and evil. It's a constant struggle as to which one will win. And one cannot exist without the other.

-    Eric Burdon

For my son, who keeps me accountable to be the best man I can be each day.

Support the author by scanning here for a free eBook bundle, exclusive news and updates and much, much more.

BREAKING POINT

OLIVER

Today was the last day Jamie would see his son.

He would remember it forever. The song playing on the radio on the classic rock station. The smoke emanating from the exhausts of the cars in front of him pumped into the crisp winter air. The sound of the scribbling Oliver was making on the piece of paper next to him that he was resting on his lap. How Jamie looked upon his boy with longing, and how he had missed so much of his life whilst in prison.

It was Friday, and Jamie had collected his job seeker's payment and picked Oliver up from Claire's house. The sight of her still made his legs weak, but the new junkie boyfriend of hers, Declan, made his skin crawl. He took a drag of his e-cig, determined to completely kick the nicotine habit by Christmas. He had ordered some nicotine patches to try and get through the withdrawal stage a little smoother. The audiobook by *Tony Robbins* that he was halfway through said that *'It was all in the mind. Change. Success. It all starts within.'* It sounded easy, but with the steam slipping through his nostrils and his mouth, he thought the contrary.

"Why do you put that thing to your mouth?" Oliver said next to him, eyeing the instrument that glittered with sparkling lights whenever his dad put it to his mouth and made a crackling *swooshing* sound. Jamie watched him with a smile, the car idling at the traffic lights.

"Because," he said, his blackened and cracked teeth forming a grin like chipped dominos. The sign of a former life. "Haven't I told you?" He leant into Oliver, a few inches from those big blue eyes. "I'm actually a dragon." Oliver scrunched up his face.

"Dragons aren't real, Dad." He could almost hear his son's eyes rolling.

"Oh, no?" Jamie said. "Then why can I do this?" Jamie put the vape in his mouth, sucked in some steam, and then blew a massive lungful of white smoke.

"That's just that thing in your hand," Oliver laughed. "I'm not five."

"You're getting too clever," Jamie laughed, before wafting away the smoke to see the solid green lights. A horn blared behind him. Jamie's eyes shot up to the rear-view mirror. He saw another man, older, his face flabby with balding snow-coloured hair gesturing at him to move. Jamie felt a flare of anger well up in his chest. He revved the engine and crept forward, before slamming on the brakes. Another horn blast bellowed as the lights changed from amber to red. Jamie eyed the guy behind him whose face and hands were going all kinds of crazy.

"What's that noise?" Oliver asked innocently, unaware of the subtleties of passive-aggressive road rage etiquette.

"Just someone being silly," Jamie said. He ruffled Oliver's blonde hair. "So why don't you think dragons are real?" Again, Oliver scrunched up his face.

"Because dragons are monsters, Dad," he said. "And monsters don't exist." The lights cycled back to green, and Jamie pondered for a moment about toying with the guy in the red Fiesta behind him, but dismissed the urge of torment. Tonight was movie night with Oliver, and they were going to watch *The Avengers* movie. The last one where they all get to fight. Oliver had gotten into the Avengers following someone in school bringing a Thanos gauntlet into class. The kid had told him all about it, and then Oliver told Jamie that following weekend. From there, the Marvel fascination was born. They had watched all of them in order, and tonight was the night they finally got to watch *End Game*. Jamie would be lying if he said he wasn't excited about it. Embracing his inner child, he had promised Oliver a multitude of delicious goodies ranging from chocolate, popcorn, bottles of fizzy drinks and hell, even some gummy worms. Jamie only had him for the weekend, and he would be returning him back to his mother and her new dick head boyfriend Sunday evening. He grimaced at the thought and hated leaving him there, but it's what the social and probation had advised, so Jamie just had to smile and jump through hoops like a trained dog.

He parked the car in the furthest spot from the store entrance and killed the engine before stepping out into the cool winter air. Oliver erupted like a cannonball from the passenger side, excitedly clutching the drawing he had been working on.

"What's that you've got there?" Jamie asked, peering over the lip of the paper. Oliver turned it to his dad and showed him.

"It's Thanos," he said, and then Jamie recognised the big hulking bald figure roughly coloured in purples with a golden fist with sparking gems on the knuckles. Overcome with a feeling of pride one can only feel from seeing their own child express such independent and passionate creativity, he wrapped Oliver in his arms and gave him a kiss.

"It's really good," Jamie said.

"Can we get some Doritos?"

"Absolutely, my mate." He took Oliver's hand, and they moved up towards the supermarket entrance. Jamie liked to park near the car park entrance for the abundance of spaces, and it would help him get his step count up to try and burn his bulging gut away.

"Hey, wanker!" The voice cut through the air, and Jamie's teeth clamped together. He turned, his hand gripping Oliver's arm tightly. It was the guy from the car behind him at the lights. He was wearing a thin beige jacket, and his face resembled someone who had tried fixing their teenage acne problem with a razor blade. "What the hell was that at the lights?" Jamie eyed him like he was a wolf lurking outside his door where his children were sleeping.

"Life goes on, pal," he bit. "Have a good day." Jamie turned away from the man before he did something he regretted. He had put people's teeth to the back of their throats for less severe transgressions. He didn't want to let his son see the part of him he locked away come back out.

"Fucking cock sucker," the man hissed. The words hit Jamie's ears like glass smashing on the ground. He stopped, his body growing tort. He pinched his nose, the bubbling of pain ready to overflow in his stomach. The *rush* was coming. That's what he called it, or more what his therapist in prison had called it. The *rush* takes over, and before you knew it, you were doused in blood that stuck to your skin like hot rain. He took a deep breath, counted to three and then continued on his way.

"Who is that man?" Oliver said, eyeing the guy in the beige jacket. Jamie focused on those words.

Who is that man? That was the question. Someone who thought it okay to openly insult and degrade a boy's father. Who was that man? Someone who he would never see again. Someone who didn't matter. Someone whose wife probably loathed him. Whose kids never visited him. Some waste of a man who couldn't get his dick hard anymore.

But someone that Jamie would be thinking of for the rest of the day if he didn't do something. If he didn't teach the prick some manners.

"Just keep walking…" Jamie whispered under his breath. *It's not worth missing another ten years of Oliver's life.*

"Yeah, walk away," the man in the beige jacket mocked. "Pussy." Sometimes in life, there are crossroads. A choice to take one path or another. To choose action or inaction. To be passive or reactive. Jamie didn't know what impact his following actions would have on his life in the days to come. But he would know soon. Oh boy, would he. Jamie crouched by Oliver, who had an etched look of worry on his face.

"Just wait by the car," Jamie said. Oliver went to protest.

"But Dad," he said, his voice deflated. "The movie!" Jamie forced the guilt down into his stomach.

"Just do as you're told, Oliver," he bit. Oliver's bottom lip began to tremble.

"But…"

"Now!" Jamie barked. Oliver ran back to the car sniffling. Jamie erected himself, his body electrified, the adrenaline pumping. He locked eyes with the piece of shit that would soon be leaving in an ambulance. "Listen," he spat with venom. "I've got my boy here. We're going about our day. So do me a favour and fuck off before you get hurt." The stranger eyed Oliver standing by the car, clutching his picture of Thanos. The sides of his lips curled outwards in a sharp sneer.

"That your kid?" He pointed to Oliver. "He's cute." The sight of this worm of a man putting his eyes on Jamie's boy. That was enough. Enough to snap any last chain of resolve that was holding the wolf in Jamie's heart from lunging and tearing his throat out. Jamie flexed his knuckles. His breathing deepened. Jamie wasn't sure if he imagined it or if it really happened, but he was sure that the guy licked his fucking lips. "Hey, little man," he said to Oliver. "What you got there? A nice picture? How about you come over here and show it to me?"

The *rush* flooded through Jamie like pouring molten iron into a blacksmith's forge. Jamie lunged forward and gripped the guy's collar and wrestled him to the ground, his body smacking the tarmac with a loud crack, expunging the air from his lungs in a violent burst. His breath rancid with the stench of old cigarettes.

"You weird fuck," he hissed. "Speak one more word to my son and I'll cut your wrinkled dick off and make you eat it. Do you understand?" The whites of the guy's eyes were bulging as he stared into Jamie's soulless irises. Through the rage, Jamie heard Oliver's sharp cries. He turned and saw him scrunching the paper to his face. The tide of anger receded. He turned back to the guy that quivered underneath him. He pursed his lips and enunciated the word *disappear,* before uncoiling his fingers from around the guy's throat like a viper strangling a terrified rat that had had a change of heart. Jamie peeled himself off the stranger and got back to his feet.

He moved to Oliver and reached his hand out. Oliver recoiled at his touch like he was some kind of monster. The man scooped himself off the floor like someone trying to dislodge a frozen dog turd from the pavement and scurried back into his car.

"Come on," Jamie said, taking Oliver by the hand. Oliver let out a shriek of pained terror.

"I want to go back to Mum!" He cried, cheeks red and snot dripping down his face. Jamie felt the familiar stab of pain through his heart. He had told him monsters weren't real, but had shown his son that they were closer than he thought.

"Come on," he said softly, trying to quell the terror that had gripped his son. "Let's go get some sweets and we can watch the movie later?" Oliver shook his head fiercely.

"I want to go home!"

"No!" Jamie bolstered, barely holding it together, his hands trembling. Oliver recoiled in shock. Jamie felt his world crumble. He put his hand to his face. "Sorry," he said quickly, trying to stuff the monster back into its cage. "Sorry," he said again, softer, crouching down to Oliver. "Let's go get some sweets, and if you still want to go home when we get back, then I'll take you, okay?" Oliver thought about it and then nodded.

"Okay."

"But you have to try to enjoy yourself."

"Okay."

"Promise?" Jamie held out his hand. Oliver queried it, before taking it.

"I promise." A smile spread across Jamie's face. Jamie pulled Oliver into his arms and kissed him on his head.

"I'm sorry, mate," he said. "I lost my temper. It won't happen again." They continued to the supermarket entrance. A car crawled past them, the driver eyeing them. It was the stranger. He eyed Jamie through the driver's side window and winked at him. Jamie felt his skin peel off his bones as he watched him drive out of sight.

The supermarket was awash with life: teenagers grabbing their booze for pre-drinks at their friend's house, laughing about the latest viral TikTok they had watched or how they couldn't believe that Ryan from Psychology sent a picture of his dick to the tutor. Elderly couples wandering around collecting hairnets and dog food, and then the new fathers who frantically searched the baby food isle with their phones glued to their ears, yammering away at whether they needed the four-month-old formula or whether it was time they started trying their baby on little pots of carrot flavoured mush.

Jamie and Oliver manoeuvred into the popcorn and confectionery aisle and filled their trolley with an assortment of sugary goodies. Jamie barely had a penny to his name, but laden with guilt and trying to put a smile on his son's puffy red face, he decided his credit card – the one that wasn't maxed out – would foot the bill this time.

"I want Oreos, too," Oliver croaked. Jamie took out two sleeves of biscuits and put them in the trolley. "And fudge." Jamie grabbed some of those too. "And also…"

"Don't push it," Jamie laughed, but didn't protest when those little fingers grabbed another packet of sweetie goodness. Jamie grabbed a small four back of his favourite beer, and hell, even took a paperback book off the shelves. One about a millionaire that gets his comeuppance.

Knowing that he had his father on the end of a metaphorical fishing line hooked with parental guilt, Oliver grabbed a children's gaming magazine with a giant Spiderman on the front cover. Jamie checked the price tag and, after a sharp intake of breath, reluctantly placed it in the trolley.

"Stop milking it," he laughed, and saw that glowing smile spread across Oliver's face. They paid, and Oliver insisted on grabbing a handful of tokens that were on the side of the till and placed them in the boxes for local charities, where the supermarket would let shoppers vote for what community project they could put funding into next. Oliver dished them out sporadically, but Jamie saw one he liked the look of. "Give me one of those," he said, holding out his hand. Oliver placed one into his palm reluctantly, before Jamie dropped it into the box for helping convicts get into education whilst in prison. It didn't have many tokens. As they exited the building, Jamie tugged on Oliver's hand. "How you feeling?" Oliver toyed with the question.

"Sad." He looked down to the floor. "Why were you shouting at the man?" What answer could he give that a child could understand? He was a bad guy? Daddy was stressed? But nothing came to mind.

"Sometimes," he began tentatively. "Sometimes, we must look after ourselves. Sometimes we have to fight things outside us, but sometimes we have to fight things *inside* us. Sometimes we win. Sometimes we lose. But as long as we learn from it, then we win in the end." He stroked Oliver's face. "Sorry I scared you." Oliver nodded.

"It's okay, Dad." They continued to the car, stepping over half-frozen puddles with the sweet treasures of the store rustling and rattling in the trolley. Oliver turned to him. "Why don't you and Mum live with each other?" The question hit him like a brick to the gut.

"What makes you ask that?" Oliver shrugged.

"I don't remember you being there when I was younger. I was just wondering why you don't live with me and Mum."

"I was away," Jamie said, his mouth drying up.

"Where?"

"Just somewhere else. But I wanted so badly to come back to you."

"Then why didn't you?" Oliver's voice was innocent, yet a slither of pain was breaking through. "Why didn't you come back to take care of me?"

"It's complicated," Jamie said, the swelling of guilt in his chest like a balloon about to explode with hungry cockroaches. "But I'm here now." He squeezed Oliver's hand. "Besides, I see you every week. This way, you have two homes. One with me, and one with your Mum."

"And Declan." The name cut him.

"Yeah," he said. "And Declan."

Jamie unpacked the shopping bags and placed them into the boot of his car. Oliver had a smile on his face as he held his Thanos picture, looking over it with pride. Jamie opened the passenger door and told Oliver to scoot in.

"I'll just put the trolley back," Jamie said, leaving his son alone by the car. Only for a moment. But that's all it took. When Jamie got back to the car, not ten seconds later, his son was nowhere to be seen.

"Oliver?" Jamie whispered, scanning the inside of the car, and casting his eye around the busy car park. "Oli?"

There's a new kind of panic that emerges when you lose a loved one even for a moment. Something that is indescribable yet so visceral. For Jamie Green, it was catatonic. His heart picked up. Sweat pushed through his skin. He said his name repeatedly, growing into a crescendo until he was screaming his name, mind going a thousand miles an hour. Every awful possibility ran through his mind like barbed wire raking over his brain.

He saw a young boy up towards the entrance. It was him. He knew it. Walking with someone else. Walking away from him to another car. He sprinted like a madman. He didn't know how fast he crossed the distance, but he gripped the boy by the hand and pulled him towards him.

It wasn't Oliver, and the hope died away.

"What the hell!" The parent – a woman in her mid-twenties – shrieked. Jamie recoiled like he had seen a ghost, the child pulled from him. He thrust his hands to his head, scanning the shoppers. Every face. Every car. Every child that passed him. He raced to another child. Same build. Same hair. Same colour coat. It wasn't Oliver, and another nail in his coffin of hope was hammered in. Jamie sprinted into the supermarket, yammering away at the security staff. Screaming Oliver's name into the crowd of worried shoppers.

Chapter One

Laura

The death of a child is the most unimaginable thing that can ever happen to a parent. We not only mourn the child we have lost, but we also mourn the adult too. We mourn the person they will never become. The stories they will tell us. The life they would have lived, or even the grandchildren they may have produced. Their wedding. The extended family. Arguments over who is to host Christmas dinner that year. The celebrations of achievement. The worry when they don't call you back. Things which we always took as a given, and never as conditional.

Laura Warburton had experienced the grief of despairing mothers as she delivered the news that their sweet daughter or son would never return home. It could be something simple or benign like a peanut allergy they never knew they had, or they had fallen over and hit their head in the playground and wouldn't wake up.

But then there were the *missing*. The children that just seemed to vanish into thin air. Most, if not all of the time, these were children in the care system that had been drawn into criminal activities by county lines gangs and were usually found getting high with their friends or getting locked up after shoplifting. But then there were the more serious cases. The children that on the face of it, came from respectable homes and were loved and cared for deeply by their parents. Their bedrooms with beds with fresh bedding, plenty of clothes, posters on their walls and food in their fridge. They attended school and had friends and were loved dearly by all those that knew them.

Laura had grown adept at recognising whether the child was from a home that never gave a shit, and reporting them missing was simply a way of keeping in line with the instruction of the social services. Then there were the cases that led to midnight candlelit vigils and mothers screaming into the TV cameras with red and puffy faces.

These families, like the case of Oliver Green, didn't like going to the police. Because going to the police made the monster real and meant they couldn't hide away from it anymore. As Laura Warburton looked into Jamie Green's eyes, she knew this was the latter.

"You have to help me," he said, barely holding it together. He looked like he hadn't slept in days and hadn't eaten anything in even longer. His skin was waxy, and his eyes were red-rimmed and bloodshot. Laura didn't think he could cry anymore if he tried. "Oliver. Oliver Green," Jamie said, taking out his phone and showing Laura photos of him quickly, tapping the screen frantically.

"Okay," Laura said, trying to sound as sure as she could. "Tell me where you last saw him." Jamie heaved a big breath into his lungs. His eyes scanned over the white room they were in with the buzzing of the lights overhead. They had moved quickly from the main reception and found an unused interview room. Laura wondered if she would be sitting in here with Jamie Green again in the future. Sometimes a missing child is long dead before they're reported missing. More often than not, it's the parents that did it. Not something she liked thinking about, but recent events had shown her that she can stare into the eyes of a killer and not even realise it.

"Earlier today. We went shopping. We were going to watch a movie together. I have him at the weekends."

"Where did you go?"

"The supermarket. Just off the main highway." Laura took out her phone, punched a few numbers and hit send. She put the phone away. "What was that?" Jamie asked, pointing to the phone with the same disdain as if he was on a first date and she had just whipped out Angry Birds.

"My job," she said, nonchalantly. "Tell me about Oliver's mother."

"She lives with her younger boyfriend," Jamie continued after a sharp breath. "We've been separated for years."

"Any reason?"

"Is it important?" Laura pursed her lips.

"It is if I'm asking the question."

"My separation from Claire has nothing to do with my missing son. Why aren't you out there looking for him? I told you he's missing!" Jamie pointed to the door as if trying to banish a bad smell.

"I'm finishing the report, and will pass it to the officers." Jamie sat back.

"So, you aren't going to look for him yourself? I asked for you specifically after seeing how you solved those murders." Laura felt a whirling of vomit bouncing in her stomach. *That* was why he had come to her? Never mind the rest of the excellent police work that went into that case or the cops that run around daily trying to keep the wheel of society from falling off. But because she was infamous. Because she had been working alongside a killer all this time and hadn't even noticed. This is not the new life she wanted by moving up here. Her mark on this place a dirty stain.

"I will see what I can do, Mr. Green," she said, pen hovering over the paper. "And the faster you answer my questions and let me do my job, the faster I will go out and find your boy. I have already dispatched a detective to the supermarket to review the CCTV, and we have created an incident. Officers will be flooding the area soon. We will do our best to find your son. Now," she continued coolly. "Tell me everything else."

Jamie told Laura what clothing he was wearing, the school he went to and even where they had parked. Addresses of friends, family and any medication he had.

She took out her phone slyly under the desk to check the time. She was late. Again.

"Everything okay?" Jamie said. Laura quickly stuffed her phone back into her pocket.

"Sorry," she said quickly. "Continue."

"There was another thing," he said after a moment, dragging the words out from between his lips like a heavy weight. Laura stopped scribbling on the pad and raised her head to meet his eye.

"Go on."

"There was," Jamie shifted in his seat, bringing his hand to his mouth. "There was a guy..."

"What guy?"

"A guy in a beige jacket. Older looking and as ugly as they come. I was slow setting out in traffic and he followed me into the car park. We exchanged some words, and then he eyed my son and tried speaking to him." Laura furrowed her brow.

"Anything happen with this *guy*?" She said. "Did you get his name? Or the reg of his car?" Jamie shook his head. "But you think he had something to do with your son going missing?" Jamie nodded.

"I think he had something to do with it, yes." He said meekly. He was holding something back. Laura could tell. Something that he knew he needed to say but wasn't willing to. Laura leant forward, the creaking of the chair under her breaking the tension in the air.

Jay Darkmoore

"Why do you think this person had anything to do with what's happened? Any information you can give me, no matter how small, can help us build a better picture." Jamie twisted in his seat. After a beat of silence, he answered.

"He was just creepy," he said finally. "You know? A bit strange." Laura pursed her lips.

"Did anything happen with this individual?"

"No." Laura sat back and crossed her arms. "I told him I was sorry for the lights," Jamie said quickly, beads of sweat appearing on his brow. "He tried speaking to Oliver, and then he just got in his car and left." Laura did not buy that he just *got in his car and left*. There was definitely something that was being left out. The only thing is she didn't know *why* Jamie was leaving something out. Maybe it was an ex-lover, and he was ashamed of his sexuality? He was cagy about the ex-wife... Maybe it was an associate that he didn't want to divulge the full details of. But Laura had already ran Jamie through the box. He was as clean as a whistle. Either way, she could smell a rat.

"One last question," Laura said, pushing her hair behind her ear. Jamie tensed up tighter.

"Anything."

"Did anything, I don't know, traumatic happen prior to your son's disappearance? Anything that may have upset him or caused him alarm?" Jamie's blood ran cold. Did she know something?

Did she know about his past?

The silence dragged on. A moment. An hour. He couldn't tell. Just her eyes boring into his. She knew what he was thinking, and an innocent man doesn't think of the answer to a question. They just snap out an answer. But here he was, thinking about the answer, and the silence told her more than his words ever could.

"No." Laura nodded slowly. She put her notebook away and stood. She passed him her card.

"We have all of your details. If you hear anything or your son turns up," she tapped the card. "Call me." He took the card from her and placed it in his wallet. The item was old, and as he opened it a small photo and some pieces of paper fell out. Jamie quickly dove to the ground and began collecting the items. Laura eyed a piece of paper and her curiosity spiked. She placed her foot over the top.

"Sorry," Jamie said, collecting the items and putting them back into his pocket. "Old thing," he said, gesturing to his betraying wallet.

"Yeah," she said. "Funny things aren't they." She pointed to the photo of Oliver in his hand. "Is that a recent photo?" He eyed the picture.

"Yes," he said. "A few weeks ago, when we went fishing." She extended her hand.

"For our investigation." Jamie eyed the photograph, like handing it over was saying goodbye to his son. "Please," Laura said. Jamie parted with the photograph. Laura placed it into her pocket. "Thank you." She gestured to the door. Jamie slipped through. Laura took the paper from under her shoe, placed it in her pocket, and followed him.

"I'll call around and see if anyone has seen him," he said as he stood by the exit, his voice hoarse. "Maybe he just went back to his mother's?" He laughed with the same heaviness as a funeral march.

"I've seen stranger things happen in this world, Mr. Green," she said before pressing the door release for the exit. "I will be in touch as soon as I hear something. In the meantime, I need to go out and look for him myself. Please ensure you pass any extra details or updates to us, even if it seems minor."

"I will." He stepped out into the cold and turned to move down the street.

"Oh, Mr. Green!" She shouted. Her voice turned him on a dime to face her, the wind and rain pelting his face. Her hair blew fiercely like a frenzy of worms. "If you do think of anything that you may have forgotten to mention today, please let us know." With that, he nodded and walked along the car park to his car. Laura watched him go before closing the door.

She emailed the information over to the force control room from her phone and updated the log. It was to be assigned to another unit, response most likely, and they would do the initial searching whilst her own team did the more complex stuff. She took out the picture and held it to the light. The boy was handsome. Blonde, big blue eyes, white and had a birthmark on his chin the size of a penny. His big smile made his cheeks dimple, and his frame was slight. He was going to be a tall boy. His dad was an easy six foot five, if not a little taller, and as large as an ox.

Laura flicked the photo in her fingers and rested against the wall. He was hiding something for sure. You couldn't make toast with the heat she was putting on him, yet he looked like he was being cooked in an oven. The worm of doubt in her head dug itself deeper into her mind. Why would someone come to the police station and report their child missing and withhold information? Again, she wondered if there was something more sinister at play. There was something about him that he didn't want her to know. Which, unfortunately for him, made him a suspect.

Contrary to popular belief, stranger abductions are incredibly rare. Even Tiger Kidnappings are very uncommon. Now suddenly, there was a mystery guy in the car park who was creepy and speaking to Oliver, of utterly no serious significance at all? Laura scoffed.

"Bullshit." Either something had occurred with this person that would give them a motive for an abduction, or there was no person at all, and the father was behind this. Either way, she would find out.

Laura took out the piece of paper from her pocket. It took a second to figure out the faded writing, but it was a phone number. The words scribbled above it almost completely gone.

If you ever need me.

She pondered the cryptic message. She made a note of the number and put it back in her pocket. She sent a photo of the picture of the boy to the control room and returned to her office.

The troops were working away. Jeremy was nursing his fourth cup of coffee and was talking about some shit he had seen on the TV to Catherine, who was halfway through a crossword puzzle.

"Anything?" Jeremy said, sitting at his desk with a backlog of files that were piled by his desk. He had been working overtime recently. His bruises and cuts had healed nicely. Laura had even given him a compliment upon his return that he had lost weight. Poor guy nearly keeled over from a heart attack. The therapy was helping, or so he said. He insisted Laura speak to them, but she shrugged it off. The locked box of misery in her mind would stay just that – Locked and drowning in alcohol.

"He's definitely hiding something."

"What makes you say that?" Laura relayed the details of the conversation. Jeremy sat back and listened. "That is strange," he said. "Do we know anything about this mystery guy?"

"Only what I've told you," she said. "We need to go check out the CCTV."

"Why?" Jeremy said. "It's a missing child. We get at least eight a day. He's probably just wandered off and the dad's overreacting." This inflamed Laura's temper, and she could feel her blood pressure rising.

"This is different," she said, sending chills running through Jeremy's body. "I can feel it." She pulled out the phone number from her pocket and passed it to Catherine. "Run that through. See if we get a hit." Catherine took the scrap paper from her.

"Yes ma'am." She turned back to Jeremy.

"I want you to do a full investigation and have a report ready by the morning." Laura grabbed her things from her desk and threw her coat over her. "Grab a detective," she said. "One of the newbies. See what you can find and get back to me."

"Where are you going?" Jeremy said. Laura wrapped her scarf around her neck.

"Date night, and I'm late," she said flustered. "I will be on the end of the phone if you need me. But only if it's urgent," she finished, enunciating the last word. She passed him the details of Green. "Do some digging on him. PNC is clear but check the local systems. Send someone to speak to the mother too. Do some detective work. See what you can 'detect.'" She smiled. Jeremy returned it meekly. Laura moved to step out of the office when Jeremy called back to her.

"Ma'am," he said. Laura turned and looked at him. "How is Celine doing?" Laura felt a stab in her chest.

"Goodnight, Sergeant." She left the building quickly, the comment from Jeremy running around her mind. Celine hadn't been herself recently. Their relationship in tatters: work stress. Relationship stress. Money. Bills. Moving in. All the shit with the murders. Laura had lost weight. Wasn't sleeping. And the bottle was calling her name stronger and stronger each night, and it was getting harder and harder to hide it from everyone.

Laura pulled a cigarette out of her pocket and placed it between her teeth. She had promised Celine she would quit, but there was no way in hell she would be able to quit while she was a cop. Coffee and nicotine practically ran a police force. It would be like kicking a chair leg away and hoping it didn't collapse. Then when she was sure the car park was clear, she opened up the glove box and took out a single of vodka and sank it in one. She pulled a face of war, but it stopped the quickening of her heart. Feeling a little looser, she put the keys in the ignition and fired up the car engine. Laura punched in her address into the sat nav. She knew she needed to figure out her own way home without it, but right now her mind was too full of bad memories to let anything else in.

Chapter Two

Laura

Laura pulled up to the driveway. The LED lights of the Audi drenching the house in radiant light.

"Shit," Laura hissed deflated. She had a bundle of flowers in her passenger seat. She wanted to stop off before the florist closed, but then a missing child ironically 'appeared' in her life. So, she had to make do with a five-pound bunch of half-dead flowers from the service station.

The lights were off in the house, and she didn't want to go in and disturb that unwelcoming darkness. She slammed her head back into the seat. So much for making amends. She pinched her nose. The job was taking everything from her.

"Don't be late," Celine's voice bounced around her mind as she sat at the kitchen bar with a cold coffee that morning. Laura had barely looked up from her work computer as Celine moved around the kitchen cleaning.

"Yeah, sure," she said vacantly, looking at the flood of emails pouring in from different units asking her to look at their caseload.

"Laura." Her name dragged her from the void. Laura caught Celine's eye. She was standing there with two bottles of non-alcoholic wine. "Which one?" Laura eyed the imposters. It didn't matter to her. They both tasted like rat piss.

"The red," she said, barely looking away from the computer. Celine shifted her weight to her other foot.

"I don't know why I'm bothering," she hissed, slamming the bottles on the counter. Laura snatched her eyes away from the screen. Celine stood at the sink, hands resting on the worktop and staring at the wall. Laura got up and moved to her, tentatively placing her hands onto Celine's shoulders.

"Sorry," Laura said, kissing her neck. Celine turned to her, her eyes glistening with tears. Laura drew in and placed her lips on hers. They shared a moment, breathing each other in. "I'll make sure I'm home on time," she whispered, running her fingers through her hair. "I promise." What she wanted Celine to say was a *thank you*, or a *see you later*. Instead, Celine began to pry at the lock box in Laura's mind.

"It's like you're never here with me anymore," she said, staring at the floor. "I feel so alone."

Laura listened to the idling engine as she continued to look at the house. She had not taken the comment well, and they argued. Celine wasn't being understanding or supportive. Laura was being a hard ass and burying everything away. The usual kind of arguments they had been having recently.

She knew she should speak to someone about what had happened, the same way she had made Jeremy speak to Occupational Health. But she wasn't great at cutting herself open and spilling everything out to a stranger. She was more adept at burying her problems and thoughts rather than letting their evil sprout and fester all over her rotting soil. Her and Celine had only been dating a couple of months, their union forever marred by murder. Their partnership was baptised in blood, the pews filled with rotting corpses. Not the best way to start.

She remembered reading a book that depression and pain is the body's way of telling you that something is wrong, and you needed to fix it. But what the fuck did she need to fix now? She had by all accounts, a good life: stability, regular orgasms, and a place to call home. But yet, the black dog of her mind was moving slowly closer and closer to the point now where it wasn't just panting at her heels, but instead was lying on her chest and trying to suffocate her.

"You should have never moved her in," Laura said to herself in that stillness. The smoke from her cigarette filled the cab. "I should have told you when I got out the hospital. But instead, you crawled right under my skin and never left." Laura killed the engine. She watched the dark clouds caress the full moon that hung in the sky. The craters forming a face. A face that looked as though it was screaming.

She took a drag of the smoke and watched the blue ribbons dance into the air. Her mind running away like a train with a sleeping driver. The flowers would have to do for now. The birthday card would have to wait. They would fight, and then they would fuck, and everything would be okay again. Just another thing swept under the rug to never be disturbed. Then, she would promise to take Celine out somewhere nice when she finally got a day off.

There was nothing wrong with Celine, not on the surface. She was amazingly beautiful, and Laura couldn't keep her eyes off her, and yet, she still felt an emptiness towards her. Towards most things. A feeling she couldn't shake.

She cracked the handle and stepped into the cold and locked the car. The jingling of her keys rang into the air. She placed the door key into the lock and opened it. The house was deathly silent. Even Bagpipe who would usually be up and about when he heard her come home was nowhere to be seen. Laura closed the door and moved through the house. She eyed someone standing in the darkness of the kitchen. Was Celine awake? Laura put the flowers behind her back, the crinkle of the plastic cutting through the still air.

"Hey," she said to the silhouette. "Sorry I'm late." She flicked the kitchen light on.

He was standing there with the knife in his hand. The blood dripping down onto the kitchen surface. The emaciated leather mask stretched and tort in an eternal scream. His clothing soaked in blood. He rushed to her, bringing the knife up high. Laura screamed, crumbling to the ground, shielding herself and ready to feel the teeth of the knife sink into her flesh.

She looked up. He was gone. The echo of her shriek still bouncing around the empty kitchen. Her heart hammered. Her breath ragged and body drenched in sweat. She touched the ground, feeling the cold tiles on her fingertips. She eyed the room. She was alone.

Laura pulled staggered breaths through her burning throat. Tears doused her face and salt filtered through her lips. After a moment, she climbed to her feet with shaking legs. The flowers now crumpled and destroyed.

The water was ice cold as it splashed onto her face. Celine thought Laura was sober, that she had thrown out her wine, but she had just gotten better at hiding her drinking. She dug under the sink and moved past the array of bottles and cleaning products and fished out a hidden bottle of red. She cracked the top and took a long drink before putting the cap back on and placing it back into its hiding place. Her anxiety melted away, and she drowned the feeling of failure. She checked the time. It was almost two in the morning. She placed the crumpled flowers in a vase and put them on the bar. If flowers could look depressed, then the ones she had bought Celine was damn near suicidal.

She took out her cigarettes and fired one to life in the kitchen. Celine didn't like her smoking in the house. In *her* house.

"I don't like breathing in your smoke," she had said one night when they were decorating her bedroom. *Their* bedroom.

"Well," Laura said, taking another drag. "Now you know how it feels to be suffocated." She didn't mean to say that out loud, and Laura saw Celine had stopped painting, her roller abandoned on the floor and was panting, her eyes growing red. Laura went to speak, but Celine moved past her like a wailing wind onto the landing. Laura followed the drips of mahogany paint to the bathroom. She could hear the faint sobbing coming from behind the door.

"Celine," Laura said dryly. "Come out. I didn't mean that."

"Just say it Laura," Celine cried, rage dousing her voice. "You don't want to be with me. I was just a convenience to you."

"No, you weren't, Celine," Laura said, feeling like the weight of the world was squeezing her from all ends. Who knew gravity was three-dimensional? Instead of just pulling someone down to their knees? "Sorry," she said, the words dry like ash in her mouth. "I want us to be happy. You helped me so much with everything that happened…"

"So, I'm just here to help you, is that it?" She hissed behind the door. "What about me, Laura? Ever stop to think about me?"

All I ever do is think about you…

"Come out of there," Laura said. "You're being ridiculous." She tried the handle. It was locked. Laura ran her hand down her face and leaned against the wall.

"You don't want me," Celine croaked. "I am trying my best for you, but you can't even do a little in return."

"Okay," Laura blurted. "What is it that you want? "

"I want you to get some help, Laura. You need the help." Laura took a deep breath. In for three, hold for two, out for four. Repeat.

"Look, why don't you come out, and we can finish the bedroom? Tomorrow, I'll come home early, get you some nice flowers, and we can have a night in. I'll even cook." Laura heard the crying slow.

"But you're a terrible cook." Laura forced a smile.

"And you're a terrible guest." After a moment, Celine emerged from the bathroom. Her eyes were red around the edges. Her overalls were stained with grey blotches of teardrops.

"I would like that." Laura aired the kitchen out and checked her phone. No missed calls. She had been working so much recently, and if the lack of sleep and bags under her eyes didn't tell you, then the lack of any real human interaction recently would. She took out a piece of paper from the kitchen drawer and wrote –

Work was crazy. I slept on the couch as I didn't want to wake you. Will make it up to you. Sorry. Again.

L x

She placed the note down and considered for a moment going upstairs and lying in bed next to Celine, but she knew that wouldn't yield anything for her. The warmth of her body was enough to knock her out, but she knew that she would just be spending hours staring into the black that slowly turned to light from the rising dawn, before crawling out of bed and throwing herself into a cold shower to wake herself up followed by a morning smoke and some muesli, if she was feeling hungry, which right now she couldn't remember the last time she had eaten anything but a quick microwavable meal from the station.

She lay down on the couch and let the consuming blackness envelop her. She stared at the vacant space above, wondering if sleep would come. Insomnia was a demon she had fought with most of her life, which is one of the reasons why she started drinking in the evening. She had often considered taking medication for it, but she was already taking enough pills for the depression. So, she lay there, listening to the empty void around her as sleep forsook her, and her mind wandered into that dark place she called home.

The morning kissed her eyelids as the clink of a cup of coffee caught her ear. She cracked her eyes open to the sight of Celine above her in her dressing gown. Her eyes were bloodshot and puffy, and her hair resembled a wire brush.

"What time did you come home last night?" She said, her voice laced with hurt. Laura sat up and touched her head. She rubbed her eyes and let out a groan.

"What time is it?"

"Six," Celine said. "What time did you come home? I waited up for you."

"I was working. You know the score with the job." Laura looked and took the cup of coffee. She took a sip and then spat it out. She eyed the defiling liquid. "What is this?"

"You should know," she hissed. "You left it out for me to find." Laura's pallet came to life. Red wine.

Shit.

"How long have you been lying to me?" Laura felt her skin beginning to crawl. She just wanted to go back to sleep. To let the world consume her, to bury her beneath the feet of men to not be disturbed until the sun died.

"Oh god," she said, falling back onto the couch and lacing her hands over her face. "Don't start. Not again."

"You told me that you were going to stop drinking," she said sourly. "And the flowers? Where the hell did you pick

43

those up from? From someone's grave? They looked trampled on!"

"I got caught up in something important."

"More important than me?" Celine bit. Laura squeezed her eyes shut.

"I didn't say that," she whispered.

"If you have two choices, and you pick one over the other, then that means that it is more important, right?" Laura stood up and stormed past Celine.

"I'm not doing this with you right now." She slipped into the kitchen and put the kettle on. The bottle of wine had fallen out from under the sink and had leaked its sticky red contents onto the floor. The thing that she was trying to hide is the thing that had exposed her. There was something poetic in that.

"Are you going to clean that up?" Celine said, following closely behind. Laura eyed the sticky mess on the ground.

"I have to get ready for work." Celine closed the gap quickly.

"You're not doing this to me, Laura." She placed her hand on the counter and leaned into her. "You're not just running away again. I'm not staying here on my own."

"No one is keeping you here Celine," Laura said, brushing her hand away to take out a mug from the cupboard. "You can leave anytime you like." Celine recoiled back, her face like she was chewing a wasp.

"What's gotten into you?" She snarled. "When we first met, I was there for you when you needed me and now, what? You don't need me anymore, so you just throw me away like I'm yesterday's rubbish?" Laura slammed the cup down on the counter and moved past Celine.

"I'm going to be late." She disappeared upstairs to the sound of Celine shouting and howling at her. Bagpipe was sleeping on the bed when she walked in. Laura petted him and wished him a good morning, before stepping into the shower, putting it as hot as she could stand, and then cranked it up some more.

Chapter Three
Jamie

Jamie called up any relatives he could think of. Family friends. School teachers. Even old doctors he knew Oliver had been to see, blowing up their phones in the middle of the night to the sound of worried gasps or answer machines.

"I haven't seen him," was the general consensus, followed by thin reassurance or "have you called the police? Do you want me to help?" Or the one he was dreading, like a piano dangling over him by a thin piece of thread – "Have you spoken to Claire?" The last question being the most delicate of tightropes to walk on.

"I'll handle Claire," he would say. "Please don't say anything to her. I need to speak to her myself. Plus, if he turns up somewhere, then I won't need to rock the boat." That was one way of saying it. Rocking the boat was saying you're going to be an hour late home for dinner when you have plans. This was a tsunami coming to destroy your home and everything you had known about the world.

You could call him, his mind whispered in his ear. *You could call him for help. He gave you his number just in case. They owe you, remember?* Jamie pushed the thoughts away. He had left the monsters of his past behind. He would handle things himself. He would do things by the book. His life depended on it.

Dawn had broken and cast the sky the colour of a melted flamingo. He rubbed his eyes, sitting in his car and turned to look at Claire's house. His mind was churning over with agony. What was he going to say? How was he going to say it? He took out his phone, hoping that the cops would call quickly and tell him that they had found his son after he had wandered off too far, chasing a balloon or something.

Why couldn't he remember the reg or the make of the car? He desperately searched his mind, but it wasn't coming, like trying to remember a nightmare upon waking. The terror was still there, but you couldn't remember why. The guy in the jacket. The one driving the Fiesta. Was he behind it? Had he done something? He had to remember him. And when the memory came back, which it would, he would track him down and make him wish he had never been born. If the police didn't do something, then he would do something himself.

He forced the thoughts away again. He wouldn't do that. Not this time. He had to keep his temper under control. Keep the dog chained up. It was *his* fault why Oliver had been taken, too consumed in his own rage and hatred. The beast inside him had been let out of its cage, and now it had consumed the most precious part of him. He had to sit back and let the police do their job. But he couldn't tell them everything that happened. If he told them the full story, then he would go back to prison, and then no one would be able to care for his son. A moral dilemma if there ever was one.

Who will take care of Oliver when you're in jail? Hmm? His whore of a mother that is dating a weed dealer half her age? Or was he going to go into care?

His mind churned again. He was being selfish. He should have told Detective Warburton. He went to her specifically. He had pled with her yet was holding back key information. This was his son that was at stake. He should call her right now. He eyed his phone and took out the detective's card and began punching in the number.

You'll go back to prison. They're all waiting for you. They'll scoop out your eyes and fuck the fleshy holes.

He slammed his fist into the wheel of the car.

"Fuck!" He screamed, his mouth arid, lips cracking. He rammed his hands to his eyes and rocked in the car seat, slamming his fist into the windows, doors and dashboard. He gripped the steering wheel fiercely, like a drowning man clinging to a life raft. Panting heavily, sweating even harder, he picked up his phone that had fallen into the passenger side footwell and placed it in his pocket. He took a deep breath, releasing it slowly. He needed to keep a lid on it.

Jamie eyed the terrace house which had its curtains permanently drawn. The bottom of the PVC door had been boarded up with a plank of wood from the last time the police had come knocking. Oliver's bike lay abandoned in the front garden, and a trampoline with more empty beer cans than happy memories sat rotting and waterlogged in the middle of the overgrown grass.

He squeezed his eyes shut and then reopened them. It was twilight. Grey clouds had carpeted the golden dawn, washing out the colour from the street. It looked ashen. Desolate. A couple walked past him, hardly a set of teeth between them. Both with cans of strong lager in their hand. An echo of a former life that he had tried to leave behind. But no matter how far he tried to run from it, it always seemed to drag him back with its hooks and claws. He stepped out into the street. One of the passers-by turned to him, a man that looked like he should have died years ago.

"Any change, mate?" The man said. He was so thin that Jamie figured he had to jump over grids in the road to avoid falling through them.

"No," he snapped.

"A ciggy then?" He said, holding out his tobacco-stained fingertips. Jamie rolled his eyes and took out a pack of smokes that he had bought whilst looking for Oliver. The nicotine beast would have to wait to die. He pulled them out and gave the letch three.

"Enjoy."

"Thanks," the guy croaked as he watched Jamie approach the front door. "God bless you." Then he was gone, flitting away like the wind. Jamie paused at the front door. Everything in his body was screaming at him not to do this. Not to make it real. But he had to. He eyed the door. Either she had been up all night drinking, now that Oliver wasn't her responsibility for the weekend, or she was sleeping off a hangover, and she wouldn't answer. Either way, Jamie knew this wasn't going to end well. He held his breath and knocked firmly. The sound echoed around the empty estate. A usual alarm clock for some folks around this part of town. Normally, it was the police coming to say good morning to them and they were going to spend the day in Casa del Custody. Jamie could hear something stirring inside. The sound of a bottle falling over. A glass rolled along the floor. He waited, his heart in his throat. The handle twitched.

"Hold on," a guy said. That was Declan. A waste of life if there ever was one. Jamie knocked again. "I said hold on!" Declan rasped, followed by a burst of wheezy coughing. The keys jingled, and the door came open. He stood eyeing Jamie like he was a rat trying to crawl into the kitchen of his established restaurant. He was topless. His skinny bald build prickling with the morning chill. He resembled a hairless, emaciated ape. His hair was long and fell to his shoulders, held together in clumps by grease. His face was swollen with large craters and red bulbous boils. "What?" He spat.

"Is Claire in?"

"She's asleep."

"Wake her." Declan tutted and moved to close the door. Jamie jammed his foot in the gap. "Now." He eyed Declan with fire. Declan let go of the handle, took out a rollie from behind his ear, sparked it up and blew smoke into the morning air. He moved from the door and slipped away, shouting for Claire.

The stench that emanated from the house was potent. A mixture of shit, weed, cigarette smoke and stale booze. The floor was littered with clothing and crumbs of food. The television hung from the wall with dust and grime smothering it. The floor, the parts which weren't carpeted with discarded clothes, was bare with floorboards that were dusty and lined with dirt. The cream leather couch had rotted into a septic pus yellow with ashtrays on the arms.

He turned his face away, both gasping for air, and also gasping at the thought this was where his boy called *home*. He had put a case forward to have his son given to him by the family court.

"There's food in the fridge and they have clothing," the social worker had said, and that apparently, was enough for a child. He stared at the door, listening to the muffled sounds of Declan and Claire arguing about being up so early.

What the hell was he going to say to her?

"Hi, Claire. So, listen, you know how I believe I am the better parent, and I am going to be taking you and your latest fuck up of a boyfriend to court for custody of Oliver? Yeah, well, funny story. There is no Oliver. Oh, the police? They're looking for him sure enough, but I haven't given them the full details of what happened because I will go back to prison, meaning I won't be able to protect Oliver from you and your latest abusive boyfriend. I know. A real doozy of a situation, aint it!"

Claire arrived at the bottom of the stairs. Her eyes were sunken into her head, and she had the last half of a joint hanging from her chapped lips. Her hair was pinned back tightly in a bobble, and her nightgown still had the price tag on from some high-end retailer. Obviously stolen, and would no doubt be sold in the coming weeks, hence the tag, but she had to get her wear out of it first.

"You bored of him already?" Claire spat. "He doesn't come home until tomorrow." She eyed him with venom. Jamie searched for the words. The most delicate way to break her heart. To make it real. Claire looked past Jamie into the street. "Where is Oliver?" She said, the horror beginning to dawn on her face. Jamie's face looked like he was chewing on a wasp. "Eric, where the fuck is our son?"

"I…" He croaked. Jamie eyed her with pain. Her expression changed, like melting rubber with a blow torch.

"What's going on?" Jamie felt the world's weight fall onto him, crushing him like an insect under its boot.

"I need to come in," Jamie said, barely louder than a whisper. "I have some bad news."

Chapter Four
Laura

Laura walked into the office with her Starbucks in her hand. She had sworn them off with the cost of a daily cappuccino amounting to more than her monthly car payments, but the 'fuck it' monster had struck, and for breakfast, she had already had a triple chocolate chip muffin and had grabbed the coffee to go. Plus, the coffee disguised the vodka, and no one ever drank out of someone else's Starbucks cup.

"Morning, everyone," she said with more enthusiasm than she would have liked. She sat down at her desk. Jeremy was working his way through some paperwork. Catherine was completing another crossword, but upon seeing Laura, she quickly stuffed it into the drawer and opened her workload for the day. The two new recruits were nowhere to be seen.

"Where are the newbies?" Laura asked, gesturing with the coffee cup to the empty desks.

"They're doing further enquiries into Oliver Green," Catherine said, before taking a drink of her herbal tea. Laura opened her emails and then took another drink of coffee. It wasn't as strong as she had liked. She would sneak out to her car during her dinner and add in an extra single.

"Any developments?" Laura said. Catherine shrugged.

"I think they'll be back soon. They went a few hours ago." Laura checked her watch.

"They're keen!"

"Early birds, ma'am," Jeremy piped up. "Between us, I think they're competing for your attention." A bemused smirk appeared on her face.

"I'll leave them to it then."

The two detectives walked into the office as if summoning the devil himself.

Laura hadn't spoken to them much since they joined the team. She had been preoccupied with the clean-up from the Straw Man killings. Between the clean-up, the daily life of a detective, her new failing relationship, and rising alcoholism, she had little time for much else. Bagpipe's worming and flea treatment was also overdue, and she made a mental note to get that sorted before the end of the week. One day, the house of her sanity might crumble under the weight of everything that had been piled onto her. She just hoped she would be shit-faced, and dancing around in her underwear when it did.

"Ma'am!" One of the detectives shouted.

"Yes?"

"I said good morning," he laughed. Francis Cline, or 'Frankie' as his old colleagues had called him. Laura had recognised him when he first walked into the office. He was a little older than the other recruit – Alice Hudson. Alice was in her late twenties, but Francis was nearer to fifty. He had done twenty-two years on the front line and thought that joining the Major Investigation Unit would be a nice change of pace. Boy, was he mistaken. But she had to give him his due. Since he had landed on the team, he had solved two frauds, a sextortion and even a cold case murder. He was good, and Laura liked him.

Alice, however, was quieter. Laura often caught her eye from across the room, and Alice would let her stare linger for a moment before looking away, letting Laura know she was watching her, but not obvious enough for others to notice. Enough to put Alice into Laura's mind. Alice was good at her job and very meticulous with her reports. She was subtle about it, not loud and booming like Francis. She was eager to impress but did it through her hard work and presentation, and that didn't stop with just her work, as her dedication was also shown through the shape of her body. She wore a tight pencil dress and black tights and heels. Her shoulders were uncovered, advertising her figure to those in the room. Her hair was like liquid gold that radiated from her head, like the morning sunshine over a winter's day.

"I got you this cat," Francis said quickly, holding out a pin of the Cheshire Cat smiling ear to ear. Laura queried the item, before pursing her lips and taking it from him. She stuck it on her monitor.

"Thanks," she said coldly.

"I thought you might like it," he continued. "You have a cat, don't you? What's his name?"

"Bagpipe," she said, feigning a smile. Francis' face looked like Laura had just done a handstand and was juggling with her feet.

"Why did you call him Bagpipe?" He said, dumbfounded. Laura went to speak, but Alice interjected.

"Because you can call a cat whatever you like, it still won't come to you." She smiled at Laura warmly.

"How did you know that?" Laura said, taken back, a smile creeping across her face.

"I pay attention," Alice said, before slipping to her desk. Laura watched her go. Her hips swayed in that dress. She turned to Francis, who was like a dog waiting for her to throw a ball. She gestured to the Cheshire Cat pin.

"Thank Francis," she said, her mind still thinking about Alice's honey sweet curves.

"It's Frankie, ma'am," he said.

"Okay, Francis." Deflated at the formality, he skulked back to his chair, opened his computer, and began furiously typing away. Alice glided through the room like a cool wind slipping through a cracked window on a hot day. She fixed herself a coffee and asked if anyone else wanted one. Laura declined. Alice made the rounds and then slipped back into the office. She moved to Laura who was reading her emails. Something from the new superintendent, Bill Bennet. He was older than Mary Dutton and was kinder and knew everyone's names in the office. Approachable. A leader. And hopefully didn't have a homicidal, psychotic son, but no one is perfect. The email has to do with some bullshit wellbeing survey. It was clearly just an arse-covering exercise, and Laura deleted the email.

"Make sure you all fill in the well-being survey," she said to the room. "It's of the utmost importance." She tried to hide her sarcasm. Jeremy eyed her from behind his monitors with a smirk. Alice approached her.

"I have the CCTV from the supermarket for the kid if you want to have a look, ma'am? I have also done some digging and have some things you might like to see." Laura got a whiff of perfume, and like hooked on a line, found herself drawn into her.

"Yeah, no problem," Laura said. Her voice caught in her throat. Alice perched her ass on the side of the table. Laura imagined what it tasted like.

Celine, she thought to herself. *Stop eye fucking the new detective.*

"I'll load it up for you," Alice uttered, before reaching her hand to Laura's coffee cup. "You sure I can't get anything for you?" Laura felt a blast of heat run through her body. There was a lot she could do for her. Laura grabbed the coffee cup, sank the last drops and tossed it into the bin under her desk.

"I'm fine, thanks," she said, pushing her hair behind her ears. Clearing her throat as she stood up. "Show me what you have." Alice eyed her from top to bottom.

"My pleasure." They moved to Alice's desk, and she took out the DVD from the plastic evidence bag labelled 'CCTV' along with the statement provided by the security guard.

"How come this has taken so long to get?" Laura said, snapping back to boss mode. Francis piped up behind her.

"Uniformed cops were having trouble working it because the security didn't know how to work the CCTV," he said. "So, we had to wait for the security to speak to their manager for us to be able to view it, get a copy, and bring it back here."

"Figures," Laura said, pursing her lips and shaking her head. "You would think that those that ran the cameras would know how to operate them." A chorus of sniggering met her ears. Alice got the footage working. It was colour, which was a bonus. People flitted and moved around quickly like out of a silent movie.

"Sound?" Laura asked.

"No sound," Francis said, leaning over her shoulder to get a look in like a child that was being left out of the party gatherings.

"Put it to the right part," Laura said, growing impatient. Alice moved the slider to the part where Jamie said he had attended. They saw his car drive into the car park. Laura pointed at the screen. "There. Can you get closer?" Alice shook her head.

"It doesn't go any further than that. He parked at the bottom of the car park where the cameras don't cover."

"Brilliant," Laura said in a frustrated whisper. They watched as Jamie and a young blonde boy got out of the car. He was holding a picture in his hand, and Jamie was pointing at it. Then, Jamie turned, agitated, and was talking to someone out of frame.

"Who's he talking to?" Laura said, pointing to the monitor.

"We can't see," Alice said. "The camera doesn't cover it." They watched as Jamie appeared more animated to the unknown other. Then, at once, Oliver recoils, clutching his piece of paper in his hand, and the team behold a silent scream erupt from his mouth. Jamie appears a short time later. His hands are wet, and his trousers and shirt are covered with grime and gravel. He crouches, trying to soothe Oliver, before pulling him away, and they walk towards the store's entrance.

"What was that all about?" Francis asked.

"Something Jamie left out of his story," Laura said sharply. "Not the quiet happy little outing he suggested." Laura erected herself, running her hand across her face.

She was sweating more than usual for this time in the morning. The shakes didn't start kicking in until at least noon. "Keep the footage playing. See what happens."

"Will do," Alice said, zooming in on Oliver and Jamie in the store.

"No," Laura waved her hand. "Keep it on the car park. He didn't go missing inside the store. We can look for wandering eyes or if someone is showing an interest in the kid later. But right now, I want to see what happens when Jamie leaves the scene." They did just that. A few minutes passed, and nothing moved. Laura grew more impatient. Then, they saw the lip of a brown shoe at the top of the frame, and then the corner of a red Fiesta move out of frame. The fiesta drove around the car park and cut in front of Oliver and Jamie as they approached the opening of the store. Jamie eyed the driver with rage before the car slipped out of the car park.

"That's the guy from out of the frame," Laura said. "Run the registration plate, then do a PNC on the driver. See who this person is."

"Do we have a suspect?" Francis said, yipping like an excited dog, before scribbling the registration plate down quickly on a pad of paper.

"Not just one," Laura said.

"What do you mean?" Francis asked. Laura placed her hands on the desk and pointed at Jamie's pixelated face.

"Strangers don't just steal kids," she said. "It happens, sure. But most of the time, the worst crimes that can happen to a person are committed by those that are familiar." Laura's heart began to feel like it was placed into a machine press and was slowly being crushed. "The ones that say they love us the most. They are the ones we really need to keep our eye on." The room fell silent. Laura snapped out of her thoughts and pushed the sound of crashing waves and the stench of sea salt from her mind. She pushed her hand into her jacket. "I've got his details here." Laura pulled out her notepad and Francis copied the scribblings down. He furrowed his brow at the scribblings. Francis began typing away. "I've run him through already. No trace. But see what you can do."

"I think this is wrong ma'am?" He said. She snapped her eyes to him.

"Prey tell?" Francis' mouth dried up.

"Well," he said tentatively. "You have written his birthday is the 17th of the 4th of 1887." Laura's blood ran cold. She could feel her body beginning to tremor internally, like someone had put a vibrating exercise plate under her feet and was turning it up slowly.

"Fuck me," she hissed. She had taken down the wrong details. That would make him over a hundred years old. Such a stupid mistake. "Right," she said frustratingly. "Run every possible combination of those with the name Jamie Green. See what comes back, and we'll go from there."

Francis didn't question it further. Jeremy peered over his monitor and eyed the inspector.

"You all right, ma'am?" He said. "You don't look so good." Laura felt like dog shit. She was sweating. Her skin had turned waxy, and her body was running ice cold.

"I'm fine," she whispered. "Just get the reg of the car and do the checks. There's a reason why Jamie hasn't told us the full story about what happened. Either he knows something and who is driving that car, or he has something greater to hide. Either way, I want to find out." Laura moved and grabbed her coat. "I'm going for a smoke." She pulled her coffee cup from the waste bin. "Keep looking over the footage. See if there's anything else we can see." She was about to leave the room when Alice's voice returned her attention.

"Ma'am," she said, gesturing for her to come and see the good part of the movie. Laura's face turned to resemble a bulldog that had been chewing on porcupine spikes.

"What is it?" she felt breathless. Clutching onto the side of the door.

"They're back at the car," she said. "We need to see this." Laura reluctantly moved back to the monitor. All of them were on their feet in the office and staring at the screen. Laura felt her clothes sticking to her like a second skin. She needed a minute to herself and badly. She expected the footage to show nothing. She was wrong.

The screen was the same: cars lined together like multicoloured teeth against the black mouth of the tarmac. They watched as Jamie brought Oliver back to the car. He appeared in better spirits. A plethora of popcorn, fizzy drinks and sweets bulged out of swollen carrier bags and a four pack of beers.

"Make a note of what they have bought and the time stamp in case we want to speak to the cashier on that day." Someone began scribbling away. Laura didn't look who; she was too busy watching the part of the movie where a child is stolen.

Jamie unlocked the car and spoke to Oliver before opening the passenger seat for him to get in. As Jamie turns away to return the trolley, Oliver's picture is caught by the wind and fly's out into the car park. He chases the picture down the car park and out of frame. A moment passes, and Jamie returns to his car. Laura watched as a grown man began crumbling into dust right before their eyes. She knew the feeling well. When your entire world is shattered in an instant.

"Fuck," Laura snapped. "Is there no better angle?" Alice quickly flitted through the cameras, but they can't see Oliver. "Wait," Laura barks. "Go back." Alice does just that and cycles through the cameras. "Stop," Laura says before stabbing her finger at the monitor. "There." All close in at what she is looking at.

"The red fiesta," Francis whispers.

"It never left the car park," Alice concurs.

"Fast forward," Laura said, keeping her eye on the car. An hour, two hours of footage later, the car hasn't moved before the night settles in, and the car is out of sight.

"Did it leave the car park?" Someone says. Laura shook her head.

"I don't know. We can't see a damn thing on these monitors. Move to the morning." Alice hit the triple-speed button, and the car was gone when the sun came back up. Laura stood upright, her back aching from bending down. "Get me the results of that check right now," she said. "And I want to know everywhere where the father has been in the last forty-eight hours. I want to know where he works. I want information on his ex-wife, I want information on her new partner, PNCs, local checks, out of force checks. Cameras to be checked in and out of the supermarket. Any back alleyways that people can walk through. I want the name of every rat that found a leftover sandwich and them brought in for questioning."

Laura moved back to the door.

"Where are you going?" Jeremy said. Laura didn't answer. The sound of waves was coming back, and she needed some quiet.

Chapter Five

Jamie

There are moments in life that people can recall with a smile on their face. When just a whisper of a memory makes the sky seem a little bluer. The happiest times of our lives. The day our children are born. Finally saving up to go on that dream holiday. Being able to finally leave that soul-sucking job. But there are also days when life descends its cloud over our lives so thick, we choke on it. Where in the blink of an eye, your world has crumbled around you, and everything you have ever known, everything you have believed, is lit on fire and the essence of what your life once was, disintegrates to ash and is scattered into the wind.

For Claire, it was on this cold winter's morning when nothing would ever be the same again. At first, she didn't say anything. The words not registering, like she was blind and was being told what colour a sunset was. She sat there in cold silence. The sound of the outside world slipping through the stale air. A numbness few people ever get to experience took hold of her. Her eyes began to sting, followed by the trembling of her lip like the vibrations of an earthquake before the ground cracked in two.

"I'm sorry," Jamie said, leaning forward on the pus-coloured sofa. Claire's mouth hanging vacant, her face like her soul had been ripped out of her stomach and was being set alight. She mouthed a response.

"How?" She whispered, her throat sewing shut with hooks and spiked barbs. Jamie tried to speak, but his mouth flopped around silently like a suffocating fish laid out on a ship deck. His eyes arid and raw. He couldn't cry anymore if he tried. "You had him," she croaked. "You had our son." The pain began to surface like a black tide filled with dead fish and bones. "And now…" She couldn't finish the sentence. To say it, meant it was real. To say the words was sacrilege. A defiance of the natural order of life. And yet, her silence said everything Jamie needed to hear.

"I'm sorry," he whispered again.

"Sorry doesn't cut it," Declan piped up behind Claire, standing over her with a rollie poking out from his rotting teeth. "You should have looked after him. You should have been there for him!" Jamie felt something snap deep inside him. In the space of time it took Declan to take the cigarette from between his teeth and pinch it between his fingers, Jamie's hand was around Declan's throat, his teeth bared like a rabid dog with murder in its eyes.

"Say that again!" Jamie screamed. "Say it one more time!" I dare you, you little rat!" Hot spittle slapped Declan's face, Jamie's veins pulsing along his forehead.

"Sorry, sorry!" Declan rebuked quickly, raising his hands, Jamie's grip around his throat the only thing keeping him standing on his jelly legs.

"You have the cheek to tell me that I should have done more when both of your kids are in care? Every breath you take is wasted air you disgusting degenerate." Jamie spat a hock of phlegm into Declan's spotted face and cocked back his fist. His knuckles the paintbrush. Declan's dithering face the canvas. His blood soon to be the paint that showed the world all of his hatred, his regret, and his self-loathing. Through the screeching of Declan and the red mist of Jamie's fury, he heard the screaming of Claire.

"Stop!" She wailed, gripping hold of Jamie. "Stop! Don't you think you have done enough?" Her words like daggers in his heart, rupturing the chains of his despair, cutting them loose. He uncoiled his fingers from around Declan's thin neck and pulled his hand back, stepping away from him like he had touched a hot stove, holding his head in his hands. Declan crumbling to the ground, moving back and trying to bury himself into the wall.

"Get out!" Claire bellowed, her voice raw, slapping and hitting Jamie to the side in his face and back. "Get the hell out of my house!" She pushed him, would have thrown him out of the damn window if Jamie hadn't made it to the front door. Jamie turned to try and say something. Say anything. But he couldn't. There was so much he wanted to unload onto her, but agony fed him only silence. She eyed him at the door. The face of a broken woman. "Find our son," she hissed. "Or die trying."

Chapter Six

Laura

Laura raced to her car and closed the door. Checking the coast was clear, she snapped open the single measure of vodka, poured it into her coffee cup, and then got the bottle of orange juice from under her seat and filled it halfway. She took a drink and let the booze work its magic, before pulling out a smoke. She eyed herself in her rear-view mirror. She looked awful and felt even worse. She took another drink and the feeling of self-loathing fell away. She checked her phone. Another way to numb herself from the world. Five missed calls and three voicemails from Celine. She deleted them all. A text message too. The girl was persistent.

Talk to me.

Laura hit delete and drank more of her juice. Her phone began to buzz. It was Jamie Green.

"Hello."

"Detective?" He sounded awful. Something they had in common.

"Yes."

"Any update on my son?" Laura scratched her head; The cigarette smoke found her nose and eyes which began to sting. She turned on the ignition and let the smoke drift out of the cracked window.

"We're following all possible leads," she said robotically. "You should call the office. Not me." There was a beat of silence.

"You passed me your number?" Laura said nothing. She heard a tormented grunt. "Are you even trying?" His voice was laced with razors. Desperation breaking through the receiver.

"We are," she said. "But it takes time."

"My son is out there, and you aren't doing anything."

"We are going through the evidence to locate your son. We have a team working on it around the clock. I suggest you go home and let us do our job." Laura heard the scoff break through the quiet.

"Go home and let you do your job…" He repeated, his voice meek. He was angry, she could tell, but he was trying to keep a lid on it, but Laura knew when someone was sharpening their tongue ready for a sword fight, and her amour was on the ground cracked and covered with bugs and mud. "How the hell am I supposed to do that?" He spat. "How the hell am I to just sit by while your damn detectives sit in your office and are not out there *looking for my boy?*"

"Mr. Green," Laura bit. "We have officers out following all possible lines of enquiry." Jamie continued to rant and shout down the phone, his resolve dissolved into the ground. Laura continued sipping her cup of juice and smoking, the phone on loudspeaker on her lap. "What happened in the car park?" Laura snapped. Jamie silenced his rant like she had cut his throat.

"I don't know what you mean."

"Yes, you do." She said sourly. "Many people have tried to make me look like an idiot Jamie, and all of them have failed. I don't like being kept in the dark. Nor do I appreciate being lied to when I try to shine a light into the blackness. So, I will ask you one more time. What happened in the car park?" Jamie went quiet. Then –

"I had an argument with someone."

"And?"

"It got heated. I didn't hurt him. We went to the store, and I saw him drive away."

You think you did. Laura thought. *But he never left. And that gives us a suspect.* She wanted to tell him this, but that would be like throwing petrol on a fire to put it out. He was desperate, and there was no telling what he might do. She didn't want to be looking for more than one body at the end of all this.

"I need you to tell me everything about the person you had an argument with. What they looked like. How tall? Tattoos, scars, distinguishing features. I need you to tell me about the way they spoke, how they walked. Their build. Their clothing. Hair colour. Everything." Jamie relayed all he could in staggered intervals. "Thank you,"

Laura said, finishing her drink. She felt a little more human. The feeling of vibration and rattling in her bones slowly subsided and was replaced by an ethanol hugging numbness that tingled her gums and made her body feel heavy. "Now Jamie, it sounds to me like you're struggling, but I need you to relax, okay? I know it's hard, and I can't imagine what you're going through. But trust me when I say we are doing all we can."

"Okay," he whispered.

"You need to come into the station and give a statement about what you told me. Okay?" Jamie didn't say anything else. Only a sigh, before he killed the call. Laura pursed her lips and let out a tight breath, taking another drag from her cigarette which had burned down to the end.

Another call came in. It was Celine. Laura flopped her head back onto the headrest. She hit ANSWER and closed her eyes, putting the phone to her ear.

"Finally!" Celine barked down the phone. Laura ended the call and put her phone in her glove box. She cracked the door and stepped out into the air. Officers were coming and going, either racing to dive into their cars and speed away with sirens and lights blaring, or they were walking in half-dead from finishing late from a night shift. Laura moved to the front door of the building.

"Detective Warburton!" The voice caught her off guard, and she turned. It was Alice. "I've been looking for you," she said eagerly. "I tried to call you." Laura righted herself.

"Sorry," she said. "I must have missed it." Alice ignored the excuse, eagerly pressing her pass to the door and holding it open like she was leading a friend to a free bar at a wedding.

"Come on," she said, smiling ear to ear. "I've got something you'll really want to see."

Chapter Seven

Jamie

Jamie stared at the phone in his hand. A growing anger bubbled inside of him. *We have officers out following all possible lines of enquiry.* What did that even mean? It was just a way for the cops to get him to shut up and go away. Something which he had never done. In a past life, he would be out there breaking down doors and cracking skulls to get what he wanted. But he wasn't that person anymore. He had to not let that beast out again, yet by doing nothing, he was choosing to let his son come to harm, like a sailor who doesn't ring the bell when he sees the iceberg coming, hoping the captain has already seen it. He couldn't bear the thought of something happening to Oliver. Not after everything Jamie had done to be in his life. The hoops he'd had to jump through. The people he had had to sell down the river. The danger he had put himself in. A thought festered in his mind, like a botfly that lays its eggs that slowly hatch and eat the host from the inside out.

They aren't going to help me, he thought. *They know who I am. Somehow. She figured it out. This is revenge for what I have done. They can travel to the ends of the earth to put me in chains, but when I need their help, they leave me to rot.*

They didn't care about him or finding his son. Oliver was just another case in their workload. It wasn't like the movies. Like the books. Like on TV where they pull out the helicopters or turn the world upside down. No. It was very different to that. He was just a missing child lost in a long list of missing children. His son was a number. A statistic. He was a priority case in a bunch of other priority cases. If everyone is special, then everyone is the same. If everyone is high risk, then no one is high risk. He needed to take matters into his own hands. Had no option but to take control. To let the beast out. Just a little.

His ex-wife. The look in her eyes when she spoke to him at the door. No anger. No happiness. Just numbness. A numbness that can only come from a place of utter and complete surrender to the desperation that has gripped you tightly with no intention of letting go.

Find him. Or die trying.

The words were like daggers into his soul, stripping everything he was, everything he could be or had ever been, right back to the bone. He had to make a choice. To act, or not act. He had abandoned them long ago and left her to fend for herself, to be used and abused by the scum of the earth. He was not going to do that again.

He got in his car and drove to the supermarket. It was blocked off by officers with tape that said 'POLICE.' It stretched along the entrance of the car park. Shoppers blared their horns at each other when they had to make a quick U-turn to avoid being caught by the lights. Jamie drove up to an officer. He was older, grey hair and more wrinkles than you could shake a stick at. The job had obviously not been kind to him, and Jamie bet he was counting down the paydays until retirement.

"Keep moving sir," he said nonchalantly. It was almost like a robot speaking, with eyes that held no humanity behind them.

"Is this about the missing boy?" Jamie said cautiously.

"I can't discuss an open case sir, now please move on." He turned his back to Jamie and began waving other drivers along. Jamie blasted on his horn. His anger a shark fin gliding through still water.

"I'm the boy's father," he said. "It was me who raised his disappearance. I want to come and help you in the search." The officer grimaced and waved him along.

"Okay sir," he said disbelievingly. How many others had tried to pull the same trick? He probably thought he was a journalist of some shitty newspaper or YouTube channel either trying to solve the case himself, show the police as being incompetent, or get an insider scoop of the scene before the news broke to the nationals. "Move along." Jamie hovered in a state of anguish, defeat and reluctance.

"I'm not moving until you let me in," Jamie said. The officer pursed his lips. He leant into Jamie's window. A blaring of car horns behind him.

"Move," the officer spat. "Move now, or you'll get locked up." Those words sobered him. If he got pinched, then he would be of no use. He needed to think about this rationally. Arguing with the police has never gotten him very far in his life. Jamie hesitated, thinking of a response. The officer flashed his handcuffs. "Now." Jamie revved the engine, reversed back sharply without looking, before vanishing down the street. He eyed the cops and the traffic behind him. The officer didn't so much as glance at him and again argued with another driver who was pissed that they couldn't get their eggs and bacon for breakfast.

Jamie parked in the car park opposite the supermarket where they normally held car boot sales early in the morning. Whereas normally, the place would be bustling with life, now it was home to only ghosts. He shut the engine off and eyed the police tape and the cops milling around the place. He had to get onto that car park. Just for a minute or two. To see what he could find. Maybe they had missed something? A clue of some kind?

He got out of the car and crossed the road. His heart was in his chest, his eyes darting in all directions. He had to be quick. Be sneaky about it. If he got caught, then it was game over. In front of him was a walkway that fed onto the supermarket grounds that was covered with high bushes on either side. The passageway opened up, and he saw an officer standing there with his phone in his hand. Not exactly a scene guard, is it? He was probably a newbie.

Not had many conflicts. Didn't know his ass from his elbow. This was good. Jamie had a good feeling in his stomach.

But then he saw past the fresh-faced officer and glimpsed to the meanest looking Alsatian on a lead he had ever seen, being pulled by an officer so big Jamie thought he lived atop a beanstalk and ate children for breakfast. His throat dried. Despite how hopeless it seemed, this was the only way in. He could see the space where he had had the altercation with the man in the beige jacket. Mr Unknown. Mr Responsible. He needed a way to get in there undetected. He thought of something. It was crazy, but it just might work. Jamie took out his phone and called 999.

"Police emergency."

"I need help," he said. This phone was disposable. Untraceable. Plus, he hadn't ever called the police from this number, so there wasn't a way of them attributing it to him.

"Go ahead."

"There's someone hanging from the roof of the supermarket. The police haven't noticed him yet. He's right at the back, dangling off. I think he's going to jump!" Jamie heard typing. His heart was in his throat, peering past the shrubbery at the lone officer. Jamie could rush him and knock him out, but he didn't fancy his chances against that dog.

"Can you describe him?"

"What do you mean '*describe him?*'" Jamie urged. "The guy's hanging off the top of the building! Get someone there now!" Jamie killed the call and waited. Moments ticked by before officers began to touch their radios, and just like that, they were rushing to the imaginary person trying to end their life.

A gap opened, and Jamie seized his opportunity.

He ducked under the police tape and moved behind a line of parked cop cars until he got to where he needed to be. His nerves were pulled tight, throbbing and pulsating a steady stream of anxiety. He saw officers moving around the building. It wouldn't take long before they figured it was a hoax, and then they would be back on guard, and he would be a rat trapped in a heating furnace. He peered from behind one of the police cars. It was cold to the touch, the morning dew covering its vinyl in slick bulbous drops. In front of him was where it had happened. Where he had last held his son. What memory would his son have of him? Would he remember him as the man he was trying to be? Or the man who he was deep inside?

He took a deep breath. He had seconds, if that. He darted out into the open, scouring the ground and the asphalt, trying to find anything that could help him. A shred of his son that he could use to get some kind of hope.

Hope, he thought. *The worst of human emotions. As it makes men believe that there is a way out of the despair they are trapped in.* But he had to try. He had to believe.

He fell to his hands and knees, searching the ground. He would not abandon his son again. They had locked him away, they had taken his life from him, and now he had a second chance to make things right. He prayed internally. Screamed in his mind as time ticked by. The officers were shouting at each other. Relaying messages on their radios. The sound of feet crunching on gravel. He didn't have long. Then he saw it. It was only small, hidden in between discarded receipts and McDonald's cups. A pink driver's license. He scooped it up between his fingers, his eyes falling on the face staring back at him. It was him all right. He would remember that disgusting face anywhere.

"Hey!" A voice called. A bolt of fear rattled through Jamie's body. Desolation stabbed his heart as he turned and saw officers racing towards him. Jamie hauled himself up onto his feet before driving towards the main road.

Chapter Eight

Laura

Laura was ushered into the office by Alice. She turned her head a couple of times, making sure Laura was following closely behind. It reminded her of a time in her early twenties when she met a guy outside of a nightclub, and she agreed to go to the bathroom with him and get to know him *better*. She was a little buzzed, the vodka and lack of sleep doing a number on her coordination. The paranoia set in as officers and senior management passed her. They nodded to her as they went, wanting to stop and talk.

"Ma'am."

Was she walking properly?

"Good morning, Ma'am."

Where was Alice taking her?

"How are you, ma'am?"

Had someone smelt the booze on her breath?

"I'll catch up with you later," she replied, very conscious of the alcohol that still burned her tongue. She focused her mind and kept up appearances. She could feel the numbness settling into her body. She thought of pretending to feel ill if someone said something.

"You don't look too hot ma'am, you okay?"

Sickness would do it. It was going around. A few people had been struck off with it. She would have drove her fingers down her throat and threw up on the blue carpet of the office right then and there, but she couldn't go home and face Celine.

Why are you drinking at work? This is getting out of hand.

I can't sleep. I can't think. I can't focus. He's gone. Gone for good. And the toxic hope I had in my heart that he would come back is gone forever, and now I can't face a life knowing that I have to live without him.

But you hated him.

Yes. And I hate myself for missing him.

"She's back," Jeremy squealed from behind the monitor. She was standing in the MIU office. She hadn't even noticed. She smiled courtly and closed the door behind her. Almost robotic. Habit.

"I don't feel so good," she said quietly, almost to herself. No one seemed to hear her. Alice had moved to the monitor that the rest of the team was staring at.

"Come here ma'am," Francis said quickly like a dog wanting her to throw his favourite chew toy. If he had a tail, it could power the entire station. She moved to them and stood a foot back, should the booze scent emanate from her without her realising.

"What am I looking at?" She peered at the monitor. It was a white document with the word 'PNC' on the top.

"We managed to get a hit on the vehicle from a camera across the street. He left a few hours later after the abduction. The ANPR confirms it too." Laura's ears pricked up.

"So, who does it come back to?" She said, her mouth beginning to water. She took a drink from the liquid left in her coffee mug. The taste was sharp, but Laura hid it well. Orange juice wasn't her drink of choice to consume poison with. But it was all they had in. She hadn't been shopping in a while. Alice flicked through the various photos and then onto the force database. She typed in the car registration, and it was linked to a nominal. A well-known nominal.

"Gary Murphy," she said. "A child murderer." Laura felt her stomach churn like a cement mixer filled with bile. This whole thing just got so much worse. So, it *wasn't* the father. Part of her now wished it was. The room fell silent. She clicked his last custody photo. He was a new level of ugly. His lips huge and his glasses thick-rimmed, making his eyes bulge out. His face was so filled with craters that she was amazed NASA hadn't tried to land a shuttle on it.

"He hasn't come to our attention for ten years. In and out of prison for theft and drug offences. Finally got sent down for manslaughter of a child. He's been out eight months."

"Does he have a probation worker?"

"Yeah," Alice said. "We've checked. Not a blip on his record since getting out."

"And this is the guy we think took the child?" Alice shrugged.

"He was at the scene. He argued with Jamie. The child was there. We saw him drive past the two of them and then park up. Then the child is gone." Laura stood upright.

"That's good enough for me," she said. "Let's go bring him in, and we can search the house." Laura turned to Catherine who was dipping a tea bag into a cup of hot water. "Any luck with that number I gave you?"

"Last time it came to our attention, it was used to call in a capsized boat eight years ago. Nothing since then." Laura grimaced.

"Thanks for checking. Keep your eye on it. It may be useful later down the line."

"One more thing," Francis piped up, reaching for the computer mouse. Alice pulled her hand away, her fingers gliding across the top of Laura's hand. They locked eyes for a moment, then Alice looked away as if nothing had happened. Francis flicked through some tabs quickly, using keyboard shortcuts none of the others knew existed. Simple things, but it sped up the process of gathering information, and when seconds mattered, that shit was impressive.

"I looked into Jamie Green's associates on the database. He doesn't have many, but he was involved in a court case with his kid a few years back. Linked to him is a guy called 'Declan Murphy'. A local weed dealer."

"Okay," Laura said, still thinking about the lingering touch of Alice.

"He was arrested last night for a domestic disturbance. Get this, the mother of the missing Child, Claire Martin. She threw him out. Shouting about someone called *Eric*?"

"Who the hell is Eric?" Laura said. Francis shrugged. "He was released without charge. Claire said he hasn't been back since. Packed his stuff and left. Something must have spooked him, whoever this Eric guy is. I think we should do some digging."

"Good thinking detective. I like it." Francis' eyes lit up.

"So, what's our next move?" Alice said. Laura ran her tongue around her dry mouth.

"What do you think?"

"We need to go and search the house of Gary Murphy." Laura broke a smile.

"There we go," she said. She turned to Francis. "Find out who this *Eric* is." Francis' eyes snapped wide.

"Well," he said meekly. "I was hoping I could come with you to find the boy?" Laura thought about this, then accepted.

"Okay," she said. She turned to Catherine. Catherine eyed her back.

"I have a lot on today," she said. Laura tightened her smile.

"Well, you're going to have a busy afternoon then, aren't you?" Catherine rolled her eyes, moved to her desk, and began typing away like a well-trained dog. "Jeremy," Laura declared. "You and Catherine head out to see Claire. See what information she can give us. Following that, try and speak to this Declan again. Rattle him a little. See if he says anything. It may be nothing, but the more information we can get out of them, the closer we will be to untangling this web."

"We already have a suspect, ma'am," Jeremy protested, nursing his morning cup of coffee. "Why are we going through all of this?" Laura let out a frustrated breath.

"Something about this whole thing doesn't seem so black and white to me. There's a reason why Jamie Green forgot to mention this guy in the car park. He's hiding something, and I want to know what, and why." She turned to Francis and Alice. "Get kitted up. We're going hunting. Grab a couple of uniform too in case he decides to fight or get on his toes." Francis and Alice eyed each other. It was game on. They moved for the door. Laura spoke. "Oh, and I would also take a dog with us too."

"What for?" Alice asked, but as soon as she did, she knew why. It was in case they needed to search for something.

Like a small body hidden in a crawl space.

Chapter Nine

Jamie

Jamie ran with the jaws of the law chasing him. He bolted out of the car park. The land shark hot on his tail, barking and snarling. He glanced behind him and saw the beast on four legs snapping at the air. Its mouth foaming, ready to rip and tear. He had no time to make it to the alleyway that he had snook in through, which meant he had only one choice. To run straight through the blockade of officers that were running towards him. The jaws of a hound behind him, and the arms of the law in front. He felt like he was being chased by the devil into a flaming building.

He dug deeper, his feet slamming against the ground as officers stood clad in black and high-vis. He had to get through them. To keep running and charge through them like it was a game of bulldog on the playground. To stop at nothing. Not only did his freedom (and life) depend on it, but also his son. There was no way that the officers would stop and listen to him now. The snarling of the hound drew closer. Jamie could almost feel the hot breath on the back of his legs. The exit closed in quickly.

Fifty metres.

"Stop!" An officer screamed. He was as big as a door and as broad as one too. He stood by the taped-off exit, ready to smash Jamie's ribs to pieces with his baton.

Twenty - Five metres.

His lungs burning. Chest heaving. Heart hammering. His mind racing faster than the adrenaline injected into his bloodstream that yammered every possibility and eventuality that could occur in this moment and every moment following.

Red dots dancing around his chest and stomach like fireflies. An officer pointing a taser at his chest.

Ten.

Teeth graced his calf.

This is it.

He darted sharply to the right, the snap of the taser cutting through the air and the crackle of electricity rattling through the air like popcorn thrown onto an open fire. The barbs of the taser went wide. One collided with the dog. It fell to the ground, howling and yipping. Its handler running quickly behind it, calling out its name and screaming for it to heel. But with the promise of blood, the hound had other ideas. It leapt back to its feet and continued its pursuit. The officer with the baton swung at Jamie, who threw himself onto the ground and rolled, the tip of the instrument narrowly missing the crown of his head. Jamie was on his feet again in a shot, propelling himself to freedom.

Against all odds, he made it to the police cordon and dove under the tape. A police vehicle sped into the street, and its brakes screeched as it slammed to a halt, the sirens blaring. Jamie couldn't stop. His legs wouldn't allow it. He leapt onto the bonnet, slamming his feet into the car which bounced and pulsed under his weight. The shocked eyes of the occupants as he dove from the roof, landing hard on the ground, stumbling forward and continuing into the busy street of cars and onlookers.

The dog was fast behind him, following his scent. Gorging on his fear. It easily launched itself over the vehicle, kicking up dirt and gravel as it pursued after him. Jamie flew out of the side street and across traffic to the sound of blaring horns. Cars swerved, crashing into each other.

He pushed through a store door and the bell rattled loudly, charging through isles of confectionary and magazines. People jumped out of the way, Jamie throwing the slower ones to the floor.

"Move!" He screamed. The dog raged through the store, jumping on top of the aisles and bounding down to Jamie. It landed on his back, pushing him onto his front, knocking the wind out of him. The animal wrapped its jaws around his jeans, snarling and growling viciously. Jamie slammed his other foot in its snout, and it released its grasp with a howl. He clambered to his feet, hauling himself up on the counter, before diving over it. The shop owner stared in horror. Jamie lunged at him, snatching the baseball cap off his head and grabbing a pair of sunglasses from the shelving. He raced through the back door and through the stock room, finally bursting through the back door where two workers were standing drinking coffee and smoking cigarettes, hardly able to pull themselves away from their phones to notice him. A small car park filled with waterlogged potholes met his eye and beyond that, a shrubbery with trees and bushes. He keeled over, panting wildly. His body in overdrive, his insides ready to paint the ground. He had to relent soon. He was redlining, the adrenaline pump beginning to run dry. The sound of shouting and then fierce barking pressed through the open back door. Jamie snatched his head back to see the two workers staring into the void. He didn't need to wait around, and he forced himself for one last push.

Jamie moved up to the small embankment of mud and clay and threw himself into the bushes and shrubbery, twigs and logs and nestles and thorns cutting and smacking and snagging him, trying to hold him in place in order to be devoured.

The back door burst open and ricocheted off the brick wall. The two workers recoiled, dropping their coffee cups onto the ground as the police land shark blasted through the opening, headed straight for Jamie.

"Fuck!" He cursed, pressing through the thorns and thickets. He moved, the dog quickly gaining on him. The sound of its panting matched the fast beating of his heart. He wasn't looking where he was going. His eyes fixed on the black spheres of malice and the dog's sharp teeth.

His foot snagged a rock, sending him tumbling into the mud and leaves. That was all it took. The hound was upon him. His face was bombarded with teeth, saliva and fur. Snarling and barking punched his hearing with its sharp tones. He grabbed the dog by the side of its head. The thing was as big as a bear. Its paws scratched at him, its jaw snapping an inch from his face. Thick saliva slapped his cheeks. The dog was heavy, and all of its weight was on his chest. He couldn't breathe, desperation gripping him like a viper around his throat that didn't want to let go until it had taken all of him to the bone. He grabbed a thick branch and jammed it between those snapping jaws. Its teeth burrowed into the wood and splintered and snapped in its mouth. He slammed his fist into the mutt's face with his free hand. The thing's skull was as hard as rock, and Jamie felt pain erupt in his wrist. He cried out in pain. He punched the beast again, but it didn't relent. The dog released the branch in a flash and snatched its jaws forward for his face. Without thinking, with blind primal instinct, Jamie raised his forearm, and the animal sank its teeth into him.

Pain flooded his body. The dog shook its head violently like it had caught an escaping rat. Blood filled the beast's jaws as it ripped and tore, coating its brown fur in copper.

Jamie could feel its teeth scraping along his bone like dull knives. His jacket soaked with burning red. He screamed. Oh, how he screamed.

Jamie felt hatred. The part of him he kept locked away. His old friend. His hunger for pain and suffering rose up and consumed him. He reeled himself up, grabbed a rock from the dirt and smashed it against the beast's skull.

It yelped loudly, its body shaking, releasing his arm and staggered back, pawing at its face. It turned out, as Jamie found out then, even animals can scream, its face coated in thick blood and gloop. The hound howling and falling into the mud and dirt.

Jamie crawled to his feet, the blood from his arm drenching his trousers. He saw officers appearing at the crest of the woodland, peering in, listening to the hellish wailing of the animal. He stumbled through the thicket, his body weak, wiping the fragments of fur and bone from his mouth. The sounds of the dog dying away in the distance. The sound of sirens fading into the air.

He didn't know how long he had been walking until he reached a wire fence. He used his working hand to haul himself over and disappeared further into the woodlands. His breath heavy. All around him nothing but dying leaves in a mushy red and orange autumn.

He stopped a moment and found refuge on a rotting tree stump. He checked his arm, pulling back the fabric of his long sleeve shirt. He nearly threw up at the sight. The blood was thick and dark, which wasn't good. It indicated that the dog had cut through veins and the blood slithered out of him lazily like a black ooze. The flesh was parted in a jagged tear, with his skin turned a bruised black and the inside of the wound bulging brown fatty tissue and red torn muscle.

He pulled off his shirt and tore one of the arms off and tied it tightly around his bicep, forcing pressure on the artery in a makeshift torniquet. The blood seemed to slow, but it wouldn't hold forever. He couldn't go to the hospital. He wouldn't make it home. The cops would be looking for him there. He was going to bleed out if he didn't get help, but help was a hard thing to find when you were wanted. He had to make the call. He had to get *him* involved. He swore he would never call on him. A ghost of his past. But he pulled his phone out of his pocket with shaking fingers. He looked into his wallet. Fear wrapped through him.

"Where is it?" The note with his number on. It wasn't there. He couldn't think where it could be. His mind fired a thousand thoughts at once, only to draw a blank. He tried to remember the number. He punched in some combinations.

"Mark's takeaway," the voice said at the end of the phone. He killed the call. He tried again. The phone rang. Jamie waited with bated breath.

"It's about time you called me," the voice said. Jamie swallowed dryly.

"It's me…"

"Who?"

"Me!" He emphasised the word. A beat of silence passed.

"I don't know who this is?" The voice sounded younger. Jamie checked the call. "Who is this? Is this Courtney?" The voice said. Jamie hung up the phone. He leant back on the dead stump. He caught his breath and tried one more time. The phone rang.

"Come on, you fuck…" The call connected. Only heavy breathing and beats of silence.

"It's me," Jamie whispered. The breathing through the receiver slowed.

"You must be in some serious trouble to be calling me up," the voice said. Jamie nodded.

"I need you to come pick me up," he said.

"Is it hot?"

"No," John said. "They've stopped looking." Jamie heard the drag of a cigarette.

"You on a burner?"

"Yeah. I'll text you where to meet me." Jamie hung up the phone. What was he doing? The number he never wanted to call, but here he was texting the GPS location to him.

Jamie moved through the thicket to a small country road. He hid in the bushes. The sound of a police helicopter flying overhead. He ducked into the undergrowth and waited. Bugs and spiders crawling over his still body, as the steel bird fluttered overhead. The day began to bleed to night, and eventually the chopper slipped away. Jamie felt the old chill his bones. Shaking and weary, he forced life into his frozen legs, and stumbled through the rest of the wood.

By the time the transit van appeared, the bleeding had finally stopped. He was ice cold. The dampness of his clothes and the winter air cutting through him, leeching the heat from his bones. He got into the van and the warm cab enveloped him. A medical bag on the centre console, along with a bottle of rum and some painkillers. Jamie shut the passenger door. Seeing him again was like staring at the face of a ghost. John Heywood passed him a black hoodie.

"Throw that over you," John said with disdain. Jamie pulled it over him. Then, John handed him the painkillers and rum. "You look like shit."

"Just get me out of here," Jamie said, sinking the drugs and swallowing a mouthful of rum. John sighted his arm. He took out a plastic bag.

"Put it in here," he said, gesturing to his arm. "Don't want the police finding your blood in my van now do we?" Jamie did as requested, then rested his head against the window. John reversed out of the country lane and set off towards home. He eyed him. "Good to see you back in the game, Eric," John said with a smirk. Jamie stared out of the window as the world passed him by.

No matter how far he ran, the devil, it would seem, would always find him.

Chapter Ten

Laura

Alice and Francis kitted up, throwing on their body armour, handcuffs, and grabbing their captor spray and radios. Alice emerged in a slick black tac vest with a shiny new taser in its holster. Francis had to stick some WD40 on his cuffs.

"It's been a while," he said with a smile. Laura laughed.

"Then let's get those babies working." They marched into the main office, and Laura approached two cops typing away on their computers.

"Ma'am," one of them said, looking up at her from behind his monitor. A coffee by his side that he had probably been trying to drink all morning and half a subway footlong that no doubt they had just bought. She hated pulling cops away from what little downtime they had, but this was important.

"You both busy?" She said firmly. They shared a look with each other. There was a hierarchy of what 'being busy' meant. If it was someone of the same rank, then it went off how much you liked them. One rank above, a little wiggle room. Any higher, and you were always free.

"What do you need?" The officer said.

"We're going to this address," she passed a piece of paper with the address of Gary Murphy. She moved away, heading for the locker room. "Meet me outside in five minutes." Like an unheard cue, both officers closed their workloads, took a last hasty bite of their food, and sank their cold coffee before throwing their kit on and moving for the front doors.

Laura slipped into the locker room and began gearing herself up. She grabbed a radio and put it on the right channel. She needed to wash her stab vest badly. It was covered in grime and dried blood. No matter how hard she scrubbed it, it wouldn't come off. The day in that room with Sheree strapped to a chair. Craig brandishing a knife. Dennis. Oh, Dennis. How he had been lured into something so horrific and toxic. His mind completely convoluted by the hopes and dreams of a better world and how he had been ensnared into the sinister plan of a complete psychopath. She felt a small level of pity for him. After the inquest and the IOPC had finished sticking their noses in everything, it transpired that Dennis had scored high on the spectrum of autism, and as such, he was an easier target for a predator like Craig. Did it excuse the atrocities that he was part of? No. But it made him seem a little more human, and less of a monster. Something Laura had much experience with.

"Laura." The voice was quiet, and not one she was expecting. She turned and saw Celine standing at the end of the lockers.

"What are you doing here?" The sight of her made her stomach churn. She couldn't figure out why, but just the sight of her made her skin crawl. It seemed that the closer she got, the more she wanted to push her away. Her therapist had described it as a defence mechanism. In reality, it was more a way of her hitting self-destruct. If she believes that no one will love her, and she pushes away anyone that tries, then that will reaffirm her belief, and thus the cycle continues. Which was why she drank. But she was self-aware in her own annihilation. Otherwise, she would be a bulldozer with no driver. This way, she could decide what to destroy.

"I need to speak to you," Celine pled. She looked like she had been crying. No. She was *still* crying. Her eyes were bloodshot. Her lips trembling. Her hair unwashed. She looked awful, and that made her even more repugnant.

"I'm busy," Laura said dismissively, fixing her kit together. Laura moved to walk past her. Celine put her hand between her and the locker, slamming her palm against the metal door, which rattled around the room.

"No," she said fiercely, holding back the tears. "You aren't right now."

"Celine," Laura scoffed. "Whatever it is, we can talk after I get home from work. Right now, I have more…" she took a moment. "I have other things to worry about."

"More important than us, you mean?" She said meekly.

"Jesus, not this again," she hissed. "Yes," Laura bit. "More important than us. Now move." She tried to push past her again, but Celine closed the gap. Laura let out a frustrated huff. "What the fuck do you want Celine? A hug? An apology? A trip to Vienna?"

"I just want to talk." She wiped a leaking tear from her eye. "I feel like I'm losing you. I feel like I am trying to help you. Talk to you, but you aren't there. Even when you are, you're drunk. Or if you aren't drunk, you're completely absent from everything, like you're dead behind the eyes."

"You're suffocating me."

"I'm trying to help you!"

"We can talk later." Laura pushed past her. If a person could break into pieces, then Celine was doing that right now. Laura moved through the locker room towards the exit without looking back.

"Don't you love me?" Celine cried as she moved away. Laura stopped on the spot. Those words. Why was she clinging to such desperation? It made her seem weak. Pathetic. The fact that Laura was busy and had things to do. Things much bigger than the feelings of a woman she had been fucking for a few months. Since the case with

Craig and Dutton, everything had moved so fast. Even when she was in the hospital, after having some time off work, Celine was there. All the time, right there in her space and in her head. No wonder she drank. She hadn't had time to process anything that had happened because she had an emotional leech sucking everything out of her and demanding her attention all the damn time. Laura span on her heel.

"You know what, Celine?" She said, the rage that had built in her stomach spewing out like vitriolic acid. "You're pathetic. I have done nothing but spend time with you, care for you and have you in my home. Now you come to my work and tell me that I am being distant and *you* don't feel heard? And then you have the audacity when I tell you I can't fucking talk right now because I am busy, you play some emotional blackmailing bullshit? It's manipulative and, quite frankly, pitiful." Laura enunciated the last few words, her voice rising. Celine looked like she was about to melt into the ground. Laura was panting loudly, looking her up and down like she was a cancer that needed to be cut out of her life. "Get your shit out of my fucking home. I don't want you there by the time I finish work." Laura eyed her for another second, waiting for a response. "Well?" She bit. "Are you going to say anything? Or are you just going to stand here crying onto the carpet like the pathetic cunt you are?"

Celine's lips were bubbling, and her body folded in two. She brought her trembling hands up to her face, grabbed her hair, and ran her fingers through her braids. Her staggering breaths finally broke from a silent scream that was etched along her face.

"You sound just like Ron," Celine croaked. "This isn't you." Laura forced down the steam train of pain that was swelling in her throat.

"Celine," she said, rage in her eyes. "You don't know the first thing about me," she hissed. "What's my favourite colour?" Celine was like a deer trapped in headlights.

"Purple." Laura's blood pressure rose a notch.

"I don't have a favourite colour. I'm a fucking adult." She looked Celine up and down with malice, and moved away, feeling the knives of Celine's gaze in her back as she moved away, trying to stop her eyes from burning from the tears that wanted to break through. Out in the car park, Alice, Francis, and the other officers were waiting.

"What kept you?" Alice said. Laura fired her a look of death. Alice recoiled.

"Just some home shit," Laura said, moving towards the cars.

"You need to talk about it?" Alice said meekly, following behind her.

"Do I *look* like I want to talk about it?" Laura spoke with fire. "We'll go in two separate cars," she said quickly, moving the subject along. "I'll cover the front, the other cover the back." She gestured to Alice. "Have you called for a dog?"

"The only dog patrol is tied up right now. Something about an incident at the scene." This made Laura's blood run cold.

"What?"

"It just came over the radio, ma'am," Francis said, butting into the conversation. "Something about someone interfering with the crime scene. Dogs in a bad way." Laura squinted her eyes shut.

You're just like Ron.

The two officers joined them in the car park, asking what their next instruction was.

Fuck, I need a drink.

"Should we wait for another dog?" Jeremy said, his long coat swaying in the wind. "We can have one here within an hour."

What's happened to you?

"Fuck it," Laura snapped, instinctively reaching for her pack of cigarettes. "We will go anyway. We can search the house later when he is in custody." Laura moved to her unmarked squad car – a sleek new BMW with all the bells and whistles. She cracked the passenger door and slipped inside. The rest of the unit stood there eyeing each other, unsure of who was going with whom. She didn't give them direction. They were grown adults and detectives. She was sure they could figure it out.

Alice moved to Laura's car while Francis went into the other. The two cops moved to the marked panda parked outside the main gates. Alice cocked the door and slid in. Her perfume hit Laura like a scented kiss. Something flowery. Fresh. Was she wearing an extra-tight dress today? She hadn't noticed, but now she was, and Laura could hardly keep her eyes off her. Alice turned to her, her hair flowing down past her shoulders.

"Ma'am," she said curtly. Laura didn't know if she was imagining it, but she was sure that Alice had just fucked her with her eyes. Maybe she was imagining it? Maybe she hoped it was true.

"Do you know where you're going?" Laura said, lighting the smoke and cracking the window. Alice eyed the cigarette. Laura caught her glance. "You have a problem with me smoking in a work car?" Alice shrugged the comment away.

"Not at all," she said. She punched the address in the sat nav and side-eyed her. "I can keep a secret."

Chapter Eleven

Laura

The roads blurred past as they blue-lighted to the address of Gary Murphy. It was on the other side of town, and the loud blaring of horns and the screeching of tyres gave a strange sense of calm, like collecting a thought during a thunderstorm. Was she too tough on Celine? Was she breaking into pieces like she said? Was she becoming like Ron? A kind of transmitted abuse? Had he infected her and turned her soul black?

"What happened with the dog?" Laura said, breaking her train of thought like she was cutting a tough rung of chains with giant steel teeth.

"Someone was interfering with a crime scene," Alice said relaxed. You wouldn't think she was driving nearly triple the speed limit through oncoming traffic. Something response cops got used to: living their lives on the edge of a razor blade so often that they didn't feel it cutting them anymore. "They chased the guy from the scene and through the street. They lost him shortly afterwards. Apparently, the dog is hurt. Badly. Officers are looking at the footage and searching for him now."

"Why was someone at the crime scene?" Alice shrugged.

"Beats me," she said, turning a hard right to avoid an oncoming car, not a bead of sweat on her head. Laura opened her phone and dialled Jamie Green's number. It went straight to voicemail.

"Jamie, it's DI Warburton," she said. "I need you to contact me ASAP." She ended the call.

"You think it's the dad?" Alice said.

"I don't know what I think," Laura said. Without thinking, she found herself digging into her pocket and fingering the measure of vodka. She pulled her hand out quickly, recomposing herself. Laura got onto the radio and asked the force control room to dispatch someone to Jamie Green's house. She passed the address, and they said they'd put it on the list when another patrol became available.

"What's it regarding ma'am?" The operator queried.

"Safe and well check," she lied. "Let me know when it gets done." She turned to Alice. "If this guy isn't here, we'll go and check ourselves." They sped through the busy streets, past the retail parks and took a right onto the dual carriageway that bled through the town and connected it to the other metropolitan cities in the county.

"I'm happy that you let me come with you," Alice said. "I wanted to work with you for a while. Since hearing about what you did? And you rescued that girl? I was like, woah. I *have* to work with that detective. I could really learn something amazing."

"Nothing amazing about it," Laura said vacantly, looking out of the window at the standing traffic as they cut through them like Moses parting the red sea. She didn't offer anymore. The adulation she was being offered fell flat on her ears. She didn't know what it felt like to be admired. She had never had it. And now that she was getting it, she hated it. She moved up to this county to make a life and a name for herself. And now she had, she detested it. She despised the newspapers that had her face on with triumphant cheers and headlines. She despised the frequent reporters that wanted to snap a shot of her on duty. And above all, she hated that she left her old life to get away from her abusive ex-boyfriend, to escape his shadow, and now she had built a life under the eclipse of his bloodline. To live forever under him, in his memory. It was like a vicious wind eroding her mind, body and soul away. Suddenly, adulation and praise didn't quite feel so good.

Her phone rang. It was Celine. She hadn't stopped calling since Laura had left the police station. She hung up the phone. Two seconds later, it rang again. And again, she killed the call.

"Who keeps blowing up your phone?" Alice giggled.

"A friend."

"Seems like a good friend," she said. Laura felt a stab of pain in her stomach. Alice was dangerously close to stepping over the line. Still, Laura let her tread over the minefield and was waiting to see if she triggered an explosion. The phone called again. Laura eyed it like a rattlesnake uncoiling and moving towards her.

"What?" She snapped, putting the phone to her ear. Sniffling met the receiver.

"You wanted to talk to me?" It was Jamie Green. Laura composed herself.

"Where were you today?"

"Looking for my son, like you should be doing." He sounded drunk.

"I need you to come to the station later today."

"Why?"

"To talk to you about the case." A moment of silence, then a slither of laughter.

"Find my son, detective. Stop looking into what I'm doing." The call went dead. Laura eyed the handset. Alice raised a brow.

"That our guy?" Laura ignored the comment. She got back onto the radio.

"Cancel the safe and well." They happily obliged. One less job for them. Laura's phone went again. She answered it after a few rings, taking every bit of her strength not to throw it out of the window at ninety.

"Go on," she said. It was Celine.

"I don't know what I have done wrong," she stammered down the phone. "All I have done is care for you. Love you. And you treat me like shit."

"We'll talk about this later, okay? I'm working. Got a lot on right now. You can hear the sirens, can't you? I can't talk right now." Laura put the phone down and switched it off. She sat back, the speeding traffic blurring past them. Alice changed the tone of the sirens from a long wail to a quick and rapid blast, telling others to move out of the way or feel the force of metal crushing into them. They reluctantly obliged. The siren changed back to a stretching scream, and they sped along the right-hand lane. ETA four minutes.

"Want to talk about it?" Alice said, peering at Laura, who was sitting back with her fingers pinching the bridge of her nose.

"There's nothing to talk about," she said vacantly, trying to stop the tears from breaking from her eyelids. She forced the ball of razors down into her stomach with the rest of her emotions, and they joined the graveyard of unsaid things and broken promises. "Just keep driving."

Chapter Twelve

Jamie

Jamie hung up the phone and stared at the blank screen with hatred. The rum had numbed his tongue. He knew he had been slurring, but he didn't give a shit. The booze made the pain in his arm seem far away, and the blood loss paired with the half a bottle of rum coursing through his veins would make for a great buzz.

"Who was that?" John Heywood said, as they drove down the busy roads, turning off to a side street and then along a country path to the outskirts of Wigtown.

"Some bitch detective I'm talking to." John snapped his eye to Jamie.

"You speaking to the police?" Jamie felt his skin prickle. John reached out his hand. "Give me that phone now." Jamie did as instructed. John steered with one hand, unclipped the battery of the old Nokia, threw it out the window and then swallowed the sim card, washing it down with a gulp of energy drink with a satisfied sigh. "No police. You're with me, remember?" Jamie nodded. He remembered all right, as hard as he tried not to.

The two of them continued down the country lane, passing sheep and old disused farms. The horizon opened up, revealing miles of green grass. The sun hung lazily in the sky, barely picking the temperature up above freezing. Jamie re-tied his makeshift tourniquet and poured alcohol gel on the wound. Even with the help of Captain Morgan, the touch was like acid, and he bit down and slammed his fist into the dashboard.

"Fuck!" He seethed, his heartbeat red lining.

"You sure you don't want to go to the hospital?" John said. "You've lost a lot of blood."

"No!" Jamie seethed through gritted teeth, his eyes squeezed shut. "Take me to the yard. I'll patch myself up there, and then I have a stop to make."

"You're talking to a cop, and you don't want to go to the hospital," John pursed his old lips, the grey whiskers of his stubble tickling his aged skin. "What trouble have you got yourself into this time?" He said with an aged laugh.

"Not me," Jamie said. "It's my son. He's been taken by someone." John's complexion dulled.

"Oliver?" Jamie nodded. "And this police bitch," John said, turning a corner. "She doing much to find him?"

"The police aren't doing anything," Jamie seethed, pressing down on the wound. "They told me to sit and wait until I hear something. Like I'm going to do that. Nearly two days now. Still nothing." Jamie felt like his throat was being clamped in an iron vice. Fighting desperately to hold onto hope.

"What happened to your arm?" John pointed at the wound like it was a fine piece of art. You take a chainsaw to it? There are easier ways to lose weight."

"Police dog got me in the woods." John let out a barrel of laughter and slapped the steering wheel.

"Fucking hell Eric," he laughed loudly. "I thought you left all this shit when Interpol got a hold of you." Jamie went quiet. A memory he wasn't fond of. Making a deal to save his skin, at the cost of many others. He was a marked man for life.

"It's Jamie now," he said. "Jamie Green. That's the name they gave me when I got out." John queried this.

"Well, my name's Twinkle Toes then," he said. "What you did put a lot of people out of business. Lucky thing we've known each other so long, or I'd be feeding you your heart." He said it with a smile, but Jamie knew John meant every word of it.

"I know who took him," Jamie whispered. John leaned in.

"Speak louder lad, my old ears aren't as good as they used to be."

"I said, I know who has taken Oliver. And when I'm done here, I'm going straight to his house." Jamie took another drink of the rum and forced it down his gullet where it exploded in a wave of heat. John turned to him, and he didn't see a man in pain, nor a man gripped by rage. But a man who had come to the resolution that there was nothing else to lose. That he was on a mission, and he would not stop until he had fulfilled that mission. He didn't try to talk him out of it. Jamie was too far gone.

John's children had grown up and had joined the business. But he knew the pain of losing a grandchild. The thought of someone taking one of them and doing God knows what to them. He would see the world burn if it meant bringing them back home safely.

"So, you need my help…" John said. "More than just for your arm."

"You owe me," Jamie bit. John turned his head, taking his eyes off the road. He pondered a response. A *fuck you* or an *eat shit*. But instead, he came to the resounding conclusion that 'Jamie Green' was right. He did owe him. "I never wanted to call on you," Jamie continued. "But yes, as much as I hate to admit it. I need your help."

"Okay," John said, turning a right down another country lane that was flanked by thick trees in every direction.

Maybe he's in there? Jamie thought, looking into the thicket. The leaves and trees blurring past. Maybe he would catch a glimpse of a child with blonde hair running for his life with monsters behind him.

"Thanks," Jamie said.

"What for?"

"For not trying to talk me out of it." Both men sat in silence then, Jamie nursing the rum. John held out his hand, and Jamie gave him a hit off the bottle. He snarled as it went down.

"Let's get you patched up," John said. "The boys will be thrilled to see you again."

A short drive later, they turned into the industrial site. A disused breakfast van outside in a lay by ironically boasting the world's 'best fried egg sandwiches,' 'fresh coffee' and of course, 'baked potatoes.'

They moved through the estate and found themselves affronted by a large metallic unit with disused and abandoned cars that looked like a creature that feasted on metal and rubber had been gorging on them. Only the skeletons of their former glory remained. Atop of those, shredded bikes and motorcycles, old washing machines and kitchen appliances, and even mobility scooters. The sign 'Grey's Scrapyard,' mounted above the iron graveyard.

The two men got out of the car and moved into the foyer. The smack of the cold country air made Jamie's alcohol levels rise and he had to steady himself on the side of the van. John rushed to him, slung his arm over his shoulder, and stumbled into the building.

A small reception desk greeted them that was caked in mud and axle grease at least a centimetre thick. An old computer blinked and hummed with keys so thick in oil and sludge that one would have to fight to type simple commands. Next to it, a stack of folders with dog-eared brown stained pages. A young man sat behind the desk reading a Marvel comic. He had grown since Jamie last saw him.

"Ryan," John said, as they stepped into the warehouse that had a plywood wall that separated the entrance from the even colder back warehouse, which led to the back yard that was fenced off, with a sign telling people to beware of the dogs, although no paws or slavering jaws were there to be wary of.

Ryan didn't budge from his chair.

"Ryan!" John blasted, an icy plume escaping his mouth. Ryan jumped up from his chewed-up swivel chair and kicked off his cup of cold coffee onto the ground where it smashed into shards of ceramic. His black cargo pants were almost as greased up and covered in soot as his hands and face. His small amount of facial hair barely noticeable. He resembled a Middle Ages knight that had been oiled. All that was missing was the feathers and fire.

"Oh jeez!" Ryan said, jumping to his feet, his eyes falling on Jamie. "Is that uncle Eric?" He rushed to him. "What happened?"

"Don't touch him with the state of your hands lad," John said. "Go and grab some bandages from the back." Ryan did so without any protesting. He bolted into the back and returned a minute later with a first aid kit that looked fresh off the shelf. Jamie was let go onto a small chair that was bolted to the wall next to a stained radiator where he slumped like a sack of meat, barely holding onto consciousness. John took the first aid kit off Ryan. "Where's your brother?"

"He's in the back. Want me to get him?"

"Yes!" He barked. Again, Ryan vanished from the reception and could be heard shouting his brother's name, reverberating around the compound. John opened the kit and took out a numbing agent, a syringe, and liquid antibiotics. He put a pouch in between his teeth and tore it open, and removed some isopropyl alcohol wipes. He eyed Jamie. "This is going to sting."

"Lay it on me." Jamie removed the bandages and marvelled at the dog bite. His bone was showing through like a slither of pale in between bulbous pink lips. Puncture wounds surrounded the gash like fleshy craters. John put on the blue rubber gloves and quickly doused the wound in alcohol. Jamie winced and managed to keep the scream at bay, clutching the side of the chair so tight his knuckles turned as white as morning snow. Quickly, John got in deep with the alcohol wipes. Finally, he removed a needle and thread and roughly stitched the wound together. Before snipping the thread, he cleaned the dripping fat and blood with another wipe. The wound was still gaping in patches like a fleshy grin. He eyed Jamie, who had turned the same shade of dirty cream as the walls behind him. He nodded. John took out the stapler from behind the counter and slammed on it, forcing the straggling flesh back together. Jamie finally let out a gasp of pain. His body doused in sweat. His head pounding to the sound of a marching band that'd had way too much caffeine that morning. Lastly, John took out the antibiotics, filled a syringe, flicked the end to get the excess air out, and jammed it into Jamie's quivering bicep. An iodine wipe later, along with some bandages, Jamie could finally release the breath that had been trapped in his lungs.

"Jesus," he said, gasping. "You get faster at that every time."

"You're welcome," John replied with a smirk appearing along his aged face. Jamie went to stand, but John pushed him back onto the chair. "You're going nowhere just yet lad," he said. Ryan returned with a cup of coffee that steamed into the cool air. "Get that down you." Jamie took it in his shaking hands. The feeling of fatigue began to wane in. "Ryan, I told you to get your brother," John spat.

"He's busy. He's out back."

"I don't care if he's meeting with the president of the USA! Go get him!" Ryan disappeared again. John let out a frustrated sigh.

"After I find my boy," Jamie said wearily. "I'll be getting this checked out at the hospital. But only when he's been found." Jamie spent the next minute recounting the events. From the argument with the guy in the car park, to the ineptitude of the police, and then to being chased around town by a shark with legs. Ryan and John sat there, needing to stop Jamie from getting out of his chair and getting behind the car's wheel to break someone's legs and iron their skin until he got the creases out.

Ryan emerged a few minutes later. Simon was stocky with tattoos covering his arms that had since worn away, now resembling an oil slick. His beard thick and black. Eyes dark like great white sharks. John looked upon his boys with proudness, like an ageing lion passing the leadership of the pride lands to his cubs. "Simon," John said. "Go upstairs and get my toolbox." Simon moved away silently.

"What about me, Dad?" Ryan said eagerly. John threw him the car keys. "Go warm the car. You're driving." Ryan went to protest, but he knew better. Simon emerged with a large duffel bag and placed it on the floor. John thanked him and zipped it open. He took out pairs of black leather gloves, balaclavas, false license plates, a crowbar and a box cutter. Jamie eyed the box of goodies like it was Christmas.

"I knew you never left the trade," Jamie laughed.

"Never know when you'll need to dip your toe back in." John donned the rubber gloves, and they cracked around his knuckles. Simon put them on too and threw a pair to

Jamie. Simon eyed the box cutter, the dried blood staining the razor edge. "Who we thinking took your boy?" John said. Jamie fished his hand into his pocket, and pulled out the drivers license and passed it to John.

"Here," Jamie said. John studied the face, and his jaw dropped. His eyes began to bulge at the image, and then the name, then a cruel grin spread along his aged face. Jamie eyed him, and a feeling of unease crept over him.

"Something wrong?" Jamie asked. John shook the grin away.

"No," John said. "You sure you're okay to walk?" Jamie forced his way to his feet. A little blood loss never killed anybody.

"I'll be fine," he said. Jamie peered out into the yard at the setting sun. "Going to be dark soon," he said. John cracked a wicked smile.

"Good," he said. "Let's go play."

Chapter Thirteen

Laura

They broke from the carriageway and sped through quieter streets. A blurring parade of blue, with roaring engines and the screeching of tyres as they cut around corners.

"All units," Laura said over the radio. "Silent approach." The deafening sirens turned mute in unison, and the blue lights flickered along the empty streets. Daylight was dying. It had hardly crossed the middle of the afternoon as the breath of winter was descending over the town. The first signs of frost appeared on the tarmac that glistened like a peppering of fine glass. They slipped into a quiet estate. Laura eyed the houses that they passed by. Only a minute or two left before they got to their destination. Her heart began to pick up.

"Kill the lights," she said over the radio. And again, like a magician whispering a spell, the lights vanished. "Headlights, too," she said. More silence. More dark.

The houses were new builds. The flicker of Christmas lights in windows. Winter wreaths hung on the front of doors. It was a pleasant estate. Not the kind of estate one would expect a child killer to live on. She always found it somewhat refreshing when she was in a respectable neighbourhood.

You knew when a cop liked the look of the house when they will sit on the furniture. You know they really like the place when they accept that drink you offer them out of courtesy. Laura almost missed the feeling of clothes under her feet and the stench of animal faeces as she stepped into a house in the back end of some hell hole estate when she was in uniform. The sights she had seen. She remembered once walking into a house to check if they had CCTV for a burglary that had occurred a few doors down and they believed that those responsible had fled past the house she was standing in. A house was one thing she could call it. But it was more accurately donned a rat den. Empty beer bottles lined the skirting boards of the floors. The carpets were non-existent, and the cushioning under her boots was of dirty clothing and even worse – old nappies that hadn't been thrown out. The mother had an infant clinging to her arm. A child with a sweet and innocent smile, in a home that would steal whatever happiness she could dream up in the years to come.

Laura made her excuses, and she requested to use the restroom. The mother – if you could call her that - with a rolled-up cigarette in between what teeth she had that hadn't been worn away by heroin, smiled and said she could.

"I haven't cleaned up, though!" She coughed as Laura made her way up the stairs. She peeked into the bathroom, and she saw what she can only describe as a murder scene in the toilet. On the floor were more clothes, used tampons, and empty bottles of wine. Blunt razors and more evidence of drug use – scrunched up tin foil, fizzy drinks cans with tin foil stretched over the top with holes punctured in them and a hole in the side for the rock to slide through. In the bathtub, there were piles and piles of soaking wet clothes that were growing mould.

Laura moved along the bare floorboards into the child's bedroom. What she saw broke her heart. A huge room, easily capable of being something of beauty and love, had walls defaced with obscene graffiti. There was a clear walkway in the middle of the room, and the walkway flanks were piled high with more bags than she could count, all filled and overflowing with empty bottles of cider, wine bottles and beer. On the far end of the bedroom was a cot without any covers that was coated in thick grime and stains.

Pain flared in Laura's heart. She marched down to the woman who was lighting another cigarette and tore that baby girl out of her arms. The mother screamed of course. Tried to claw Laura. To fight her. To protest that her child was the most important thing in the world to her, as the baby's nappy overflowed and soaked into her uniform. Laura tried to hold the tears back.

"Your baby is coming with me until you sort your life out," and she left. Laura never heard from the woman again, and the child was put into the care system.

Sometimes children can recover from a bad start. Sometimes they are too damaged, and the world they have survived is imprinted on their minds. She pushed the memory away as they pulled up to the target house. Alice killed the engine.

"Lights are off," Alice said, eyeing the darkened house. Laura eyed it too.

"It doesn't mean anything." She pointed to the driveway. "That's our car." She eyed the red fiesta on the driveway. It was the car, all right. Down to the registration plate and the colour of the bird shit on the bonnet. They eyed the darkened house. Bats flitted around the twilight sky.

Let's bring this to an end, she thought. She touched the door handle. "Let's go." They cracked the door and got out of the car, Alice following Laura to the front of the vehicle. The two uniformed officers met them, and so did Francis. "You two," Laura said, pointing to the uniformed officers, their breath permeating the air that danced away into the night sky. "One of you at the back, the other at the front with me and Alice. Francis, head to the back." None protested, and they moved to the darkened house. "Grab a key out the back," she said to the officer, who eagerly trotted to the back of his car. The shuffling of weight and the sound of something heavy dragging onto the tarmac. It was time to get loud.

He returned a second later with a large red ram with a handle on top with chipped paint revealing the brown steel underneath. Its head flat, where an officer had written the words 'KNOCK KNOCK' on the smooth face. She leaned her head to the door and listened for any signs of life. She could hear the faint sound of a television coming from inside, and then the flickering of light from behind the thick curtains that lined the windows. The street was silent. Only the wind dared a whisper.

"Draw your kit." Alice drew her taser, Laura, her baton. Laura turned to the officer with the ram. "Open it." The officer heaved the heavy ram and swung it into the air. It collided with the far side of the door which rattled loudly. The sound of the slamming broke the silence of the night. Birds exploded from trees into the night sky. The officer struck it again at the top corner. The door began to come away from the hinge. Another heave and the top corner blew away, clinging onto the frame weakly. The second hinge came away, and with a final mighty swing, the last of the door fragmented and blasted onto the ground. They converged into the house, screaming like marauding barbarians converging on a castle.

"Police! Stay where you are!"

"Don't move! Officer with taser!"

The officers raced through rooms. Laura moved to the back door and let the other cop and Francis in. Francis bounced upstairs. She heard him moving around above. Footsteps on floorboards.

"Clear!" Francis shouted.

"Clear!" Alice shouted from somewhere in the house. The other officers shouted too. The silence of the house returned, and Laura heard it then. A small scraping sound, like someone dragging nails across drywall. Her mouth ran dry.

"Doesn't seem to be anyone home, Ma'am," Francis said as he walked downstairs. Laura held up a finger, and Francis fell mute.

"You hear that?" They listened to the ensuing quiet. "Someone is in here." The officers silenced their voices like snuffing out a candle flame. Laura stepped lightly on the bare floorboards. The quiet chattering of the television filtered through the house. She moved into the living room. Nothing but a television set and a single seat with a lamp. A few nudie mags strewn onto the floor. Beer bottles. Overflowing ashtrays. Laura turned the television set off. The sound of scraping grew louder, then she heard the groan of a voice. "Hello?" Laura cried. The other officers looked amongst themselves.

"What is it ma'am?" An officer asked. Laura held up her hand, like driving a dagger through his questioning. She moved to the kitchen, the sound growing louder. The kitchen counters were stacked with filthy pots and pans and plates with food welded onto them. Flies buzzed eagerly around the mess. The bins were overflowing and stuffed with takeout boxes. The team followed behind her. Laura took out her torch and shined the beam of light along the room. She saw what appeared to be a broom closet, but upon closer inspection, she found there to be a padlock. Laura fingered it. She pressed her ear against the murky door. The sound of scratching grew louder. She could hear something moving inside. Her heartbeat picked up.

What was in there?

She shot the officers a look of worry. Was someone down there? *Something* down there? Hiding in the dark? Her mind swelled with a cesspool of terrible possibilities. She needed a drink. God, she needed a drink so badly. She could hear breathing on the other side, and it pulled her closer to the door.

Hello?" She whispered. The sound of scratching stopped dead. A blanket of silence fell onto her. Then, the tiniest whisper.

Help me…

Laura recoiled back from the door, her heart bouncing around her chest.

"Open it," Laura barked to the officers. "Now!"

An officer moved to the door and jammed his baton between the door and the lock and pried it open. The lock popped from the door and rattled on the ground. The door yearned open and revealed a black mouth. Laura took out her torch and shined it into the gaping maw.

"I'm here," she said breathlessly. "It's all over now."

Laura felt her body turn to ice.

The emaciated woman sat in rags, her bloodied fingers carving something into the wall. Over and over again, her fingers worn down to bloodied stumps.

Laura Warburton. Laura Warburton. Over and over and over again.

"Oh… God," Laura said, the rasp of air escaping her throat. Photos of her and Ron dangled from the ceiling.

"You didn't save me," the woman hissed. "You didn't save any of us." Laura went to speak, to scream, to cry, but terror clutched her throat. The withered woman, with black wiry hair, half-dressed in a soiled nighty turned to face her. Her eyes were missing, just two fleshy holes of abyssal black staring back at her.

"You should have saved me!" The wretched creature screeched. She opened her mouth, and out poured worms and maggots and beetles that flopped onto the floor, matted with strands of hay. Behind her, the Straw Man appeared with the mask of the dead woman, its eyes sewn up, its hair hanging loosely over his face.

"Kiss kiss, baby."

Laura screamed.

Chapter Fourteen
Jamie

"Holy shit," John whispered as they watched the house of Gary Murphy from across the street in their van. They sat silently, watching the police break down the door. At first, they thought they were too late. They needed to drive away and abandon the mission. But the sight of the detective, no doubt the 'bitch' detective, getting dragged out by a cop in uniform and screaming like a banshee into the night, gave them hope that things hadn't gone quite to plan.

"That's the one in charge of looking for your son?" John said sourly to Jamie who sat quietly, watching the scene unfold. Jamie nodded. John tutted and rolled his eyes. The van fell silent, not a single noise coming from the other men. Simon and Ryan sat quietly in the back, the small door in the bulkhead open so they could get a good view like sitting in the back row of a movie theatre.

"Pathetic," Jamie scoffed, eyeing the insanity in front of him. Laura was being dragged into a car, screaming until her lungs gave out, thrashing like a squid on fire.

"This is why we don't speak to the police, isn't it dad," Ryan said from the back. John nodded.

"Precisely," he said "Just a bunch of tits who don't know their arse from their elbow. Throw you in the slammer for a tick on a piece of paper. You know that oath they swear to? Complete horse shit."

"Where is the guy?" Ryan whispered to the front. "Shouldn't he be in there?" They eyed the house and then the car. Simon's jaw tightened, the knuckles of his leather gloves cracking. John pointed to the parked vehicle on the driveway.

"You sure that's the car?"

"Dead certain," Jamie whispered.

"Let's just hope the pigs disappear before he comes back. Then we'll snatch him. Nice and quiet like." All nodded in agreement. "For now, we wait." The four of them sat quietly. Time stretched on. They searched the house, fixed the hole in the door with a large piece of plywood, and then left. They ducked their heads down as they drove past, the headlights gliding over the van.

Ryan began playing on his phone, and John snatched it from his hand and scolded him.

"No light," he hissed. Ryan slunk back into the darkness. Simon kept his eyes fixated on the dark house. Jamie didn't think he had blinked once. John felt a bubbling of excitement in his heart. He hadn't had to do this for a while. To sit and wait for the target to come home. Something he had missed doing. He wasn't like other men. He was the best at what he did and was proud of it.

Jamie was fixated on the empty house. What was he about to do? But he had no choice. Desperation, it would seem, is more powerful than the morality of men. Desperation will drive men to do the unthinkable. What little conscience he may have, he knew that John was dead behind the eyes. One may touch his hand and feel the warmth of flesh. May see his smile and think there is a human being behind his smile. But you would be mistaken. His reputation precedes him, and why his name was whispered in the darkest corners of the underground clubs and backroom poker games, when those that had no faces needed something to be done.

John saw something moving in the darkness.

"That him?" He said, pointing to the fat figure stumbling jovially drunk down the street. Jamie tensed up. He could still call the whole thing off. But the sight of him. The man responsible for his pain, made his blood run cold. He wanted to inflict pain on him. Pain that even the cruellest hearts in the depths of hell would be envious of. He wanted to watch this man boil in a bathtub of his own blood.

Simon saw him. His jaw tensed and his teeth cracked. He dove for the door, but John turned and grabbed his leather coat and eyed him intently. He shot his eye to the open passenger door. Jamie was already out and marching towards Gary Murphy. The metal bar in his hand.

"Shit," John hissed, before diving out of the van, followed by Simon. Ryan stood in the open doorway. Simon turned to him with murder in his eyes.

131

"I don't want to…" Ryan quivered. Simon grabbed him by the arm and dragged him out into the street.

The target turned to his house and stopped a moment, pondering in his drunken stupor where his door had gone. Jamie closed the distance, practically running, his knuckles tightening around the bar. John rushed to him. He was going to blow it.

"Hey!" Jamie called as he approached Gary. Gary *mother fucking* Murphy. The man from the car park. The face he had seen every time he closed his eyes. The man that invaded every second of his thoughts. Gary turned to Jamie's voice, and his jaw was met with a crack of cold steel. Gary's head bounced back like a pinball, him smashing into the cold pavement.

"Fuck!" John called. Jamie raised the bar above his head, lining up Gary's skull like he was holding a nine iron at the final shot at the Ryder Cup. John gripped hold of the metal rod.

"Don't be stupid!" John urged, wresting with the pipe. Jamie fought him, both men caught in a battle of pain and fury.

"Just let me…" Jamie hissed. "Just let me! Just one more time. Just let me!" John overpowered him. For a man twenty years his senior, he tore the pipe out his hand like a gorilla tearing the wings off a bat. The weapon landed loudly on the ground, rattling into the dead night. Jamie faced him and John slammed him hard to the chest, knocking the wind out of him. He doubled over, catching himself on a garden wall. Simon joined the affray. Ryan holding back with his hands over his mouth.

"Is he dead, dad?" Ryan squirmed. John held up a hand, panting smoke.

"Shut the fuck up!" He hissed. He pointed to Simon. "Check if he's breathing." Simon wandered over to Gary and felt his pulse. He nodded.

"You fuck," Jamie wheezed. "You should have let me –" John wrapped his hand around Jamie's throat, pulling him to his feet.

"You stupid prick," he spat. "Use your fucking head." He let go of Jamie who gasped for air. John ran his hands over his shaved head. "This is not how this is done. Do you want a murder on your hands too? You want CCTV? Witnesses? Forensics?" John pointed to Simon and Ryan. "Grab him." Simon took hold of his shoulders, pulling him off the ground. Ryan shook his head, folding his arms, the cold biting into him.

"I can't," he quivered. John charged to him like an enraged bull. He grabbed him by the scruff of the neck.

"You listen here," he hissed through clenched teeth. "You're going to do as I say and grab him with your brother, and put him in the van." The tears glistened off Ryan's cheeks in the streetlight.

"Dad…" he croaked. John threw Ryan to the floor.

"Pick him up, right now boy!" Ryan dithered to his feet, taking hold of Gary's legs. The two of them staggered and grunted back to the van and placed him inside. "Put him in the recovery position," John hissed, checking the empty streets. Simon nodded. John took out a rag from his pocket and passed it to him. "Stick this in his mouth in case he wakes up." Simon did. Ryan put his hands on his head. John grabbed him and thrust him into the darkness and slammed the door shut. He could hear quiet sobbing filtering from the back. John eyed Jamie who was still holding onto the garden wall. "You coming?" Jamie eyed him. His anger now subsided. He moved and picked up the metal bar and moved quickly to the van. In the absence of agony, a new feeling crept into his bones. Nestled in between the joints with the biting cold, he felt it.

Fear.

What was he doing? He had lost his head, and *Grey's Scrapyard* had cleaned up after him. They owned him now. He had called upon the devil for help and now he owned his soul. From this moment on, his life would never be the same again. The two men piled into the cab of the van.

"Ready?" John said. The stench of stale cigarette smoke pushing from his breath. Jamie didn't reply, his face turning a sheet of white. John fired the van to life.

"Where is my boy?" Jamie croaked, staring at the house. He was supposed to be here. They were supposed to look.

John put the van into gear. Jamie's hand snatched hold of his wrist. "Let me go in," he begged. "I just need to check." John's fierce eyes eyed him. He could protest, but the look on Jamie's face told him that it would be no use. John banged on the bulkhead with his free arm.

"Ryan!" John called.

"Why Ryan?" Jamie said, tears gracing his eyes. "Let me go in."

"After what you've just done? No chance."

"What?" A quivering voice pushed through the dark.

"Got a job for you." Jamie went to speak, but John snatched the air from his lungs. "Ryan's the only one who will get let go if he gets locked up. He's the only *clean* one out the lot of us. Plus, he's smaller. He'll be in and out in a minute. I can't risk you pulling up the floorboards." Jamie wanted to scream, but found his vocal cords severed. John eyed Jamie's grip around his wrist. "Now get your fucking hand off me."

Jamie sat in silence as he watched Ryan pull the plywood off the front of the house with a crowbar. He vanished into the blackness, and after what seemed like an eternity of wishing that he would emerge with a lost soul in his arms, Ryan returned empty handed. Jamie felt the tight air in his chest deflate, and he wanted the world to swallow him whole.

"Anything?" Jamie barked, his head leaning out the window. Ryan shook his head and then jumped in the side door before rattling it shut.

"Sorry," John said after a moment, throwing the van into first. Jamie said nothing. He had hoped more than anything, more than life itself that Ryan would find him. That Gary Murphy was keeping him inside the house. But he wasn't, and the black hole growing in Jamie's heart was devouring what ember of hope he had left of finding him alive.

Unless he's already dead? Buried in the garden. Jamie swallowed such thoughts. He couldn't risk losing hope. It was all he had left.

John turned the van around and pulled out into the street and headed back to the yard with their prisoner. Back to the workshop where they wouldn't be disturbed, and Gary could scream as loud as he liked while they worked on him. He turned the radio on. Something old and classical. He began to tap on the steering wheel lightly. "I love this one," he said smiling, turning the radio up and began singing along. John side eyed him, keeping his nose pointed towards the rolling black tarmac.

He had met many people that he would describe as a psychopath in his time. Callous. No empathy. Ruthless. But John Heywood. He was the only person that he would truly describe as insane. Beyond redemption. The only man that he ever felt the chill of fear run through his blood.

They drove for a few minutes. The world spun in Jamie's mind. He didn't realise he said it until the words left his mouth.

"Are we doing the right thing?" Jamie croaked. John pursed his lips and crimpled his brow.

"What?" He asked. Jamie repeated the question.

"Are we doing the right thing?" John slammed on the brakes hard and curtailed the van onto the pavement. The sound of bodies slamming against the bulkhead. Jamie turned to John with fear in his eyes. A slam of white rattled his vision and the back of his head bounced off the window as John slammed his fist into his jaw. John converged on him, held back by the tort seatbelt, gripping Jamie by the ear and leaning into him.

"Don't be going soft on me now lad," he hissed. "You asked me for my help. You came to me. You knew what you were getting yourself in for. You want to find your son? You want to get answers that that bitch detective won't give you? Then shut the fuck up and do as I say." He released Jamie who staggered his breathing. "We clear?" He asked, eyeing him how a starving wolf eyes a lone rabbit. Jamie nodded.

"Yeah," he said, putting himself back together. "We're clear." John righted himself.

"Good," he said, pulling out a cigarette. "This is the guy. I know it." John lit up the cigarette and offered Jamie one. He took it with shaking hands.

They drove further, turning onto the main highway.

"Look," John said finally. "You're worried. I get it. You've been out of this game for a while. But you need to trust me. We'll make this piggy squeal." They came to a set of traffic lights. Jamie felt a stab of anxiety in his chest.

"Shit," he whispered. John matched his eye. He was looking out of John's window. John followed his gaze and eyed the police car sitting next to him.

"Ahh fuck," he whispered. The two officers eyed them curiously. John waved at them, grinning ear to ear. Jamie's mind fell into darkness. John's voice pushing through the black.

This is the guy. Trust me.

"John?" Jamie said. "What do you know about him that I don't?" John turned to Jamie, his eyes cold.

"The less you know the better," he said. He returned his gaze to the solid red light in front of them. The lights turned green. John waited for the cops to set off first, but they didn't. They were waiting. John squeezed the steering wheel tighter, his leather gloves cracking. Jamie ran his gloved hand over his face. He noticed it then. He had blood on his jacket and hands. If the cops saw...

He quickly took off his gloves and threw them to the ground, stuffing them under the seat with his feet. The temperature in the cab seemed to plummet. The cops cracked their doors open and stepped out, the flickering of their car's rear reds peppering them in sinister shades of dull rouge.

"Fuck…" John hissed. He clenched his jaw tight.

"Just drive," Jamie whispered. John shook his head.

"And have a car chase? Great idea. Why didn't I think of that." The cops moved to the van. "Just play it cool. I'm picking you up from work. Give them joey details. Give them my address. Say you're Ryan. I'll say I'm Simon." The officers moved towards the window. One arriving at John's side. The other eyeing the van. "Keep your fucking mouths shut," John called to the back. Nothing moved or made a sound. An officer's face appeared at John's window. John wound it down. "Evening officers."

"Noticed you didn't set off when the lights went green," the cop said. He was older. Heavy bags under his eyes. John raised his hand.

"God," he said laughing. "Mustn't have noticed. Been a long day, you know?" The cop tightened his lips.

"Where're you going? A little late to be out and about, isn't it?" The officer said. He was smiling slightly, but his tone was serious. He was trying to play it coolly to not raise John's suspicions. But when it came to the law, John was well versed in police etiquette. They were onto him. He knew it.

"Just picking my mate up from his shift," he said casually. He strained a smile. The cold air numbed his face. His nose began to tingle with the sharp wind. The officer eyed him. The traffic lights ran through their cycle before turning back to a solid red. The deep light casting both of their faces in a shade of shadow and blood. The officer nodded. His eyes fell onto the black gloves that were tightly gripping the steering wheel.

"Cold?"

"Freezing."

"Where are you heading?"

"Just back home," John said. They were going to check the registration plate of the van, and last time he checked, he wasn't driving a Nissan Micra registered to Ms. Doris. "I'm picking my brother up," he said, pointing to Jamie who was facing away towards the window. The officer pulled out his torch. The sound of his radio chattering in his ear.

"Do you have your licence on you?" John shook his head.

"No sorry. I don't have my wallet. Like I said, just came out to pick up my brother." The officer peered into the cab.

"You're fuel light is on. You didn't think to bring something to pay for fuel?"

"I have Apple Pay." The officer pursed his lips and nodded.

"Well, what are your details?" *Do I have to tell you?* The question lingered on John's lips. But he knew the score. If they were asking, it meant they could. If you protested. Well. That wouldn't end well.

"Ryan Heywood." He pointed to Jamie. "And he is —"

"I'll ask him his details, thanks." The officer said with finality. He leant into the window.

"What're your details, sir?" Jamie felt a stab in his chest. The other officer was shining his torch around the van.

"Why is there blood on the van?" The officer called from the side of the vehicle. Jamie felt the world closing in. He could make a run for it right now. Disappear into the night. He held it together. His life, quite literally, depended on it.

"I hit a fox earlier. Just ran out from behind a car. Need to get it cleaned off." John said quickly. The officer narrowed his eyes and shined his torch into John's face. He recoiled from the beam, raising his gloved hand.

"You been drinking tonight?"

"No officer. Like I said, I was picking my friend up from work and we're going home." The officer took a step back.

"You said he was your brother?" Blades raked across his nerves.

"Brother, friend. You know how it is." The officer took a step backwards.

"Step out of the car please. I'm going to search the vehicle."

Jamie shot John a worried look.

"Look," John said, raising his hands out submissively. "Is this necessary? I'm tired. It's late. We both just want to go home." The officer shook his head.

"Now," he said. "Get out of the car." The cop reached for the small black box on his body armour and flicked on the body camera. It blinked and beeped to life. John's face looking back at him with a blinking red light on a tiny monitor. John turned to Jamie. His eyes said it all.

Get us the fuck out of here.

"Look," John said. "Have I done something wrong?"

"Last time," the officer said, his patience wearing thin. "Come on." He reached for the door handle. "Get out of the car. Now." John stretched himself out, pretending to move for his seatbelt.

"They check this van," he whispered to Jamie, "I'll cut your throat. *Do something.*" Jamie had seconds to think of something.

"Look," Jamie barked, his mind racing. "Is this necessary? Have you nothing better to do? You have no right to search the van. We've told you what we're doing. This is harassment. I'm calling my solicitor." Jamie took his phone out his pocket and put it to his ear. A moment went by. The cop didn't waver. Jamie waiting for the imaginary lawyer to answer the phone. Waiting for John to peel his eyes from him. "Hi," Jamie barked down the phone. He relayed the details of their stop. "They want to speak to you." Jamie reached over John and held the phone to the officer. He held his breath. The officer holding a hard stare at the phone. An endless moment stretched by.

"It's fine," the officer said, gesturing Jamie to take the phone back. The cop stepped back, calling to the other officer who was checking out the van. "Have a good night." The cops moved away from the van. Jamie dared to breathe.

Something groaned.

The officers stopped dead and turned; their heads pointed to the noise like a gundog hearing the firing of a shotgun.

"What was that?" The cop said. He moved to John's open door. "Out the van now –" John exploded out of the cab like a wild animal, fists slamming into the cop.

"John! No!" Jamie called. The other officer ran to the melee and grabbed a hold of John around the throat, pawing, gripping, and yanking on his clothing. The older cop fell to the ground, grunting, struggling. John atop of him, screaming into the night –

"Boys! Get out now!" John screamed. The back of the van burst open, and Simon converged onto the two officers in the middle of the road. Ryan screamed, holding his hands to his ears. Simon speared the second officer that was reaching for his taser and pummelled him onto the floor. John struggled to his feet and drove his boot into the older officer's ribs who let out a bone-crunching wail of pain. Jamie watched in shocked terror. Does he help to get away? Does he help the police?

John pulled his fist back and smashed it into the officer's nose which exploded in a burst of crimson. Simon wrestled with the taser officer who collided with the floor. The taser officer managed to unclip his weapon and jammed it into Simon's stomach and sparked the barbs to life, sending a burning shock through his body which made him recoil onto the ground like a frenzied eel ripped out of water.

The taser officer scrambled to his feet, his face bloody, his breath ragged. He pressed the emergency button on his radio. "Urgent assistance required! Urgent assistance required!" He lined up the dancing red dots quickly onto John who was headbutting and pummelling the officer into the tarmac. His face and fists doused in steaming blood. His finger pressed on the trigger.

Jamie speared the officer in the ribs and sent him slamming into the ground. The barbs flew wide. The crackling of electricity rattling through the sounds of screaming. Jamie reeled his hand back, his face covered with the balaclava. Simon got to his feet. Jamie bit down and punched the cop to the face. The cop brought his free hand up, twisting his body under Jamie and the punch slammed into the tarmac. He let out a murderous scream and looked at the road rash on his knuckles. His face exploded in a pouring of blisteringly hot pain as the officer pulled out his spray and doused Jamie's eyes with Captor. He fell back, his eyes slammed shut as he clutched his face that burned like acid. He heard quick footsteps and then a heavy slam, like someone striking a ball with a baseball bat. The sound of weight crashing to the ground. Hands gripped him, pulling him to his feet and fumbled him back into the passenger seat of the van. The slamming of a door. The revving of an engine.

"Fuck!" Someone shouted, maybe John. Maybe an officer. The hit of cold air and the shuffling of feet. Jamie pulled the balaclava soaked in captor spray from his face and forced his eyes open. He looked out of the open door. John was wrestling with someone further down the road. The back of the van wide open like a black mouth. It was Gary, trying to stumble away into the night like a walking corpse. He screamed bloody murder into the night as John dragged him back and fumbled him back into the van.

John screamed at Simon who was standing over the two officers. The first cop groaned, twitching onto the ground, trying to crawl back to his car. The second, the one with the taser, wasn't moving. His face unrecognisable, as Simon stood vacantly holding the metal pipe dripping with blood.

"Get in the van now boy!" Simon paused a moment like he was watching the best scene of this favourite movie. He turned on his heel and moved to the crawling officer. He kicked him onto his back and raised the pipe again. Jamie screamed at him. A terrible scream. One with no words. No comprehension of language. But a scream that symbolised the end of life as they knew it, as he smashed the end of the pipe into the officer's head, and all returned to stillness in that cold black with sirens approaching in the distance.

Chapter Fifteen
Laura

Back alone in the MIU office, Laura sat staring into a cooling coffee. The harsh lighting above her burning into her retinas. Her eyes stinging and her head pounding. It was well past midnight and she had been due to go home several hours ago. But she couldn't. The memories of the house like hot pins in her brain.

He wasn't there. It was impossible. But she saw him. But her terror had to be silenced. Held behind sewn lips. Her terror hers to own. Whatever she had to say to stop them from asking questions. Whatever they wanted to hear – a large rat. A goddamn spider with a Swiss army knife. But not the truth. No, she couldn't ever tell them that.

Absently, her fingers found the inside coat pocket and she was cracking the lid of the measure of vodka and sank it in a breath. She snarled at the taste, putting it back into her pocket and pulled out a second. Her hands were beginning to shake. She needed her poison. If she didn't have it, then her day would get much, much worse. She welcomed the numb that it brought. It levelled her out. Kept her demons drowning. But she needed more. They were learning to swim. The booze coursed through her veins. It made her forget. Just for a moment. A breath in a world where she was suffocating. Ron. Craig. The drugs for depression. Anxiety. Insomnia. The incessant abyssal tomes of self-loathing that plagued her thoughts. The way she felt when she looked in the mirror. Her failures as a detective. Her failures as a lover. The adulation and the despair of her infamy. Oliver. Jamie. Jamie fucking Green. All of it. The booze made it go away, if for nothing more than a blip. The booze never judged her. It never told her to stop. It never questioned her. It never criticised her. It gave her a warm hug that she so desperately needed, but equally resisted with teeth, fists and claws. She had once rather wished to be in pain than feel nothing because it showed she was alive. But now, she was tired of being in pain, and she just wanted the voices in her head to quieten down for a little while. Laura cracked the other bottle and sank it. She was halfway through when Jeremy kicked the door open. Laura withdrew the bottle and placed it into her pocket and quickly sank the coffee. His face red like a squozen plum. He needed to get healthy. His lifestyle was going to be the death of him.

"Did you speak to Claire and Declan?" Laura whispered, her eyes turning red.

"Yeah," he said breathlessly, pulling up a chair and parking his ass in front of her. "No joy. Won't tell us anything."

"Have you thought about –"

"I beg your pardon, ma'am," he said, scowling. "But what the hell is going on with you?"

"I'm just tired," she said. "I'll tell you what I told the others. It's stress. Things aren't good at home." Jeremy chewed on the words.

"Bull shit," he spat. His temper flaring. "You might be able to fool them, but not me Laura." He leaned forward to her. "We need to talk properly." Laura stared into the empty coffee mug.

"I'm not in the mood."

"Well, you need to get in the mood," he spat. "I don't care if you're my boss. I'm not holding my tongue anymore."

"I said I'm not in the mood."

"At the house? At the goddamn house boss. You freaked everyone out. Started screaming the house down like you had seen a ghost or something."

Seen a ghost is exactly what happened Jeremy, she thought. *But you wouldn't understand. You haven't been through what I have, and I pray to God you never do.*

"I just have a lot on my mind," she said. "I'll be okay."

"I can't risk that." He said with pain in his voice. "You may outrank me, but I have been with this unit for ten years."

"And look where that got us." Laura said sourly, slowly bringing her eyes to meet Jeremy's. They were wide. Wild. The capillaries pushing through the white. He looked like he was about to have a heart attack. "When I came, the last inspector had resigned. You had two damn murdering sons of bitches working under your watch. You had a superintendent that was complicit. A unit on the verge of being disbanded." Laura could almost smell the sulphur of the match she had lit, ready to throw it on the last bridge she had to burn. Her words sliced through Jeremy's pain like an axe through brittle wood.

"That's utterly unfair," Jeremy blurted, rising to his feet. "This was failing through institutional corruption. When we cut the head off the snake and got the unit back to rights, who the hell do you think looked after it when you were in the hospital? Who put the unit back into shape? Who had to speak to the reporters? The bosses? Who the hell do you think solved the missing person cases? The frauds? The homicides? It wasn't you, was it?"

"Who saved your life when you were tied to that chair, screaming for your mother." The words drove a knife through Jeremy's heart.

"How dare you," Jeremy said, his voice closing up. "I got help. I took what I was offered. I didn't come to work each day late stinking of stale wine." Laura wanted to reply, but the wind had gone from her sail. The booze was kicking in, so she took the punishment. She almost liked it. "The very fact that you can sit in that chair is because of what I and *my* team did in your absence. I will take at least *some* of the credit for that and I will not allow you to completely derail it because you're having a breakdown." Laura stared at her cup, his voice miles away. Her eyes were heavy. She longed for sleep. An endless sleep she wouldn't wake from. She stared at the remnants of black tar in the cup, unable to recognise the reflection staring back at her. Jeremy let out a long breath, and his hands interlaced with Laura's. His touch warm. His hands smooth. "I don't know what's happening in your head, but you can talk to me." His voice was soft, kind. *Loving.*

Laura felt something breaking through the numb. It started in her throat, then moved behind her eyes. Her eyes began to itch and then sting. The tears dripped onto the desk like slow rain, before flowing more freely. She wanted to feel something again. She leaned forward, reaching for his lips. Jeremy recoiled.

"Woah," he said, raising his hands. The tears broke through finally, and she ran her hand through her auburn hair.

"Sorry," she croaked. Jeremy stared at her in astonishment, his heart beating through his chest.

"What's going on boss?" She fought with the words. The seal of her lips tightened, her tongue shrivelling away. She wanted to tell him. She really, really wanted to tell.

"I…" She croaked. The vodka was churning in her stomach. "It's…"

It's the fact that every time I close my eyes, I see him standing there and he's trying to cut my eyes out.

Jeremy waited. Waited for her to say something. But the silence dragged on.

"I'll be fine," she whispered into that empty air. Jeremy's face twisted. He went to speak as Alice burst into the office. She was frantic, throwing her body armour back on.

"Code zero!" She hollered.

"What's going on?" Laura barked.

"Two officers. One transmitted a code zero shouting for urgent backup. We haven't been able to reach them since." Laura shot to her feet and steadied herself. Jeremy eyed her cautiously, moving to help her.

"You okay?" Alice said quickly, reaching out to catch her before she fell. Laura steadied herself.

"I'm fine. Get a car." They raced out of the building and were greeted to the bellowing of a hundred sirens and lights and speeding tyres. Alice's radio was on loudspeaker, and they could hear officers screaming for updates, locations, and trying desperately to reach the officers that had hit the panic button. Laura grabbed Alice's radio.

"Detective Inspector Warburton."

"Go ahead ma'am," the radio operator said.

"The first officers to land need to transmit exactly what they find and the condition of the officers. I need them to press their red buttons for a clean and uninterrupted string of transmission. Also, they need to activate their body-worn video cameras before they get to the scene to preserve the integrity of any scene or incident."

"Roger," they replied. "All units. You heard the boss. Cameras on. First one there, button it and tell us what you can see." A myriad of confirmations and affirmatives followed, and the sirens spilled out into the night. The radio blared loudly on the dashboard as Alice hit three numbers on the speedo. The air was tense.

"Keep trying to reach the officers," Laura said into the radio. With each request for the officers to reply, the ensuing dead air weighed heavy on Laura's heart.

This isn't good, she thought.

"Despatch an ambulance," Laura put over the airwaves. "Send it to the location." The operator did. The radio operator tried again to reach the officers. The sporadic blast of the code zero repeating on a cycle. "Answer damn it," Laura hissed. She knew that this was bad. Usually, if a button goes off, then it's for one of three reasons.

The first was an accidental activation which was quickly rectified following the cajoling of the offender and them bringing in cakes for the team. The second kind of activation was when the button and noise erupts in the officer's ear quickly followed by screaming and shouting, and calls for assistance. But this was the third kind. The type no one wants to hear. Number three. When urgent assistance is requested, and then all communication goes dead, with the cavalry on its way with their hearts in their throats, waiting for the worst to be discovered.

The town blurred by. The other detectives also on their way in another car. Alice banked hard on the wheel. The stench of the clutch and burning rubber permeated the air. Laura was certain Alice hadn't pressed the brakes once. Then, another alarm was raised. It cut through the air like a foghorn over misty water.

"On scene," the officer said. He relayed his call sign and collar number. He hadn't been in the job long. Possibly his first ever blue light run, and probably one he will never forget for the rest of his life. Laura's heart quickened. They heard the sound of his car door opening and him stepping out into the cold followed by harsh breathing. "Their car is here," the cop said. "Rear reds on," he said, "they have their lights on. I can't see them –" The way his voice trailed off said everything. "Oh god," he cried. "I need an ambulance now!" He shouted down the radio. "Derek! Brian!" He screamed, rushing towards them. Alice pressed her foot to the floor. Red mist engaged. Flying through red lights and stop signs. The officer's screaming through the radio. Screaming that they were both bleeding, and that he didn't know so much blood could pour out of the human body.

More voices in the background. More transmissions. More cops landing at the horror scene.

"Secure the scene," Laura said over the radio "ETA three minutes. Begin CPR." A cold voice broke through the rabble of transmissions. The voice knocked the breath out of Laura's lungs. Jeremy's face dropped. Alice's face turned a shade of pale. Her foot relaxing from the accelerator.

"They're dead ma'am," the cop said. "Both of them."

Chapter Sixteen

Jamie

They pulled into the scrap yard, and John jumped out of the driver's side with the engine running. He unlocked the thick padlock, unravelling the chains and pulling on the gates they opened with a long, yearning creak. He was washed out in bright light, and the hum and clinking of the van engine vibrated through the quiet night. The exhaust fumes and John's breath elicited a ghostly white vapour that resembled a thin mist, before it dissipated into the black star-filled sky above them. There was no moon tonight. But if there was, Jamie was certain it would be red with the blood of their sin.

The van crept into the compound and John locked the gate behind him. Jamie hadn't said a word since Simon had done what he did. He wouldn't know where to start. He was as guilty as they were. Their lives were over. He could still hear that sickening crack as their skulls caved in…

John killed the van engine, and he slipped out. Ryan was sobbing quietly in the back when he pulled the side door open. The sharp hit of vomit assaulting his nose. Simon stepped out and dragged Gary towards the warehouse. John slipped into the dark building and emerged with a black bin bag and pulled Jamie's door open.

"Your clothes." Inside the bag were already blood-soaked garments. John standing there completely naked. His body not addressing the cold. Jamie wondered what was going on behind his eyes. What was he thinking? The *Butcher*. Was this just another day in the office for him? Jamie took the bag and went to move, but John stood in front of him. "Here," he said. He eyed him like a maggot in his beef stew. Jamie wearily rose his hand to Simon and Ryan, the sound of screaming still racing around his mind.

"What about them?" John thrust the bag into Jamie's chest.

"They're not finished yet." Simon and Ryan vanished into the maw of the building, dragging Gary's limp body with them. Jamie heard tape being pulled tort. Grunting. Shouting. The sound of a chair being scraped along concrete. With John's gaze burning into him, he stepped out of the van onto the gravelly yard and peeled away his top layers and stuffed them into the bag. Then came his trousers, his socks, his boots and finally his underwear. John threw the bag of clothes into the back of the van. Then, he pointed to a large filthy bathtub that stood next to the scrap heap of chewed metal next to a large grid. "Get in there." Jamie did, the cold biting every part of him. Sounds of toolboxes being opened. A flash of a light coming to life. John slapped Jamie across the face. "Focus," he said. He pulled out a long hosepipe from behind a pile of broken steel and rubble and fished it into

157

the tub. Then he moved his naked form to a small lock box that was fixed to the side of the warehouse and entered a combination. The metal doors ached as they opened, and John took out a pack of scouring sponges, the kind you would use to scrub thick grease from a pan and took them in his hand. He took out a large white bottle with more warning symbols than Jamie could count. Finally, a pair of goggles each. John turned on the faucet at the base of the building, and the hosepipe gurgled into life. The water was ice cold around Jamie's feet. The tub quickly began to fill. "Put these on," he said, passing Jamie the goggles. Jamie put them on and snapped them around his head so tight his brain hurt. Next, he passed Jamie the sponge. He uncapped the bottle and poured it into the spiralling black water. "Scrub until you bleed," he said. "And try not to breathe too much. That stuff will corrode you from the inside out."

"What is it?" Jamie asked.

"Just do it." He spoke with finality. A tone that said, *don't ask questions or ill rip your tongue out.*

Jamie plunged the sponge into the icy water and began to scrub himself thoroughly. His skin felt like it was on fire. He winced, trying to hold his breath the best he could. The ice-cold water and the burning of his flesh sent his senses all kinds of crazy. The water on the dog bite made him scream through gritted teeth. John slipped into the tub next to him, both of them scraping and scrubbing any part of them that had flesh, helping each other reach the parts the other couldn't. Inside their ears, under their fingernails. Along their hairlines, beards, in between their toes, butt cracks and anywhere else that the wind could touch, or possible forensics could be found.

Jamie started to feel woozy. His feet almost slipped from under him. John pulled out the hose and doused him head to toe in icy water, slapping him back to reality. After what was an agonisingly painful few minutes, Jamie stepped out of the tub redder than a sunburnt lobster. He picked up a towel and a set of grey joggers, a pair of black pumps and a grey jumper. The kind you would find in a custody suite after being arrested. He eyed the garments like it was some kind of joke, but then saw John putting them on too, him shaking and dithering so badly Jamie could hear his old bones creak and rattle.

John tipped the water away in the drain next to the tub, and then heaved the empty vessel into the back of the van and tossed the towel in there too, along with the goggles and scrubber pads. He got the hosepipe, wrapped it up, and tossed it in the back of the van. Finally, he slipped inside the warehouse's closed doors, emerging a moment later with a large canister, and began to pour the fluid inside and outside the van. He threw the canister in there too. The sharp smell of petrol found Jamie's stinging nostrils. John took out a match and cracked it to life, the new flame hissing into the air. John tossed it inside the van.

It went up in seconds. The explosion and cracking of heat made Jamie forget about the cold nestling into his bones. He watched as the flames, like a million glowing locusts, converging and ravaging the vehicle like it was a fresh plantation of crops devoured in the plagues of Egypt. John took Jamie's arm.

"Never whisper a word of tonight to anyone. Ever." Jamie stared into his eyes. They looked vacant. Dead.

"Those cops…" Jamie whispered. "They would have had families."

"They were going to make sure that you never saw your family again, Jamie," he said, his breath a stream of hot air.

"But," he said, his head facing towards the heavens that spiralled above, staring down at the damned. Not a whisper of the sun on the horizon, signalling to him that only darker times lay in his future. John grabbed him by the shoulders.

"We do this together," he said. "We're in this together. I'm helping you find your son," He pointed to the closed door. "And he knows where he is." Jamie's body ripped in two.

A parent throws away their old life with a smile from the moment their child is born. It didn't matter what dreams you had before, what plans. Any issues you had and anything that mattered before the baby opened its eyes for the first time became inconsequential. The world changes. You stop living for yourself and start living for the baby in your arms. Nothing else matters, nor will it ever matter to you as much as your child's life, happiness and safety. That is your responsibility as a parent, and Jamie knew that. When he fled from the law, his son's eyes newly opened, he knew that he had to change his life for the good. He did what was required.

He helped to bring down an empire, and in return, he earned his freedom. But as he was finding out, that freedom was exceptionally conditional, and as he stared into the eyes of the man that he had considered a friend for so long, the devil was alluring and elusive at the same time. That your soul, once sold, is always in the devil's back pocket. He just loans it out to you from time to time, letting you believe that you have escaped the pit of his requiem of savagery and darkness. John cracked a twisted smile.

"Come on," he said, moving Jamie to the door. "Let's see what tune we can make this canary sing." They stood behind a closed door. John moved for the handle. Jamie grabbed him.

"Shouldn't we cover our faces?" He said. John cracked a smile.

"No," he said. "He won't be leaving here." They moved through the door which slammed closed behind Jamie with a hard thud, rattling around the large warehouse. They were in a back room of sorts. A place where the broken utensils go to rot and die. It seemed fitting for their current situation. They were broken members of society, and they belonged to be locked away from the world for good.

Ryan sat on an overturned crate and was smoking a cigarette. Simon was silent, his hands matted with blood. His dark hair pulled back and tied to the back of his head in a ponytail. He wasn't smoking, but instead just standing, flexing his knuckles that were swollen. His breath permeated the air. A sheen of sweat broke along his forehead, illuminated by the harsh strip lighting above them. The hum of the light a drone underneath Gary Murphy's broken and staggered sobs.

"Please…." He croaked. His right eye was heavily swollen. It bulbous and black. Simon wondered what would come out if he cut that tight flesh with a box cutter or punctured it with needles.

"Where's the boy," John said, standing in front of Gary.

"I don't know…" Gary mouthed. "I don't know where he is. I told you," he dithered, blood and saliva dripping down his chin. "I went to the store, and I drove away. I wouldn't hurt a kid." He spoke in staggered bursts, trying to force out the words with what little breath he could suck in through his bloodied nose and swollen lips.

"You're lying." John spat. He matched Simon's deathly gaze. John nodded. Simon moved to the back of the room. The sound of tools being moved. Gary tried to strain his neck to see what was happening. John clicked his fingers and whistled. "No, no," he said, pulling a chair from the corner of the room and placing it a few feet from Gary. "You keep those eyes on me. You don't get to see." He gestured to Ryan, who sat quietly in the corner. John held out his hand. Ryan put his hand in his pocket and passed John a cigarette. John lit it up and offered one to Jamie, who couldn't pull his stare away from Gary. This was him. The man who had taken his son. A look of murder in his eyes. "Now," John said, sparking up the cigarette between his cracked teeth. "There's only one way you're getting out of here, and that's by telling us what you have done to that poor boy. Nobody knows you're here. So, we've got as long as we need." Gary began to shake. A dark patch grew around his trousers, then the trickling of liquid down his leg. John watched the offending fluid leak onto his floor. He took a drag of his smoke. "How tall are you? About five-nine? Did you know that your small intestine is longer than you are tall?" He looked around the room. "I reckon by that count, we could stretch yours around this room once or twice. Also, the brain doesn't have any nerves. I could peel your skull open and cut bits of your brain out and cook them in front of you, and you wouldn't feel a thing." He pursed his lips. "Did you also know that a person can live without their skin? Sure, infection and blood loss would need to be considered. But so long as we peel it away slow enough, you could lose up to eight pounds in weight by the time we're done." A silence filled the room. Then suddenly, John began laughing.

"But it's not me you have to be worried about," John barked, slapping his leg. "No. No, the one you need to *really* be worried about is my oldest boy. The one who is playing around with the tools back there. He was the black sheep of the family. Wanted to go to school and make something of his life rather than learn my trade. I wasn't happy about it, but after his mum died, I figured he should be able to carve his own way in life. And he did too. Got a good job. Got a good girl, and they had a little boy. Born two months premature! Didn't think he was going to survive, but he was a fighter. A real fighter, and my boy and the family cared for that kid until he was old enough to fend for himself." He stood up and moved closer to Gary who flinched at the sounds coming from behind him.

"It was really tragic what happened to that boy. A fishing accident. Nobody could see it coming. Boat was defective. The day we buried that boy, something broke in my son. Went within himself. Stopped talking. He became a shell of himself and returned home to me once his marriage broke into pieces. Had to stop him from tying a rope around his neck on one occasion," John shook his head.

"Grief can do that to even the strongest couples, you know? Tear even the strongest of people apart."

"Let me go," Gary whispered. John teased the cigarette between his teeth.

"There is nothing worse to a family than losing a child. It tears people apart. So, you have two choices: repair the pain you have caused, and we let you go. Or, continue to lie to us, and you will know what true pain is." Gary scanned the room. His face bloodied and wild. He swallowed hard.

"I haven't done anything," he said, tears seeping through the swollen eye. "I haven't. I haven't, I promise. I swear on my life."

"His name was fucking Oliver!" Jamie screamed, raging, storming to Gary. The memory of the atrocities of the night subsided. Desperation and fury taking their place. The sight of this man. *This* man, lying and worming his way out of what he had done. The truth was behind those disgusting lips and he would do anything to get it out. He gripped him by the blood-soaked shirt and drove his fist into his face as hard as he could in quick succession. "Where is he!" He screamed another blast of rage and knuckles drove into Gary's mouth. Teeth cracked and dislodged. His head cocking back like a spring. His brain slamming against the inside of his skull like a softball smashing against the wall of a squash court. "Where is he!" He was murderous. He couldn't hold it together any longer. Any reservation he'd had, had since disintegrated after being set alight like the burning van outside. John grabbed Jamie and pulled him away. Jamie shrugged him off and stepped away to the back of the room, snatching the pack of cigarettes from Ryan's hand and sparking one into life. He turned away from them. Gary stammered, unable to speak. A scream unable to escape his lips. Locked inside his lungs.

Simon appeared behind Gary. A tool in his hand. His eyes vacant. John looked at Gary who sat with his eyes closed, mouthing something, heaving broken breaths. Flexing his fingers that were bound to the chair. John eyed Simon, his focus snaking to the power drill in his hand.

"Do it," John said. Simon's face twisted into a sneer. Simon let off a quick revolution before drilling into Gary's kneecap. Gary found his scream after all.

Chapter Seventeen

Laura

Laura arrived on scene to a sea of blaring blue lights and high-vis jackets. Ambulances arrived on scene, paramedics diving out of the backs with oxygen tanks, stuffing tubes down the two officer's throats. Bodies grabbed and pulled, removing the coats and body armour. Paramedics cut off the officers' shirts, placed their heads in large red braces, and attached beeping mechanisms to their fingers. The sound of ribs cracking as cops drenched in sweat continued CPR. Blood spouting out from the officer's cold and still lips, thick and black. One of the officers was carefully rolled onto a red plastic bed, and others helped to heave their dead weight into the ambulance.

"Close this road," Laura ordered, pointing to an officer who was directing traffic. He nodded in response, ran to the back of his car, and took out some tape that read 'POLICE. DO NOT CROSS,' and stretched it from one end of the road to the next. A car blared its horn and Laura turned to it. The driver gestured to her. Laura stormed over to the car, her face like thunder. In the car, a woman, around age forty-five. Her haircut had Karen written all over it.

"What's happened?" She barked.

"Shark attack," Laura said reflexively. The Karen's face wrapped in confusion.

"Can I get through? I only need to go down there."

"Turn around," she said firmly. "Road is closed." The Karen went to argue further, but Laura turned away and stood in front of the line of traffic and gestured for them to turn around. She approached another officer. "Get your car and block the road at the next junction. Tape it all off. I want the whole thing shut down. This is a crime scene now." The officer didn't utter a sound, his face etched with horror and shock. He jumped in his car and sped off to the bottom of the road, then pulled out signs from the back of his car and began taping off the entrance to the junction.

It was early morning, the lip of dawn breaking over the horizon and this was a hell of a road to close down at rush hour, but Laura didn't care. Two of her colleagues had died tonight. The public could complain all they wanted.

Jeremy and the other detectives were speaking to the officers first on the scene. One of them sitting in the back seat of their car with a bottle of water. He looked like a broken man.

"He's alive!" A cop shouted. Laura sprang into action. Other officers moved to them. The cop on the floor was coughing. His face was covered in dried blood. Some of his teeth were missing. The crown of his skull concaved like a dented car bonnet, and one of his eyes bulging out its socket. He reached his hand to the sky. Laura crouched by him.

"You're okay," she said, and gripped hold of his hand. His strength was waning. He didn't have long. The officer looked around. His eyes bloodshot. His lips hypothermic blue and skin a pasty white. His wires attached to his chest than a fuse box.

"Where am I?" He coughed, eyes blackening, darting around wildly.

"You're safe," she said. His fingers were ice cold. She was looking into the face of a dead man. She knew it. She just hoped he didn't. "Can you tell me what happened?" The cop searched his mind. His voice was barely louder than a whisper. Laura leaned in close. "Who did this to you?" She pleaded. They locked eyes. His tears gave the illusion that he was bleeding from his eyes. His breathing picked up, and he coughed fiercely, his bones bending and cracking with the movement. He winced in agony and let out a long cry. He squeezed Laura's hand, his hands icy to the touch.

"I…I don't want to die," he cried. "My son. My wife. I don't want to die…" His throat began to close up, silencing the cry of despair. Laura let go of his hand.

"Get him out of here." The cops and paramedics lifted him onto the back of the ambulance. Laura directed two cops to make sure they had their body cameras activated at all times until she personally told them otherwise. They did just that. "If he says anything of use, write it down." The officers dove into the back of the ambulance and slammed the doors. The wagon flicked on its lights and sirens and sped off into the night. Laura directed two officers to follow them to the hospital. They did so without a word of protest. "Who the hell did this?" Laura asked the wind. "Who the hell…" This wasn't a car accident. A hit and run. The blow to the officer's head. The discharged barbs of a taser on the ground. The transmission over the radio. The bruising and swelling to the cop's knuckles and the gravel engrained into his scoured flesh. They had been attacked. Viciously, by more than one person.

It was doubtful it had been a targeted attack. Somewhere so open. The cops had seen something, and whoever was responsible didn't want them to find out what they had to hide. The wound on the officer's head was made by a blunt instrument, too rounded to be from a fist. The suspects were probably male, and probably know the area. Their vehicle large enough to carry multiple passengers and weaponry. A van, maybe? Either way, this was now a murder investigation. They needed everything in place and everything to be done right. The cold nipped at Laura's hands and face, sobering her up. Officers took photos of the blood stains. Others stood talking. Some just stood staring into the night. Others collapsed to the ground, crying into the asphalt.

"I've called for CSI," Francis said, approaching Laura, his face awash with horror. Laura felt a stab in her heart. *Celine.* She would be attending, and she was the last person in the world she wanted to speak to right now.

"Good work," she said. "I need you to go and take the names of every officer here and get the first account off them. Then, I need you to go back to the station and update the incident log." Francis nodded and then got to work. Jeremy was speaking to the officer that was first on the scene. Laura joined him.

"I just can't..." he said, staring at the black tarmac. "Both of them. I didn't know what to do. It seemed like I was on my own forever. I only had one pair of hands. I didn't know who to work on." The officer was in a state of complete anguish. He had cycled from shock, to vacancy, to complete despair.

"You did your best son," Jeremy said, touching him on the shoulder, and crouching by him. Jeremy had a body camera on, speaking to the officer. "You helped them before anyone else got here. You should be proud of yourself." The officer sniffled and sobbed some more. Laura leaned in.

"What's your name?" She asked. The cop looked up and met her eye. He straightened himself.

"Ma'am."

"Fuck that ma'am shit. Its Laura. What's your name?"

"Jake," he said. "Jake Foster." Laura crouched by Jeremy.

"Jake, you have done an incredible job," she said. "You were faced with the worst that this world can possibly throw at us. You did what you could. You transmitted and directed us right to where they were. If it wasn't for you, then we wouldn't have gotten here so fast. One is awake. The other might still pull through." Laura knew the truth. Both cops would be dead by sunrise. "You did good." She took out a notepad and a pen. "I need you to tell me," she continued. "What exactly did you see when you got here?" The officer's face twisted. The tears flowed again.

"Erm," he said, trying to find the right words. "I got here… and both of them were just on the floor. They looked like mannequins. Not like *people*." His eyes had a film over them. A man lost in his own war. "There was so much blood," he whispered. Agony washed over him again.

"It's okay," she said. "Take your time." Jake composed himself. He was young. His glasses thick and his face was peppered with acne. He couldn't have been over twenty years old.

"One of them woke up, only for a moment." Laura's ears pricked up.

"Go on."

"He said that there was a van. A dark green or black van. That the driver was older. Bald with leather gloves. He said he recognised the passenger."

"Recognised the passenger?" Laura said. The cop nodded. "He didn't say much more than that. Just that they attacked them." Laura sat back on her heels. The mystery growing. She looked at Jeremy. "Put out all local patrols to look for a van. Tell the control room to check every car that hit the ANPR in the thirty minutes before we got the distress call, and then every car thirty minutes later." Jeremy stood and moved away, speaking into his radio. "What else happened?" She continued. The officer drew a blank.

"I don't know," he said. "It all happened so fast. He stopped talking and began to slip away. I started CPR. The rest of the cars turned up a little later. It felt like forever. On my own, two people needed my help. Only one pair of hands." Laura touched Jake's hand.

"You did incredible."

"I got this, though," he said, reaching into his pocket and taking out both officers' body cameras. "I kept them recording." Laura eyed herself on the small screen. She put on some rubber gloves, took them off Jake, and placed them into an evidence bag.

"Go back to the station for a debrief," she said. "I'll get Francis to drive you back." Laura gestured to Francis, who was taking details from officers. He moved to the vehicle and drove Jake away. Laura watched him go and disappear into the breaking dawn. It only takes a day for your entire world to change. Laura saw Catherine standing by the scene. Pools of blood were by her feet.

"Who could do this?" She said, speaking to the wind.

"I don't know," Laura said. "But we're going to find out." Laura handed Catherine the evidence bag with the body cameras in. "Go back to the station and watch these. Let me know what you find." She took them and moved away. She stopped.

"Oh ma'am," Catherine said. Laura turned to her. "I was going to say earlier. The number you asked me to run through. We had a hit." Laura nodded her head.

"And?"

"It was an incoming call. Only a minute long. I cross-referenced the number. Same person that called in the hoax jumper at the supermarket crime scene. The same person that fled from police." Laura felt her skin prickle. She knew exactly who had made that call.

"Great work, detective," Laura said. "Now, please," she gestured to the squad car. Catherine slipped into the driver's seat and drove into the night.

With a murder, there is normally a somewhat sense of morbid enthusiasm. A sense of cracking a big case. Sending someone down for the rest of their lives and bringing justice to the world. This felt different. A sense of numbness crept into the bones of everyone in uniform.

Soon the press would be here. Someone will make an official statement. Her name will be in the papers again, and more pressure will be on her to find out who did this.

This time it was different, though. It wasn't a drug dealer that had been axed off by a rival gang or an abusive husband who finally went too far after sinking a bottle of vodka. This was two of their own. Two cops. Two members of the public that took up the vocation of keeping the world safe from monsters. Laura felt something shift inside her. It slipped through her numb flesh and nestled like a burning fire in her heart.

Rage.

"I will find you," she said, staring towards the red and blue horizon. "And I will make you pay for this." The CSI van arrived shortly afterwards. Two officers got out and began to pull out their tent, putting on masks and overalls. Taking out cameras and evidence tags. Just like you see in the movies. Laura eyed them, her brain beginning to fail her. She needed to sleep. She had been working for over twenty-four hours straight. Celine must have gotten the message. She hadn't tried to contact her in hours.

But she was here, no doubt. She was on call for the night, and that meant another uncomfortable conversation. Laura bit down and moved to the investigators rummaging in the van's back. She eyed them, and confusion slapped her.

"Where's Celine?" She asked.

"Phoned in sick," the investigator said.

"Phoned in sick?"

"Yeah. Not like her. The girl runs track and takes vitamins every day. I've never known it." The officer stopped and eyed Laura like he had stumbled on a celebrity. "Hey, aren't you –" She cut him off. She moved away and pulled out her phone and dialled her number. It went straight to voicemail. Her mouth ran dry.

Shit.

"Something is wrong," she whispered. Celine was dedicated to her job. Laura felt the bubbling of worry rise in her chest. She tried again, but the same robotic voice asked her to leave a message. "Celine, call me when you get this." She hung up the call. Then the notifications came through. She had missed calls. Tons of voicemails. All from Celine. Laura pressed play and held it to her ear. It was quiet, then a voice bled through. "I've taken something." Laura terminated the call and looked around at the insanity around her, her heart racing. Panic flooded through her bloodstream, infecting her from the inside out.

"Something wrong?" Someone said. It was Alice. Her nose red from the cold. Laura eyed the phone.

"Take me home. Now."

Chapter Eighteen

Laura

Laura had her phone glued to her ear all the way home, Alice cutting through traffic with sirens blaring. Laura's mind was spinning. *If something has happened to her,* she thought, *I couldn't forgive myself.* What was this feeling brewing in her stomach that ran through her body? Was it love? Was it pain? Were they not the same feelings? Laura couldn't tell anymore.

Laura left another three voicemails. Each ranging from firm, to pleading, to hate. The foundation of her world crashing and crashing into the spiralling ocean. She was so tired. So exhausted, but she couldn't rest. Not yet. She had so much to do and so little knowledge of how or where to even begin with picking up the pieces of her fragmented life.

They pulled into the cul-de-sac where she lived. The house was still. The curtains drawn. Celine's car was still on the driveway, a layer of frost along the windscreen. At least she hadn't left the house and wasn't hanging off a bridge somewhere. She hoped. She had lived through enough tragedy in her life to not to get complacent with first appearances.

"Wait here," she said to Alice, before stepping out of the car.

"What's going on?" Alice said, but Laura was already walking down her driveway. The air was still. The sky turned from the gold and blue of a winter morning to an overcast blanket of thick grey. The sound of the engine rumbling under macabre bird song.

She touched the handle and tried the door. Locked. She put her key in. It wouldn't turn. She must have left her key in the door. Why would she do that? The dread crept into Laura's chest again. She needed to get inside her house. She looked through the letter box. All was still. She could see Bagpipe sleeping on the floor in the hallway by the foot of the stairs.

Laura looked around for some way to get in. Had she left a window unlocked? How about the back? Laura tried all these options, but none were successful. She banged hard on the door and the windows, shouting through the letterbox as loud as she could. No answer. Nothing moved. Not even Bagpipe stirred. She felt like she was lost in a dream, the kind where the monster is chasing you and no matter how loud you screamed or how far you ran, no one came to help you.

Fear gripped her. She banged on the door loudly again. Bagpipe stirred, jumped from the bottom of the stairs, and moved back to the kitchen before disappearing out of sight. Laura saw it then. The empty wine bottles on the breakfast bar and on the counters of the kitchen. She counted three in total. Either Celine had poured them away after finding her stash, or she'd had one hell of a party.

Laura had no time to waste. She grabbed a rock from the grass of the front garden and smashed the windowpane of the front door. She heard the slamming of a car door behind her. She turned. Alice was marching to her quickly. Laura wrapped her coat around her arm and drove her elbow through the glass, then punched the broken glass lose, fragments shaking free and rattling on the wooden floor of the hallway. She reached in and fumbled with the key in the lock, turning it and unlocking the door. She pulled her arm free, shaking off the fragments of glass that clung to her coat like sharp diamonds. She turned to Alice. "I said stay in the car."

"The hell with that." Laura didn't have time to argue. She pushed the front door open and rushed inside. The living room was empty, and she fingered the empty bottles in the kitchen. They were bone dry. Nothing in the sink or spillages on the ground to indicate that they had been poured away.

"Celine?" Laura called into the void. Alice eyed the bottles, her face wrapped in both confusion and pity. Those she looked up to. They had their own demons too. Their own flaws. Laura moved past her like she was a ghost. She stood at the foot of the stairs and called up to the upper layers, hoping, desperately hoping for some kind of answer. But none met her ear. She swallowed dryly. She placed her foot on the bottom step. She wanted to run up them and see what horror awaited her. But something inside her made her slow down, like walking through an invisible bog of thick and putrid water filled with crocodiles and leeches. She waded through the space, taking one step at a time. She reached the top of the stairs and found her bedroom door to be closed. She swallowed dryly.

"What's happening?" Alice called. "What can you see?" Laura fingered the bedroom door.

"Celine?" She said lowly. Laura slipped from Alice's view. She pressed her head to the door. Dead silence met her ear. She pushed the door open, its bottom catching the carpet. Daylight bled through the red and cream drapes, casting the room dull pink. She saw Celine, and Laura's world detonated in an eruption so loud that she would never recover from it. She saw the pills and the lifeless arm dangling off the edge of the bed. "Call an ambulance!"

Chapter Nineteen

Jamie

Simon pulled the bloody drill bit out of Gary's twitching legs. He had fallen silent after the second drilling. The pain terminated his scream fiercely like someone had turned out the lights and left the world in blackness. The blood from Ryan's face had drained away.

"What happened to him, Dad?" Ryan asked, ready to throw up.

"He's passed out, son." He said, moving towards Gary. "It happens sometimes. We'll give him a minute. Wait for him to wake up." He looked at Simon. "Grab a clotting agent," John said. "Don't want him to bleed out." Simon moved to the utensils, took out a paper pouch, and poured it onto the wound like applying a dusting of flour to a worktop.

"Can't we just wake him up?" Ryan said. John shook his head.

"It's best to take things slow."

"But what about the police?" He said, his voice growing with worry. "What if they come looking for him?"

"Oh, they'll be looking for him all right. But first, they have to find the van, which they won't because it will have been chewed up by the crusher." He took another cigarette from Ryan. "And our friend here will be long gone by the time they come knocking." He looked at Ryan and fingered his clothing. "You need to go get cleaned up. Just like the way I told you. Just like the way Jamie and I did." Ryan eyed him, a flash of worry across his face.

"Naked? In the cold?"

"Jesus fucking Christ," Jamie blurted. He was sitting, hands laced together and nursing his knuckles with an ice pack. "Just do it, will you? Do you want to get caught?" Ryan froze. Jamie's eyes stared at him through the twilight of the encroaching dawn. John turned to Jamie, and then back to Ryan.

"Go on," he said. "Simon will show you what to do." Ryan nodded, and Simon emerged from the back of the shelving, stripped down to his boxer shorts. His body was streaked in blood. His knuckles swollen. Simon grabbed Ryan by the scruff of the neck and frog-marched him outside. John turned to Jamie, his eyes lit up like pits of fire.

"What?" Jamie said, taking a drag from his cigarette. John stormed to him and slapped the smoke out of his hand.

"You know Ryan is *slow*," he said. "You know he takes a while to understand things. Kids got the damn mental age of a nine-year-old." Jamie did know this, but hadn't thought to remember that detail knowing that the police would be breaking down the door any minute and they were going to prison for the rest of their lives.

"Sorry," he said nonchalantly. A man exhausted beyond belief. "Slipped my mind." John eyed his friend. At one point, he would have cut out the tongue of any man who would disrespect his family so openly in front of him. But Jamie Green wasn't just *anyone*, and this wasn't just any *old day*.

"I'm going to go get rid of the van," John said. "Then, we wake this fucker up, and he tells you where your boy is."

"What if it isn't him?" Jamie blurted, his fingers bridged like a chapel roof, pressing into his lips. He stared at the broken body of what was once a man. His body marred and scarred beyond recognition like a road map had been carved into his flesh. He would beg for death by the time they were through with him. All of them had taken their turn on him in between Simon's drilling: burning. Hammering pins under fingernails. Placing a hot iron on his arms. Boiling water on his neck. Anything they could to get some little nugget of information out of him. They knew how to hurt men, him and Jamie. Only Ryan didn't partake as he said he didn't like the sight of blood, but John made him watch anyway. Even handed him a hammer to smash in one of Gary's fingers. He threw up when he heard the crunch.

But Gary still screamed the same words, over and over.

"I haven't touched him! I promise! Let me go!"

"What if it isn't him that took my son?" Jamie reiterated. John's face contorted.

"He's lying." John spat.

"How do you know?" Jamie said. "What we've done to him. I'd have confessed by now." A silence drew out between him and John.

"Because there is nothing more insidious in this world than those that hurt children," John said cooly. "Crimes of violence. Power. Lust. They are of the flesh. Emotion. But harming a child? It's unnatural. Goes against every fibre of humanity. To admit that to yourself is one thing, but to look in the face of the man whose child you have harmed is to condemn yourself as a real monster." Jamie shifted in his seat.

"What if he's telling the truth?" This time, John did slap Jamie across the face. Full palm against the cheek.

"Now, you cut that out, okay?" He hissed. He pointed back to the broken man. "You know what he's done. He knows what he's done. We just need to make him tell us. I've got a few more things we can try." Jamie touched his mouth. The taste of copper seeped onto his tongue. He felt his bones rattling with pain. With fury. Unbridled and unchained. Murderous.

"You seem really certain." Jamie hissed.

"What?"

"When I showed you his license, your face lit up." He pointed to him. "You know him, don't you." John shook his head.

"Don't be stupid."

"Then what if he's telling the truth."

"He isn't."

"How do you know?" John lunged and grabbed Jamie's arm and wrestled him onto the floor.

"You either believe me that I don't know this son of a bitch, or you can walk him down to the cop shop yourself and go join our friends inside and let that bitch detective take charge." He gripped Jamie's face, bunching his cheeks together. "Is that what you're going to do, eh? Fucking grass me up? You rang me, remember? You fucking rang me for help." John seethed through clenched teeth. "You going soft on me? Going to grass me up to that cunt detective?" Jamie heaved heavy breaths, forcing them through his nostrils.

"No," Jamie croaked, chest pounding. John squeezed his face tighter, his hand like a dog bite.

"We got an understanding?" Jamie nodded. The two men glared at each other. John released him, pushing Jamie onto his back before straightening up, running his hand over his shaved head. "Now, if there's anything else?" John said, waiting for an answer. When none came, he turned on his heel and slipped out into the back of the scrap yard. "Come get me when he wakes up," he said, before disappearing out into the cold.

Jamie got to his feet and touched his face, massaging out the fingerprints that lingered in red blotches. It was just him and Gary. He looked over to the door. He heard staggered shrieks as Ryan was scrubbed raw, and the sound of sizzling as the burning van was extinguished, followed by an engine roaring to life, and the sound of broken metal being dragged away by a forklift.

Jamie moved to Gary and began to dig his knuckles into his collarbone. He didn't stir. Jamie drove his thumb into the drill wound. Gary stirred awake, then a scream rose from his throat. Jamie smothered his hand over his mouth, Gary's eyes swollen, but his eyeballs showed unrelenting terror. He should shout for John, but he found his lips remained still. Gary's eyes darted like pinballs under swollen, bruised lids.

"I'm going to move my hand," Jamie whispered. "And when I do, you're not going to scream, are you?" Gary nodded, tears trying to break through. Jamie pulled his hand away.

"Where am I? Am I dead?" He cried. "Oh god. I'm sorry. I'm sorry. Please don't hurt me anymore…"

"Shut up!" Jamie hissed. "How do you know us? Not me, but, how do the others know you?" Gary searched the room, waiting for knives to come out of the dark.

"I…" he staggered. "I killed him…"Jamie felt his world fall through the ground.

"Killed who?" Jamie said, trying to remain calm. He was getting somewhere. "Killed who, Gary? Just tell me," he said. Jamie could see the war raging in Gary's mind. He wanted to say something, to get something off his chest. A dark secret he had been hiding away. "Just tell me," Jamie said softly, a glimmer of humanity in his voice. Humanity, and desperation. "I need to know." Gary sucked in a sharp breath, his lips erupting in sharp, stabbing sobs.

"I killed that boy," he said, his face erupting in a flush of red. "I killed him. I didn't mean to." Jamie staggered back, nearly falling over the chair, his world falling to the ground like a detonated hall of mirrors. He had been right. John. He had been right all this time. He had killed his son. The words dragged out of his mouth like pulling teeth.

"My son?" Jamie stammered. "He took out his wallet, pulled out a photo of Oliver, and held it to his face, hands shaking. Spit flew from his mouth as he spoke. "Did you hurt my boy?" Jamie's throat began to seal closed. Gary closed his eyes, looking away. Jamie gripped his face, digging his fingers into his cheeks. Gary cracked his eyes open. "Look at it!" Gary forced himself to study the photo, then slammed his eyes shut.

"The boy," Gary stammered, swallowing hard. "I killed him. I killed that boy."

Chapter Twenty

Laura

The pills were scattered along the floor and Laura had turned her into the recovery position before she choked on her own vomit. Celine was out cold. She had found Laura's anti-depression medication and sleeping pills and had swallowed them like they would make her shit out a money tree. Medication designed to stop people feeling sad by making them feel nothing at all. The irony wasn't lost on Laura. How someone was trying to end their life with the same thing that was designed for exactly the opposite.

Celine's face was pasty and ashen, her caramel skin taking on a lighter tone like she was a slab of bleached leather. Her hair was matted to her face and the red wine had stained her skin and the bedsheets. The vomit, chunky like cold soup clung to her mouth and her hair.

Laura shook her and screamed her name. She pulled her eyelids open and shone her torch into them. Her pupils dilated lazily, but Celine didn't stir. How long had she been here? Did she take them last night after she had seen her at the station? Even if she survived, there was no telling what damage she may have done to her internal organs. Liver and kidneys to name a couple.

Alice was on the phone to 999. Laura told her not to call up on the radio. She didn't need more attention on her than what was needed. Laura barked Celine's details in between screams and slaps. Alice relayed the information, her voice vacant.

The ambulance arrived a few minutes later and the paramedics rushed in, carrying bags of medical equipment. They ushered Laura out of the way and Alice moved to her and put her arm around her. Laura stared at the paramedics as they dragged Celine off the bed and attached diodes and wires to her and stuffed tubes down her throat. They strapped her to a plastic gurney before hauling her down the stairwell. Laura watched her go. Staring absently at the space where she had once been.

It's all my fault, she thought. *If only I had answered the phone to her. If only I had listened to her.* She felt the burning of tears stinging her eyes, but they didn't come. She forced the pain down and fought with it in her stomach.

The ambulance doors slammed shut, and the engine fired to life. A senior paramedic returned to the house and passed Laura some paperwork in the bedroom, a large green piece of paper with a hundred different boxes, most of which were filled out. She completed them without much thought, lost in a valley of grief.

"Is she going to be okay?" Laura said. The paramedic's face was grave. He pursed his lips.

"I won't lie to you," he said. "She's taken a lot of pills, and I would say most, if not all, are working through her system along with the alcohol." The paramedic picked up the discarded bottle on the ground. "Are these hers?" Laura shook her head.

"They're mine. If I find any other drugs missing, I will let you know." The paramedic nodded and took the empty bottles of Venlafaxine.

"Is she taking anything for her own diagnosis?" Laura furrowed her brow. She played coy.

"Yeah," she said. "But I can never pronounce it. Remind me again what it's called?"

"I have checked her records with our control room. She has a recurring prescription for Quetiapine." Laura felt like she had been punched in the chest. She had no idea.

"Oh," she said, trying to hide her surprise. The pain in her stomach began to subside. "I haven't seen her taking those; we've been together for months."

"She hasn't mentioned her BPD to you?"

BPD?

"What's that?" Alice questioned, saving Laura the trouble. The paramedic looked over his shoulder like he was going to let the two women in on a big secret.

"Borderline Personality Disorder," he said. "It's a cluster B personality disorder found in the American DSM5, and the British ICD for psychiatric disorders." Again, Laura lied.

"Yes of course," she stammered. "I've heard of that. She had mentioned it in passing, but I didn't think she was taking anything." The paramedic shifted his weight.

"Well, she is. Without overstepping the line, if I may ma'am," he said. "This is a common trait with people with this disorder when they stop taking their medication. Suicide attempts. Outbursts of rage. Depressive symptoms and emotional dysregulation. Have you two had a fallout recently?" Laura felt like she was in a counselling session. She nodded, exposing vulnerability.

"She thought I was going to leave her," Laura whispered. *And I thought I was too.* The paramedic nodded slowly, as if the pieces were falling into place.

"BPD is characterised by a fear of abandonment. They may treat a partner horrifically but then be destroyed when they think they will be abandoned. If you two have had an argument, and she hasn't been taking her medication, then I would think that this is what caused this attempt." Alice chirped in.

"Sorry," she said. "Do you think she was faking it? Like this was some sadistic cry for help?" The paramedic shrugged.

"I don't know," he said, "And I wouldn't like to say. There were a lot of pills missing, and the alcohol was completely gone. Plus, she was unresponsive. Her blood pressure was low." He checked his watch. "What does she do for a living?"

"CSI," Laura said. Then the penny dropped. "So, she knows about chemistry and chemicals."

"Hmm," the paramedic said. "I'm sure you are aware, those that make a genuine attempt at ending their life will usually leave a note or disappear without any way of getting in contact with them. Men, more than women will make preparations. Women, statistically speaking, are more prone to impulsive acts of self-destruction. But they are more likely to use it as a *cry for help*, like you say." The three heard the sound of the ambulance sirens firing to life. "I need to go," the paramedic said. "If you can find her medication, or find any kind of indication of how much she has consumed, or how long ago she took them, then that will help us greatly." He moved to the door. "Do you want to come with us?" He said. Laura barely heard him, the new information like sharks swimming in her mind.

"We'll be okay," Alice said, filling in the space. With that, the paramedic nodded sympathetically before moving down the stairs and heading into the ambulance, which sped away with a blare of sirens and flashing lights. Alice and Laura sat staring into space, with just the sound of their own breath for comfort.

"What's Quetiapine?" Laura pulled away and got to her feet.

"It's an anti-psychotic," she said, bursting into the bathroom. "A strong one too." Alice followed behind her. Laura was opening the waste bin next to the toilet and poured it onto the ground. Old razors. Tampon wrappers. Tissues and used makeup wipes.

"What are you doing?" Alice asked. Laura frantically looked through the mess, mind going haywire. Not finding what she was looking for, she stood and pulled the lid off the top of the toilet. She had done many drug busts in her time. She knew where people hid the things they didn't want to be found. Her stomach tied in knots. Right there, floating on the top of the toilet basin in a plastic bag. A box with Celine's name on it and the word *Quetiapine* written in bold letters on a nice pink and blue coloured box. Laura ripped them out of the standing water and pulled the bag open. She took out the blister pack of drugs and found all of them to still be in there. The front of the box said twenty-four pills, and Laura counted two blister packs of twelve.

The blood drained from her face. How could she lie to her like this? Maybe she had a reason. *Hey baby, so I might get a little weird if we ever separate. Might try to kill myself. I'm on medication for it, but I won't take it. Where's the fun in controlling chaos anyway?*

Laura snapped open the blister packs. Celine had taken advantage of her. She let her into her home. Into her bed. Into her heart. She had built the highest walls imaginable that even the boom of God's trumpet wouldn't be able to make them crumble. Celine had entered her life when she was vulnerable. When she was confused. When a goddamn killer was trying to communicate with her by leaving memorabilia of her abusive ex-boyfriend at the scenes of mutilated bodies. Celine had prayed on her. Laura was vulnerable and wanted someone to hold her and comfort her. She was in pain, and Celine could smell it like a bloodhound trying to fish out a rat from the undergrowth. And when Laura got sick of her clinginess, her shit, her need for validation at all times. When the fast-burning flame of their romance began to slow and settle, that's when she noticed the problems appearing. The fights, the lack of intimacy. Sure, Laura had played her part, but she was the head of a Major Investigation Unit and she had reporters snapping photos of her every second of the day. She needed support, not the withholding of it. Which is exactly what had happened – Celine wasn't getting the crazy excitement that they'd had to begin with. They weren't fucking three times a day and five on weekends anymore. Normal life had settled in. That was when she began to push Laura away. Withholding a kiss. Being passive-aggressive but then begging her not to go to work so they could *talk*. Making her feel terrible about working so much even though she said she admired her dedication to the job when they first got together.

Staring at the proof now made it all make so much sense.

She knew that when someone leaves an abusive relationship, they are at high risk of jumping straight into another one. Swept up with the excitement and fast pace of a new lover. But those things happen to everyone else, right? Not to her. Not to a police officer. She should know better, surely? But she was just a human with trauma and pain and a broken life, just like so many others. She was like a beacon to these kinds of people, and with each one, they took a piece of you with them, and then you wonder why you are a wasteful, withered shell of your former self, only to be more vulnerable to the next using predatory piece of shit that gives you some attention, and thus the cycle starts again.

Laura thrust open the toilet lid, ready to flush the pills away. Celine wouldn't need them. Hell, she wasn't taking them anyway. The paramedic was right. There had been no note. No venturing off into the cold night with no way of tracing her. As if needing one final point to prove that her girlfriend was a using, attention-seeking piece of shit, she pulled out her phone and checked her voicemails.

"Five new messages," the robotic voice said. "First message."

"Laura," Celine said. "I don't know what I have done wrong. You have been so distant since you got out of the hospital. I need you to speak to me. I think I am losing you." Laura hit delete. She was lying. *Celine* was the one that had grown distant. She played the second message.

"Fine," Celine blurted. She was angry. Her voice raw with pain. "Be like that. Ignore me. After everything I have done for you, this is what I get? I wonder if they knew about the wine bottles you drink each night, if they would still think you were this incredible inspector who actually *didn't* have their shit together." She was trying a new tactic, the patterns of these people were always the same. They try what works, be it threatening, fawning, fighting or abandoning you. It was all the same, and for one goal. Manipulation. *Do as I say, or else.* Laura hit delete. The third message began to play. She was crying this time.

"I don't know what to do," she said. "I tried calling you over and over, but your work is clearly more important than what we have and what we have built together." Celine liked this tactic the best. Creating ultimatums. "Me and you Laura," she continued. "We were so strong together, and I know we have been through a lot in the past few months." Eliciting a euphoric recall. *We have been good, haven't we baby? Okay, I'll do what you want.* "I don't blame you. I really don't. You mean everything to me. You don't want me to leave you. Not really. I know that isn't true, because I would never want to be without you, and I know that you love me, and you're just confused. And that's okay, because I am too. I think we should take some time off work and go away together. How does that sound? Call me back. I love you." Laura felt knives dragging along her bones and stabbing into her heart. She hit delete. The fourth message began. Celine sounded vacant. A little drunk.

"So, I have had a few drinks. I really like red wine. I can see why you do too. I didn't know you had so much!" Laura heard the clinking of a glass and the sound of the bottom of a bottle being dragged along the kitchen counter. "Listen, just come home. I'll still be up. I know you're working, and I love how hard you work. I do. I know how dedicated you are to your job. You help so many people. More than I ever have." *Idealisation paired with self-defamation. Nice Celine. Very nice.* "I think that's why you want to be at work so much. I think you find me disappointing to be around, that you don't actually care about me that much because of how great you are." She was slurring her words. "But you know that anyway, don't you?" Her voice was becoming more agitated. "You know how much I have tried for you. To make us work, and what do you do for me? What reason should I even be with you, Miss high-and-fucking-mighty? Huh? Have you even told people that we are together? Or am I your little secret? Is that it? You're embarrassed to be with me, even though I do everything for you? I hate you, Laura. I hate you! Why can't we ever do things together? Why can't it just be me and you? Why can't for once, we just -" The call cut off. Laura hit the next message.

There was silence. The sound of shuffling. Breathing.

"I don't know how much I have drank..." She whispered. Laura's heart seemed to stop. "I think I have had some of your tablets to help me feel happy. I think I took too many. But I suppose this is what you want. Me out of your life. Fine. You got what you wanted. I think…" The call falls into silence before cutting out.

"End of messages," the robotic woman said. Laura stared at the phone. She didn't know for how long.

"Boss?" Alice said meekly. Her voice sounded distant. Laura saw the hand with the pills in was a tight fist. She uncoiled it, the pills crushed to powder and crumbled blister packets.

It was all a game to her, Laura thought. *All of it. It was all a game.*

"You're just like Ron," she had said. *An abuser. But it wasn't her. No. It was projection. Celine knew what she was doing, and Laura had fallen for it.*

"Laura," Alice squeaked again. "Are you okay?" The words fell dead in the air, like arrows blown away by a strong wind that crashed to the earth. Laura lost in her own mind. Drowning in a black abyss with sharks looming underneath. She needed some sleep, a shower, and the bottle. She could feel the shakes on the horizon. She lifted the toilet seat and looked into the water. She was about to drop the meds in when she saw something at the bottom of the basin that made her stomach do backflips. It was a tablet. A little round pill tucked just before the U-bend.

"No…" she mouthed. She rolled up her sleeve and plunged her hand into the water, careful not to let the pill be swallowed into the pipes. She pinched it between her fingers and lifted it out. It was worn, the water eroding the front, but she recognised it. She had been taking them for years. It was one of her own pills. A depression tablet. She had flushed them. Not taken them. It was all an act after all.

"What is it?" Alice said, eyeing Laura with a face of worry. Laura crushed the pill between her fingers that disintegrated like white ash. With that, her love for Celine dissolved and what little feelings she had for her hidden behind the tall walls she had built around herself were thrown into a pit of snakes where it they were devoured and destroyed. She stood, rectified herself, then wiped the tears that were encroaching on her eyelids. She turned to Alice who stood there, the morning light casting her in golden radiance. She rushed to Alice, grabbed her face between her hands and slammed her lips against hers. Alice recoiled and the two shared a stare.

"What are you doing?" Alice said, taken back, breathing heavy. Laura eyed her up and down, a rush of adrenaline flooding her body. Her pussy pulsing, yearning for comfort. She grabbed a handful of Alice's hair and nestled it in her fingers. Alice let out a small moan and that smile grew larger.

"Moving on," Laura whispered. "Now stop talking and get on the fucking bed."

The pair lay there. Laura stared up at the ceiling as Alice cuddled into her bare breasts, sweat dripping from the pair of them.

"Where did that come from?" Alice giggled. She traced her fingers down her stomach. "I know they say don't shit where you eat, but when it's that good…" Laura didn't respond. Instead, she fixed her eyes on the single point on the ceiling. The weight of the orgasms making her sleepy. The world that had felt a million miles away now rushing back in around her, and yet she still felt absent from it. Laura sat up, shrugging Alice off.

"We need to get back to work," she said, before getting dressed and heading downstairs.

Chapter Twenty-One

Jamie

John walked back in with something in his hand that made Jamie realise that humanity had long forgotten this place. In one hand, he held two large crocodile clips with jagged teeth, with a long cable that snaked to the car battery in his other. On his face an inhumane grin. One of malevolence, like he was finally getting an invite to the VIP suite at a dinner party that was serving children for the main course. He pulled out a small table, its wood chipped and gnawed, and slammed down the battery.

"Where's Ryan?" Jamie asked. John sneered at Jamie.

"He doesn't need to see this next part." He slapped Gary across the face, jolting him awake from his daze. "You know what I have here?" John said, rattling his fingers along the beaten-up box with dials missing. The make of the instrument long eroded away. The faint hiss of the battery acid leaked from the bottom. A beat of silence came and went. Simon emerged from the shadows with a box cutter and sliced Gary's shirt open, peeling it away like performing an autopsy, revealing the bloodied pink below. "You have one last chance," John whispered. "Where is he?" Gary looked at the box, and what little blood he had left in him drained from his face, his flesh turning ashen. He shook his head.

"I don't know…" John pursed his lips and shrugged. He slapped the top of the battery.

"I call this the 'Jukebox,'" he said with a peal of cruel laughter. "Because it gets everybody singing." John took out the crocodile clips and attached them to Gary's flesh, the metal teeth biting into his flabby body. "Now, you're going to tell me where you put that boy and what you did to him." John moved for the dial. Jamie watched with anguish in his heart.

"I don't know!" Gary erupted in an ear-shattering scream. "I don't know! For God's sake, I don't know! I never did anything to that kid, I swear to fucking god! I didn't! I'm begging you. I'm begging you please don't!" His eyes flitted sporadically between the humming battery, John, Simon and Jamie. "Please, I promise. On my life! I saw the kid, got in my car, and left!" In the absence of his plea, his heavy heaving breath, followed by a fit of coughing that rattled around the small room. All stood silently watching him, like a bird with broken wings in the road, wondering whether to leave it be or crush its skull with the heel of their boot. Gary fell into silent sobbing, thick spittle dangling from his bottom lip like a drooling dog.

"You're lying." Gary looked where the voice was coming from and saw Jamie with eyes of fire. His glare bored into

him from the shadows. "You told me you killed him."
Gary snapped his head to John.

"You said what?" John said to Jamie, not taking his eyes
off Gary. "When?"

"Earlier. When you left. He woke up. He said the words,
'I killed him. I killed that boy'." John reeled into Gary, his
face an inch from his.

"You kill his boy?" The sound of the humming of the
battery. The hissing of the acid. The stench of the tobacco
breath. "You just kill him, or did you do something *to* him
beforehand?" John spat in Gary's face, a knob of phlegm
slapping him in the eye. "You fucking disgust me." Gary
fell silent, falling into himself. John eyed him like a shark
hungry for the lone swimmer lost in the deep, then
snatched his hand to the battery and turned the dial.

Gary's body stiffened. His face contorted like hooks
were pulling every part of him tort. His swollen eyes
peeled open. His mouth stretched like a twisted clown. His
fingers splayed. The bulb in the darkened room began to
flicker and dull. The sound of the battery whirling like a
funfair ride. In the movies, there are sparks flying, lights
popping and even screams. But in real life, it didn't happen
like that. It was silent, and Gary couldn't scream if he
wanted to. Locked in a state of hellish torment. John shut
the machine off. Gary let out an ear-shattering scream and
began to sob violently, rattling on his chair, kicking his legs
like a wailing toddler at the dinner table.

"Now," John said, Gary's screams and wails sporadic like sharp stabs in their ears. "The human body can experience up to ten volts before a complete cardiac arrest. Before that, it's cardiac disruption, muscle cramps, spasming, irreversible organ damage and," he sniffed the air, the stench confirming it. "Third-degree burns. Now talk." Gary mouthed a reply. John leaned in closer. "I can't hear you," he said. "Speak up!" Gary fell mute.

John hit the switch again. Gary exploded into a contorted starfish. Smoke began to come from his stomach as the clips cooked his flesh. A few seconds later, John turned the machine off. Another round of ear-splitting cries.

"One more time," John said. "Give me something. You killed…" He gestured Gary to continue. "What did you do to that boy? After you saw him in the car park. What did you do? You said you killed him. Did you mean to? Was it an accident?" Gary continued to sob. John righted himself, stretching out his body like he had been sitting at a monotonous desk job for the last eight hours. He crouched in front of Gary, his voice soft. "Look," he said in a soothing voice. "I don't want to hurt you anymore. But you have to help me." John pointed to Jamie. "The boy you hurt. That was his son. Now, you're lucky it's me using the Jukebox. If it was him, he wouldn't turn it off. He is the one that hit you outside your home. If I hadn't stopped him, he would have bashed your brains all over the street. He's crazy. I don't want to give him control of the Jukebox. He'll let you fry. But I will, Gary. I will if you don't start talking. Let me help you." Gary closed his eyes tightly, leaning his head back.

"You'll kill me if I tell you," Gary spat.

"I'll kill you if you don't!" Jamie screamed. "Where is my boy!" Jamie shot up from his seat and raced to Gary. Simon charged him, wrestling him, pulling him away. Jamie thrust himself free, holding his hands up in the air. Simon eyed him with venom, before turning back and joining his dad. John didn't take his eyes from Gary. He reached his hand out and touched Gary's dithering face.

"Just tell us what you did." Gary eyed John with a strange feeling of terror and love, like the master who beats the dog, but gives it a treat afterwards.

"I'll tell you," Gary sobbed. "Just please, don't hurt me anymore…" John sat back with a satisfied sigh, crooked his neck, and eyed Jamie. "At my house. He's hidden." John's tobacco-stained teeth peeped through his stretching maw.

"See," John said, returning his gaze back to the bloodied and broken crying man. "That's more like it."

Chapter Twenty-Two

Laura

Laura marched into the office, the weight of Celine's treachery bubbling in her stomach like she had sank a bottle of putrid water filled with bugs and leeches. The office was all go. Cops racing around like headless chickens, the radio going crazy in their ears. The CID department chattering away and fingers rattling furiously on keyboards, rows upon rows of empty coffee cups piled on their desks.

Laura moved into the MIU office. Jeremy and Francis were eyeing a computer screen with pads in their hands. Catherine was looking over CCTV stills. Alice moved in behind her, her smile gone from her face. Her fingers and lips still lingered with the taste of their captain. She liked it. This feeling. That it was just *their* secret. A secret she was going to use to her advantage when the time came.

"What have we got?" Laura said as she moved to the computer with Jeremy and Francis.

"I thought you were going home to get some rest?" Jeremy said, eyeing Laura like she was an uninvited guest that had made herself at home on Christmas morning expecting a slice of turkey and was helping herself to the selection of wine.

"Not when there's so much going on," she said, pulling up a chair next to them.

"You just upped and left at the scene," he said. "Everything all right?"

"Everything is fine," Laura said nonchalantly.

"Is Celine okay?" An innocent question. A reasonable question, but a question Laura regarded with a slight of malice.

"I said everything is fine," she bit. Jeremy rebuked and shrunk back to his work. He knew better than to poke the bear when it was trying to focus on its honey pot, so he let the thread of conversation die. "What do we have?" Laura asked, eyeing the screen of data in front of her. Francis piped up.

"So, the guy who we think took the child, Gary Murphy."

"Lives in a shit hole?" Laura said.

"Yes ma'am," Francis said. "We ransacked his home. Nothing of note. The boy isn't there or in the grounds. But following us leaving, a call came in from a neighbour saying that they heard shouting coming from the same address. Said she saw a van parked outside his home and that there seemed to be a struggle going on."

A van, Laura thought. *Looks like my suspicions were right.*

"Were any checks done by the officers before the code zero came in?" Laura said.

"Yes," Francis said, "but the vehicle came back to an elderly lady. The operator didn't get a chance to relay it before the alarm was raised." They must have been driving on false plates, which would suggest motive, pre-meditation. Possibly even OCG involvement. They were carrying something in the van and didn't want to get caught. What was Jamie Green up to? Laura's blood ran cold. The crime scene wasn't too far from the house of Gary Murphy. Had he kidnapped him? But that didn't make sense. Jamie Green was clean. The team had run him through PNC, local and national databases, and tried every combination of personal details. So how could he have a connection to organised crime? And what did they know about Gary Murphy that they didn't?

"Okay," Laura said, keeping her thoughts to herself. "Then what?" Alice arrived a second later with three mugs of hot coffee. She handed Jeremy and Francis one each, then handed Laura's to her. Laura took the cup, and Alice graced her fingers as she took it from her, her gaze lingering on Laura's. Alice smiled. Laura felt revulsion course through her.

This was a mistake, she thought. *A mistake that should never have happened. I'll have to speak to her later. Tell her it can't happen again. Let her down gently. That I don't see her that way, and our relationship would be highly inappropriate.*

"Thanks," Laura said. She leaned into Alice. "I need to speak to you later."

"Back at your place?" Alice mouthed, practically screwing her with her eyes. Laura ignored the question. She returned her gaze to Francis, who was lost in his world of cops and robbers, like a Springer Spaniel playing with a new ball. Laura lifted the cup to her lips. Alice lingered.

"I made it *just* the way you like it, ma'am," she said. Laura eyed the coffee with disdain.

"Go see where the CID are up to," she said to her, dismissively. Alice's face soured, and she left the office without saying a word.

"The two officers – PC Harrison and PC Fahey," Francis continued, his tone turning heavy. "The two that were assaulted."

"What's their condition?" She asked.

"Harrison is critical. We have officers with him in case…"

"In case he dies," Laura said bluntly. Francis eyed her like the air had been sucked out of the room.

"Yes ma'am," he said. "In case he dies. We have the family liaison officer on standby. Next of Kin have been informed." He ran his hands through his thick hair. "But PC Fahey is alive. Seriously injured, but alive." Laura wanted to feel happy at the news. Wanted to feel anything. But all she felt was numb.

"Finally, some good news," Laura said. "One body instead of two." Jeremy tore his eyes away from the data on his computer and fired her a look of disdain.

"Laura..."

"It's *ma'am*," she bit. She focused on Francis. "Carry on." Francis took a second. The room filled with a suffocating silence. The harsh strip lighting boring into their eyes. Laura let out a breath. "I mean it's awful," she said into the void. "He may never work again. Get a pay-out. Maybe get a civilian job. It's tragic. It really is," her voice was rising. "But pardon me for not wanting to sit here wallowing. We need to find out who did this and get them in handcuffs. I'll cry later." Laura took a drink of her coffee, as if signalling the end of the conversation. She pulled it away, eyeing it curiously. Francis grabbed his notes.

"Harris and Fahey attended the initial report and saw the house and area to be empty," he spoke robotically. Laying out the facts. "They met the informant, who passed a vague description of the vehicle and the offenders. The officers did an area search and sighted a possible match." He thrust his paperwork onto the desk. "We know what happened then." They did indeed know what happened then, making each of them fall silent.

"Ma'am," Jeremy blurted. "Are you listening?" Laura stared into the cup of black in her hand. She turned her head, searching the room for Alice. "Ma'am!" Jeremy said.

Laura snapped her attention to him and Francis that were looking at her like she had taken all her clothes off and smeared shit on the walls.

"Yeah," she said, nodding quickly. "The description of the van," she waved him on. "Carry on." Francis continued to speak. ANPR hits. Cell site masts. Witnesses. Dash cam footage. His voice sounded miles away, like someone was placing their hands over her ears. Laura eyed the coffee cup, her hands beginning to tremble, eyes flitting to the door.

She knows.

Laura looked like she was paying attention: she smiled at the right parts. Gave the right responses. Gave her own verdict and thoughts. They agreed with the OCG involvement and decided to look into historic tiger kidnappings with similar motives. The mood in the room picked up. Became excited. An air of determination flowed through each of them. But her mind was elsewhere. The taste of vodka in the drink making her gut bounce.

How did she know?

"And if you look here," Francis took out some CCTV stills taken from a neighbour's Ring doorbell. "They were parked up watching the house when we were there."

I'm ruined.

"They must know him. They must have a connection with him. Do you think it's an associate of some kind? I'll look through his records, see if anything stands out."

If she knows, then she can end everything.

Her fingers searched the inside of her coat pocket. The vodka bottle. She had one left, and it was gone. The realisation slammed through her head like a truck through a hall of mirrors. She eyed her desk. After they searched the house. Sitting at the desk. Jeremy burst in. She must have dropped it. Alice must have grabbed it. At her home. In the car. At the scene. She had it on her, waiting for her moment. She felt like she was going to throw up.

What the fuck have I done?

"You okay, boss?" Francis said. Laura was anything *but* okay.

"Just continue," she said vacantly.

"We have looked at the body-worn video. It's not great, but I managed to take stills of the suspects and play around with the resolution." He clicked on a tab. "The first one, the younger one, we are running him through all the facial recognition tech we can get our hands on. So far nothing. But the second one —" He clicked on another image. A picture of a pair of eyes behind a balaclava. Eyes that were filled with hatred. Eyes that held nothing but malice and contempt for mankind. "Simon Heywood. His son died a few years back. Age nine. A boating accident. Never came to our attention before then." He flicked onto Simon's record. His face in full view. A dash of stubble, and those same hateful eyes staring back at them. "His father is John Heywood." Laura had heard the name before, but her mind was a fog filled with barbed wire.

"Explain," she whispered.

"John Heywood. Known for GBH, attempted murder, kidnapping, torture. You name it. They're an old organised criminal group. The *Heywoods*. Inventive, I know. But they were part of something much, much bigger. Remember on the news a few years back? Interpol busts around Europe and took millions of pounds worth of cocaine and heroin off the streets?" He tapped his screen. "This was them. Word on the street was that someone snitched and gave some information to the right people, which led to the busts. OCG's dragged out of their beds in dawn raids and thrown into prison to rot. Somehow, John didn't do time for it, and they have been quiet ever since." He looked over his notes.

"I think that this Murphy was the pig that squealed, and the Heywoods are getting their revenge for him destroying their criminal enterprise." Laura managed to pull herself out of her narrative of self-destruction for a moment, the information like banging on a drum covered with moss and dirt, bouncing it off into the stratosphere.

"We think they took Gary?"

"We do ma'am," he said. "But that's not everything." He flicked back to the stills. He beckoned Laura over. She stared at the still image on the screen. He hit play. Laura watched as the officers moved to the driver. His face clear as crystal on the footage. "That is John Heywood," he said, pointing to the screen. "Nicknamed '*The Butcher*.'" Francis ran his hand over his face. "But there's more." He fast forwarded the footage to the point where the assailant dives out of the car. He turned the volume up. "Listen." They sat there listening to the shouting and screams. Each with their hearts in their throats. And then, cutting through the chaos, the sound of someone shouting a name.

"Did I hear what I think I heard?" Laura said. Francis nodded. They played it again. Right when the driver attacked the officers, someone shouting a name.

"John! No!" The team shared a collective sigh.

"John, no." Laura said. "So, we think this is John Heywood and his gang?" Francis nodded. "If Interpol did a bust, why is *he* not behind bars rotting with the rest of them?" Francis flicked through some more tabs, his tongue running riot.

"It was tough to find, a lot of sensitive intel around him and his profile. On the face of it, it looks like he's hardly known. But if you have special clearance," he pressed more button combinations than Laura could count, before opening up another menu on the system that she hadn't ever seen before. Jeremy too looked both perplexed and somewhat impressed. Francis hit a button, and the occurrences linked to John Heywood began to appear, the system flickering as it tried to load them.

"Jesus," Laura said, reading some of the captions, from armed robbery to murder intel.

"Yeah," Francis said. "He has a hell of a rap sheet. He is one of the most prolific enforcers in the UK database." Francis zoomed in on the photo of John and his greyed wrinkled face. "We find the van, we find him and his crew, and we find Gary. Bring him in for questioning, whatever is left of him, and then we find Oliver." Laura studied the pixelated face on the screen.

"What does this have to do with Oliver?" Laura queried. Francis smiled.

"Because," he said. He pointed to the screen at the figure in black. "At first, I couldn't make it out, but if you play with the settings…" Francis completed wizardry, and Jamie Green appeared before their eyes.

"Fuck me…" she hissed, staring at the face. "I don't believe it." Laura stood up straight. "What the hell is he doing with them?"

"I questioned that myself," Francis said. "We've ran him through, Jamie Green. He's squeaky clean. Not a mark on him. But then I thought of aliases. I called my old friends in the NCA and got some extra, juicy intel clearance." Francis' fingers moved so fast she was waiting for smoke to come off the keyboard. Jamie's face emerged on the screen. He looked much younger in the photo. "His name isn't Jamie Green. It's *Eric Dorsey*, and he was the most wanted man in Europe at one point."

"I'll be damned," she whispered. "Head to his associates," she said. Francis did. And just like that, she saw the name John Heywood. "Fuck…" She couldn't believe it. It was all falling into place. But that still didn't solve the question of Oliver.

"Why is it so encrypted?" Jeremy asked. "Why not just have it out for us to see?"

"That's why," Laura pointed to the screen to a tab saying 'PROJECT HYDRA.' "Click on it." Francis did, and a world of secrets unravelled before them with more agencies she could shake a stick at: MI5, GCHQ, NCA, INTERPOL. Laura leaned in.

"Project Hydra. An international effort to bringing offenders and members of the Chaser Gang to justice." Laura read further. Jamie Green was no ordinary man. That's why his record was hidden. It was all protected. He was a man on the inside of the organisation. He had been a career criminal until he was facing a lifetime behind bars. He struck a deal to be an informant, to take the criminal gang down from the inside. He did just that. Some of the biggest names in the criminal underworld were arrested in dawn raids around Europe and parts of Central America.

"I remember hearing about this on the news," Francis said. He spoke in awe of what he was seeing, like it was Christmas day and he had finally got that special gift he had always wanted but never knew how badly.

"So, Jamie tries to start a new life. His son is taken, and he calls upon his old friends to repay their debt for keeping them out of the big house," Jeremy resounded.

"But why?" Francis asked. "If you had so much to risk, why would you go back to such debauchery?" Laura eyed him.

"Some people are monsters through and through," she said. "All it takes is something big enough, like your child going missing, and the chains of society and consequence disintegrate away. People will go to the ends of the earth for their children, and they will walk through the inferno no matter how badly it burns." Laura stepped back. Catherine burst into life. She had been sitting silently, looking over documents and information. Laura hadn't noticed she was there.

"I found something!" She shouted like a giddy school child. She ran to the rest of the team with a stack of photos and papers in her hands.

"What is it?" Jeremy asked. She slapped down the stack of photos of a dark green van driving along some of the main routes, several days, even weeks apart. "That's our vehicle."

"How do we know that?" Laura said.

"I cross-examined the ANPR hits with the CCTV hits. Took forever, but I managed to find a date when they were stopped by an officer, and the driver was given a ticket for not wearing a seat belt. The officer took the registration number. The driver came back no trace."

"So? How do we know it's the same people?"

"Because I ran through the VIN number. The registration plate is a clone and comes back to someone on the other end of the country. Now, most people only change the registration number because *that's* what's picked up by the cameras, but the officer took the VIN number too and filed the ticket. I found the paperwork, and I ran it through. The registered keeper comes back to John Grey."

"So, we need to find John Grey?" Laura asked, perplexed.

"Not exactly." Catherine said. "I thought it looked like an old van. Something beat up. So, I started looking into local recycling businesses, trade firms, and building supplies. Nothing. So, then I contacted the local dealers to see if anyone had had any recent purchases of this kind of vehicle that came to mind. Then I found someone who did recognise the name. Got really upset actually. A dealership on the other end of town. Said that someone called John Grey had been into their business and purchased a vehicle and never paid. Believe that they faked the background checks and credit reports."

"How would someone do that?" Francis said. Laura eyed him.

"It's easier than you think: a dead relative, an old spouse. You just need documents that look real enough to not raise any suspicion. Have you never heard of 'fraud by false representation' before?" A whisper of laughter. Catherine continued. "They said that the van was bought on finance but never paid. Now, thankfully the business had some brains and asked for a guarantor for the loan. The guys said that the person buying the van was pretty young and a little uneasy. He put down the name 'Ryan Heywood,' on the credit agreement. I ran the name through the box and there isn't much other than mention of him on a log of a child death in a local river."

Pieces began to fall into place. Laura was nearly salivating at the mouth.

"I asked if they had CCTV footage. It was a long shot, but he said he always backed up anything that didn't sit right. He emailed me over a photo of him from the CCTV. He was with another guy too. Taller. Broader. Didn't say much." Catherine produced the still. There in front of them was Simon Heywood. Clear as crystal. Next to him at the counter was John Grey, AKA his brother, Ryan Heywood, who was linked to him. He had inadvertently signed his own name. Dumb son of a bitch. They had them. They had their suspects. John, Simon and Ryan Heywood and Jamie Green AKA Eric Dorsey. "That's not the best part," Catherine continued, smiling. The room was silent, like waiting for the big reveal of a magic show. "I did some digging into local businesses. John Grey is listed as the owner of 'Grey's Scrapyard,' on the outskirts of town." Laura could see it now. A clear paper trail that had tried to be covered up with fake names and lies. But if you could wade your way through the mud, you found the fine flowers trying to bud underneath them. Laura felt a swelling of pride appearing in her stomach. They had the vehicle. They had their suspects. Their motives. And now, they had a clear trail linking them all together. She eyed Catherine proudly.

"Good work, detective." If Catherine had a tail, it would be wagging. She turned to the team. "Get your kit on," Laura said. "We're going hunting."

Chapter Twenty-three
Eric

Gary wished for death.

John and Jamie sat in the front. Ryan to his right. Simon to his left. The five of them encroached back to Gary's home address in complete silence in the cramped Ford Focus. The seats were lined with plastic which crinkled under Gary's weight as he moved and groaned. Gary went to speak, but the feeling of the knife pressing against his abdomen by Simon kept his lips firmly shut. His head was spinning. He didn't know how much blood he had lost or how long his wounds would take to start to fester. All he knew is when they discovered what he had in store for them, they would cut his throat and spill him out onto the pavement.

The streets were sleepy, only a few cars passing them on their way. They avoided the main highway routes and took the back roads instead. Shortcuts. Lesser used roads that didn't trigger ANPR cameras and that were less likely to run into the law. Jamie sat pondering, lost in his own mind.

At my house, Gary had cried. *The police wouldn't find it. But I'll show you.* That's all he had said, and before Jamie knew it, he was in the car and en route. What was he taking them to find? Was he going to find Oliver? Was he still alive? The weight of that possibility began to consume him. Finding his son locked away in the dark, his supple body bent and contorted, his face fixed in a final scream for his dad. Jamie shook the thought from his mind. He didn't want to let such atrocities plague him. He had to hold what little was left of his resolve to prevent him from diving into the back of the car and repeatedly plunging the knife into Gary's stomach. Jamie eyed John. His grey whiskers shone in the golden ray of the rising sun. The Nina Simone song came into his mind as he stared out of the window up to the blue and purple sky.

It's a new day. It's a new dawn. It's a new life for me...

What that new life consisted of however was uncertain, like plunging yourself into the black abyss in the dead of night, while monsters circled below you in the deep.

He had been on the run for the best part of eighteen months when his son was born. He fled to Europe and settled in Prague. It was nothing new. He learned enough of the language to get by and to blend in. Be ordinary. Easily miscible. Eric Dorsey got a job as a taxi driver for a local firm that paid cash and a small apartment building that didn't need proof of ID. A complete hell hole, but one he couldn't be traced to. The days stretched to weeks, that bled into months. The eye of the law always searching for him, but he kept his head down. After so long however, the mind starts to wander, and those rotten thoughts begin to ferment.

He had become a father. Claire was pregnant when he left in the night, leaving her twenty-five grand in cash and a note that said *forget me.* But the guilt ate away at him like an insect that had burrowed deep in his brain and was feasting on the soft parts. He had a son back home, and he had abandoned him just as his own father had done to him. He didn't even know his own child's name.

Thoughts infected his mind each night as he lay in bed staring at the damp-ridden ceiling. The next-door neighbours screaming at each other in foreign tongues. He began drinking to block it all out, until one night he couldn't take it anymore. His blood saturated with cheap whisky, he fished out his burner phone and called Claire.

"Hello?" She said, sleepily. He paused. His mouth drying up.

"It's me," he said, his gums and tongue numb.

"Who?"

"*Me.*" He hushed. He heard Claire stifle over the phone.

"What the hell do you want? Where are you? There are police always knocking on our door. They make the neighbours nervous and make the baby cry." *The baby cry without his father there to protect him.*

"I'll figure it out," he said. "I'll find a way to come home. I'll get some of my people to drop some money off for you. I don't want you struggling."

"He doesn't need money Eric," she hissed. "Oliver needs a father!" She raised her voice, and then the sound of a baby's cry pushed through the receiver, the sound splitting the dead air, carving out the ocean and the land that separated them like he could run uninhibited to the child's aid. "Great," she said with a frustrated sigh. "You've woken him up." She killed the call.

Eric stared at the phone and continued to sit at his dinner table, his tears mixing with the amber liquid in his mug, the single bulb above him flickering. He had all the money in the world tucked up in safehouses and tied into businesses as a front to his empire. He had more cars, women, and expensive clothes and jewellery than the Tinder Swindler. And yet, the sound of that little boy crying for someone to hold him made him feel like the poorest man in the world. he stood up, stumbling and catching himself on the lip of the table. He moved to the sink, poured a glass of water, and sank it in a breath. The chemicals made it taste like cheap perfume, the conversation running around his mind.

"He doesn't need money Eric."

His legs turned to jelly, and the glass slipped from his fingers and exploded onto the ground. A sober thought filled with panic plunged his stomach into the pits of dread.

She said my name, he thought. *I made a call, and she said my name.* He turned around on a dime and clung to the back of the sink basin. He heard the sound of footsteps on the stairwell. He eyed the door, waiting for cops to burst through at any moment with rifles trained on him.

He had to leave. Right now.

Eric grabbed his belongings and stuffed what he could into a duffel bag. He took out his fake passport and ID and a few thousand Korona, Euros and Dollars hidden in a shoe box under his single, squeaking metal framed bed. He burst out of the room and fled down the stairs, catching the eye of a drunk man in a shirt and tie fighting with the key to his room.

Outside, the Czech air bit him. It was mid-November, and the snow had begun to fall. He turned down the busy streets, moving through a thicket of people out doing early Christmas shopping and partygoers out for a stag do or weekend away. His leather coat swung as he moved. He turned his head to check if he was being followed. He couldn't see anyone, but he knew they were onto him. Like a deer moving through the forest can taste the air of a wolf nearby, he knew in his heart that they were closing in. For the first time in forever, he felt fear wrap its icy fingers around his heart. But the scariest part was, he didn't know what they looked like or when they would strike. He turned his head again. Through the myriad of souls and faces, he saw two people in dark clothing moving with an air of determination, their eyes trained on him. He could be being paranoid, but that didn't mean they weren't after him. He took a sharp turn down a side alley and continued walking. He crouched behind a large dumpster, waiting for the maw of the alley to fill with bodies. The two men in dark clothing stood at the foot of the alley. Eric's heart in his throat. They turned towards him.

Eric was hot on his toes and could hear his pursuers gaining ground, calling for him to stop. He raced to the end of the alleyway and along a busy road, cars slamming on the brakes and skidding on the fallen snow. Blaring horns split the night as his feet pounded underneath him, readjusting the bag around his shoulder. He had to shake his tail before they threw him behind bars for the rest of his life.

He charged along the pavement, knocking people out of the way like a speeding bowling ball scattering loose pins. People hollered and screamed at him. Up ahead, he saw police cars speeding down the street and above, he could hear the familiar hum of a helicopter with a large spotlight flying overhead. Adrenalin frenzied, feeling like a hare chased by bloodhounds, he darted quickly into the building next to him, heaving open the heavy glass doors into a showroom awash with bright lights.

Sports cars ranging from Lamborghini to Porsches, Ferraris to stylish Mercedes. The police congregated at the foot of the door, Glocks in their hands. They burst through the door and saw Eric vanish into one of the back rooms. They shouted to each other, the customers in the building freezing in shocked horror. A salesman held a clipboard with a pen hovering over the top of the dotted line, no doubt about to secure the big sale.

Eric turned and lifted the Beretta, squeezing the trigger, sending explosive rounds through the air, which shattered the showroom glass. The cops recoiled, diving for the ground, returning fire. The bullets went wide, smashing lights, sinking into walls which exploded in brick and dust. Eric ducked behind the sales counter, seeing a redhead with a black pencil skirt cowering behind the desk. He snatched out his hand and grabbed her, her screams and shrieks cutting through the room. Police trained their weapons on Eric, and he gave the officers another round of fire. The wailing bitch wrapped tightly in his arm screamed in a foreign tongue, and he pulled her through to the back door with him.

The cops fanned out. Police vehicles screeched to a halt outside, and the side door poured bodies clad in black armour and weaponry like a troop of ants armed to the teeth.

Eric rushed into the back of the building, dragging the receptionist with him. His breath heavy in his chest, heaving in the expensive perfume which emanated from his captive. His body drenched with sweat. He had to get out. Had to do something fast. He eyed a key safe hanging on the wall and released the prisoner.

"Open it!" He screamed, at the dithering wreck in front of him. She was only young, maybe twenty. An engagement ring on her finger. Mascara drenched and smeared along her cheeks. Eric trained the gun on her. She screamed, lifting her hands, hoping they would stop her face from eating a bullet. Eric fired into the ground. The popping of the barrel making his ears ring. "Now!" He raised the gun back to her. She took out her keys, hands trembling furiously, trying to stab the key in the lock. Eric looked back to the foyer door. The police would break through any second. "Hurry up!" The woman dropped the keyring. Eric shoved her out the way where she crumpled to the ground. He aimed the gun at the lock box and fired, it exploding open, ricocheting off the wall, revealing a set of dangling keys to the toys on display outside. He took a handful of them and rushed through the back entrance and was led into another showroom that was shrouded in darkness, the windows blacked out, no doubt where they kept the best cars that were only available to those that *really* had the money to go playing.

He moved quickly, hearing shouts and calls from police that were closing in. The cars in the showroom were covered over with thick blankets like bodies in a mortuary. He clicked one key. Nothing happened. The calls of the law getting closer. Eric tossed the key to the ground. The world growing smaller with every second. He clicked another key, the darkness of the room growing so thick he was practically chewing on it. Nothing chirped. He heard an assembly behind the showroom door. He clicked another, and one of the cars chirped amber lights that cut through the darkness. He raced to it like a burning man to water. He pulled the shroud off.

To say he didn't feel a beat of joy would be a lie as he stared at the motor. He jumped over the door and into the driver's seat of the Maserati GranCabrio and stabbed the keys into the ignition. The beast roared to life just as the back-room door burst open that severed through the blackness. Eric fired up the ignition which roared a devilish growl, the red glow of brake lights meeting the officer's eyes.

"Stop!" They screamed. Jamie eyed them in the rear view.

"Fuck off." He slammed the gearstick into drive and smashed his foot on the accelerator. The back wheels screeched loudly, carving into the marble flooring and spewed out thick white smoke into the air. Eric released the handbrake and propelled forward, the sound of the exhaust roaring like Satan's cry itself.

The car smashed through the showroom glass and Eric exploded out into the busy street. Sparks flew as bullets ricocheted off the body of the vehicle. The suspension screamed with the impact sending a flurry of sparks onto the ground as he shifted into sport mode and took off into the night, the engine screaming like a banshee.

The cops weren't far behind him, and his rear mirror was flooded with flashing reds and blues in a matter of seconds. The chopper above him kept up with him, dousing him in harsh light as he blasted down the Czech highway. He came to a junction to join the main highway and turned on a dime, snapping the wheel to the right and joining the busy carriageway on the contravene. Cars raced towards him, their headlights resembling that of a train flying down a tunnel with someone strapped to the tracks.

Eric moved onto the hard shoulder, stabbed back into the lanes, and wove between traffic. He turned his head and saw the chopper above him dancing in the air, weaving around powerlines and telephone poles. The sound of distant sirens blasted through the fierce air that enveloped him in the convertible.

Cop cars joined the carriageway behind him, clumsily weaving in and out of traffic. They didn't have the experience Eric did. He was the man when it came to this shit. Hand brake turns. Limit points. Splash gear changes. He knew how to drive. Pair that with prison, bloodied knuckles with gangsters and cops alike, and a hell of a shot, and he was one of, if not the deadliest man walking God's green earth. Even Genghis Khan would shit a brick. His employer would not be happy if he didn't go down without a fight.

A cop swung out to his right, the stream of oncoming traffic abating. An officer leaned out of the passenger window, the wind and snow pelting his reddening face as he steadied the pump action shotgun aimed at Eric's tyres.

Eric trained the Beretta on the car and let out a spray of rattling lead. The tiny teeth chewed away the windows and the body of the car in a flurry of sparks that danced onto the black highway. Eric caught one of the tyres and it erupted, shredding into the road. The cop car slumping and the rim of the wheel carving into the ground like a circular saw carving granite. The driver desperately trying to keep control of the wheel as his passenger clung onto the window he was hanging out of.

Eric's front windscreen exploded, and part of his seat was blown away. A shower of glass doused him like rain made of razor blades. The rear-view mirror was torn away and rattled onto the carriageway. He snapped his head back and saw a cruiser car right on his tail. It rammed him to the back, making Eric grab the wheel with both hands, dropping the Beretta onto the ground of the Maserati, narrowly missing an oncoming HGV which blared its horn.

Eric had an idea. It was risky, but crazy enough that it might work.

He swung out to the outside lane when he saw a gap in the traffic. Quickly, he grabbed his weapon and snapped on the handbrake, forcing the back of the car into a deadly spin. He curtailed a one-eighty, headlights of the cop car blaring him in the face as he lifted his Beretta and let hellfire rain.

The police car swerved, the windscreen exploding and the car spasming like a toddler had grabbed it and was shaking it on the ground. It collided with the central reservation before spinning out of control, its wheels lifting off of the ground as it got airtime. The roof of the car kissing the asphalt. Windows smashing. Metal crunching. Eric righted the car and left the trail of chaos behind him. The lights of the cop car dying away as he drove full speed to freedom.

The chopper followed him above. He turned the Beretta and fired a flurry of bullets into the sky which bounced and pelted the helicopter, sending it veering away, only to return a moment later up higher and out of range. Eric kept the accelerator glued to the floor. The speedo shaking, buried into the red. The seemingly straight road turning into bends. The sound of his wheels scraping along the ground, desperately trying to hold on with their rubber feet and the stench of burning hit his nostrils as he flew down the highway. The chopper above veered off into the darkness, its drone vanishing away into the black sky. The flow of traffic stopped, and just endless black road appeared in front of him. He dared to think he got away, but as he moved around a bend, he knew that the law didn't give up that easily.

In front of him in the far distance, Eric saw a wall of flashing blues and reds as he drew closer to the blockade. His heart sank. This was it. The end of the line. He had one choice. Not of surrender or of defeat, but to go out in a blaze of glory. To drive head-first into that blockage of guns and metal. He would leave his son with his mother, and he would be remembered as a hero amongst thieves. A feeling of sanguine nestled along his freezing wind-bitten flesh. He was happy with that. His choices in life, how he could have chosen a different path. How he could have done better at school. Stayed away from the bad crowd. Not gotten into this game of cops and robbers. A desire to have his time again without the debauchery and sin.

He screamed as the wind pounded him and his blood ran so hot the snow almost turned to vapour. The blockade drew closer. Officers raised their weapons like he was charging towards a firing squad. The car exploded all around him as the officers opened fire. Windows shattered. Tyres burst. Metal rims scoured along the hard ground. Sparks like a dragon's breath fountained around him as the engine ripped apart like a child tearing into Christmas presents. The stench of petrol sharp in the air. Eric felt something hit him in the shoulder like a punch from a giant. Then again in the chest. Knocking the wind out of him, forcing him over the wheel, his foot slipping off the accelerator. The Beretta fell from his hand onto the highway. His mind became clear. Through the chaos. Through the storm of his life.

He wanted to live. He wanted to be a father. He wanted a new life.

He felt the adrenalin shake in his body. Another punch of a bullet into his stomach. He let go of the wheel, staring up at the dawn that bled into the sky above before he met the roadblock in a smashing of crumpled metal and body parts before the world around him went black.

Jamie emerged from his deep thought. The world had passed him by, and John grabbed him by the shoulder.

"You alright?" He said. They were at the front of Gary's house. The street dead silent.

"Yeah," Jamie said quietly like he had been sleeping with his eyes open. John cracked a crooked smile.

"C'mon," he said with a hint of compassion. "It'll be over soon." He opened the driver's door and stepped out into the crisp morning air. He moved to the back and opened the door. Ryan stepped out too.

"Why are we here, Dad?" He said with a tone of innocence in his voice.

"You know exactly why we're here, son," he said, grabbing him by the shoulder. "You're going to help us find that boy."

"But I looked before," Ryan said. "I couldn't find him."

"Now you have us with you." Ryan felt a sharp pain in his stomach. Why was his dad doing this to him? He didn't want to be part of this anymore. Simon was the bad one, not him. He didn't want to be like the two of them, and here he was, doing bad things with them. Ryan's lip trembled.

"I don't want to do this," he said. "I don't want to do this anymore." John's face turned to hatred, and he slapped his palm against Ryan's cheek and his mouth filled with the taste of rusted brass.

"*You have to*," he seethed. "You're in too deep. Now come on." Jamie slipped out of the car. He turned to Simon, who still held the knife to Gary's side.

"He makes a noise…" Jamie said. Simon made no reply. He didn't need to. He knew exactly what to do if Gary began to squeal. And he really wanted him too. Jamie stepped out into the street. Nothing moved. He made it a little past five in the morning. A plume of ghostly breath escaped his throat.

The injuries from the car chase had left him in the hospital for a month, guarded around the clock by officers that spoke in foreign tongues as they smirked and cackled at his broken body. When Eric could finally eat unaided and walk with a little less help, he was visited by someone that had given him nightmares ever since.

"Eric Dorsey," he said. He sat with his legs crossed over. His shoes were so polished, Eric could see his reflection in them. His suit was a slick silver, and his hair was combed to one side. His glasses were thick, and his face perfectly smooth. His chin hairless. "How are you?" He said with indifference, yet a warm smile along his face. Eric didn't say anything, pondering the man's being. "Not a talker?" He said. "It's okay. I don't take offence. I try not to come into this with a preconceived notion that people wish to speak to me." He was holding a copy of War and Peace in his hands. "Just doing some light reading while you slept. But seeing as you're awake..." He slapped the book closed and placed it on the chair next to him, patting the top cover down so it lined up perfectly with the other pages. "I suppose we'll get down to business." He stood, righting himself. He was tall. One of the tallest guys Eric had ever seen. He corrected his suit and took out a bundle of papers from his satchel and zipped it closed. He sat back down, crossing his legs over, and took out the papers from the folder, before placing the folder next to the book. He flicked through the pages, his face like stone. The room was silent. Eric wasn't sure if the guy was even breathing.

"Who are you?" Eric croaked. His throat arid. The man lifted a finger to silence him.

"I asked you a question before, and you didn't wish to speak. Now you wait." Eric was taken back. If he was able to move, he would have kicked his ass. But even as he thought that, he felt the regret of such a thought. Something about this guy: the way he moved. Spoke. The energy coming from him. It was that of danger. That he could be invisible in an empty room, then snap your neck when you weren't looking. "Let's have a look." The man said. He began to rhyme off the proposed charges. "Murder," he tutted. "Oh dear. That's life imprisonment. Conspiracy to commit murder. At least you didn't go through with that one. Concerned in the importation and supply of Class A, B and C substances. Hitting all the alphabet. I'll give you that. Perverting the cause of justice," he looked up to Eric. "I always wondered why when dealing with criminals, the courts are so surprised that they are liars too? I'll have the predisposition to violence. The overdrive of the adrenal gland. Lack of empathy and consequential psychopathy. But they are always so surprised when they figure out that this marauding murderous animal tells lies." He cracked a smile. "You know that the deepest circle of hell is reserved for the treacherous, don't you?" Eric looked to the blank wall of the hospital ward. "Oh," the man in the suit said. He was standing by the foot of Eric's bed. Eric didn't hear him move. "You don't believe in hell?" He sat on the chair by his bed. "Wait until you see the inside of a Russian prison. Then tell me that hell doesn't exist."

Eric thrust out his hand to try and grab the man's throat, but the handcuffs stopped his arm dead. The guy didn't flinch. He pursed his lips and nodded.

"Like I said. The propensity of violence." He shook his head. "I don't blame you entirely. Father walking out. Alcoholic mother. Abused by your headmaster when you were sent off to boarding school. In and out of care. You never stood a chance Mr. Dorsey." Eric felt his heart plunge into a pool of ice.

"How do you know that?" He whispered. The man's face showed no emotion.

"I know everything there is to know about you, Mr. Dorsey." He smiled. A smile that was the most insidious and malevolent grin he had ever seen. He did believe in hell. He was looking into its eyes right now. The suited man flicked through more pages. "Robbery. Theft," he put the papers down as if overcome by an urgent thought. "Do you know why treachery is the worst of all the sins, Mr. Dorsey?" Eric stayed silent, afraid that this guy would cut his tongue out if he uttered a syllable. "I'll enlighten you." He leaned forward. "Humour me a moment, if you will. When God made men in his image, he did so with giving us free will. The ability to choose our own path in life. Therefore, the most animalistic sins – violence, lust etc are the animal part of us. They are what God himself imprinted into our DNA. We are animals, and God loves watching his children kill each other. He loves violence, which is why there is so much of it. God made men like you to kill others. To make other men bleed in his name. Gets him all excited. Now, he reserved the worst circles of hell for those that go *against* his blood lust and take advantage of his gift of free will. Those that corrupt, steal, defraud and lie to further their own position in the world he made of us. He finds such acts of defiance and insults deplorable. And as such, we condemn those around us for doing so. Which would you rather be known as in society? Violent, or a liar. One is an attack against flesh. The other, an assault on truth." He snapped the booklet shut. "And that is why you're never going to see your son again." The suited man eyed Eric for a long second, as if wondering whether to eat his heart or his liver first. "You're going away for the rest of your life Eric," the man said. "Say goodbye to booze, women and even sunlight. Say hello to grey walls, hugs in the showers and," he smiled again. "All your rival affiliates that have been caught already. Oh, how much fun they're going to have with you when *I* send you to where they are. Like I said. You will know hell on earth. Have you ever had your eyes scooped out and fed to you? I have seen it happen, and I can assure you, you never forget the sound of those little gelatinous balls popping." Eric felt like the hangman was placing the noose around his neck, hand hovering over the lever for the trap door.

"What do you want?" Eric mouthed. The suited man let out a wheezy laugh. It was hard to gauge his age. Eric thought him young, but his aura shone black. Older. A man who had seen the worst of humanity.

"As much as I would love to see what the inmates would do to that flesh of yours," he said, sitting back down and leaning back in the hospital chair, "You are of use to us." He stood up, took some pictures from his folder, and placed them on Eric's hospital bed. "Do you recognise any of these people?" He eyed the black and white pictures of his associates standing outside of clubs, smoking cigarettes outside their homes or even at a dinner with martinis, cigars and prostitutes.

"No," he said. The suited man gave a slight smile. He stood over his bed and peeled the hospital duvet off of him to reveal his bloodied broken body. The man took a pen from his jacket and slowly pushed it into a healing bullet wound in Eric's thigh. Eric went to scream but the suited man smothered his wail with the palm of his hand, locking those dark eyes to Eric's as he squealed. Eric rattled the cuffs against the hospital bed, a muffled scream trying to break free. The man stared into his eyes unblinking. After a moment, he released him, pulling the pen out, blood and flesh clinging to it. He cleaned it with a handkerchief and put it back into his pocket. Eric sat sweating, gasping for breath.

"Let's try another angle," he said. "Your son," he said, running a comb through his hair. "A little boy. Barely a year old?"

"Fuck you…" Eric gasped. The suited man shook his head.

"You should really improve your vernacular. So primitive. Dysfunctional. An echo of a former life, Mr. Dorsey. One we should make haste to quell from this world." He collected up the strewn photos from the bed and put them back neatly into a pile then placed them along with the papers into the folder, tucking it neatly under his arm. "I can help you, Mr. Dorsey," he said. "You will be skinned alive in prison. You will never see your son. You can have a new life if you cooperate." He moved his way to the door. "I will be back tomorrow morning, and we can negotiate more." With that, he slipped out of the door and left Eric alone with his thoughts.

As the sun rose the following day, Eric was awoken by the nurse doing the breakfast rounds. The man was sitting by his bed again. Book in his hand. This time, he was dressed in a dark suit with not a single piece of lint blemishing the fabric.

"Good morning," he said in a toneless voice. He took out a pen and twiddled it in his fingers. "Now, about what we spoke about." Eric struck a deal with the suited man. He would give them as much information about the people in the photographs in exchange for a ten year sentence, eligible for early release after seven, and housed in a lower categorised prison. From there, he would have a new identity and would be allowed to move back home. He would be given some money to start his new life, and from there, he would be on his own. However, the caveat being that should he return to his old ways, he would be sent to the hellish place he had been promised with everyone he had put away. The suited man also passed him a photo of someone else. Eric recognised him immediately. It was *John Heywood*. "And him?" Eric tried to hide his worry. There was treachery, and then there was betrayal. Eric denied all knowledge of him. Said he kept himself to the shadows. That he was faceless but very feared. He didn't know if he bought it, but the man decided not to pry any further. He had the information to bring down an empire, even if that meant an enforcer getting away. They all fuck up and come to light eventually. They needed to get lucky every time, but the law only needed to get lucky once. And that was the nature of the game they played.

As Eric finished talking, the man stood up with his notes and photos. Location data, importation and county lines numbers, dead drops and meeting places. He got it all.

"My associates will be in touch," the man said as he made for the door. He clasped his hand around the door handle. "And Eric, or should I say 'Jamie,'" he laughed lightly. He pointed to himself. "Remember. I was never here." Jamie furrowed his brow. Seeing his confusion, he spoke again. "It's not only you who works in the shadows." He cracked the door.

"Don't forget your book," Jamie said, eyeing the copy of War and Peace. He had placed it on the mattress by Jamie. The suited man regarded the crinkled paperback.

"It's for you," He winked and left. Jamie turned and fingered the book, picking it up. Every page was blank. He put the book down, a chill running over him. The suited man was gone; that was the last time Jamie ever saw or heard from him.

Jamie stepped into the house, and John moved to the front along with Ryan. They eyed the plywood across the door.

"Go in through the back," John said, his tone heavy. The three of them moved towards the back of the house and hopped over the back gate which rattled under their weight. The back garden was overgrown and littered with dog shit like landmines. At the bottom of the garden was an old shed with its door hanging open, the lock had been no doubt popped by Wigtown's finest.

"Dad," Ryan croaked. "Can I wait in the car?" John shot him a look of war. Ryan rebuked quickly, and they moved to the back of the house. The back door was unlocked. John shot Ryan a fierce look, before stepping inside. Jamie followed slowly behind. John turned and looked him dead in the eyes. His face was ashen.

"Whatever we find in there," John said. "I'm sorry." Jamie gave a tight smile. In a world filled with monsters, compassion could still shine through those serrated teeth.

Oliver

Oliver watched as his dad moved away from him, clinging to his picture of Thanos and the Avengers. The wind picked up suddenly, and the sharp gust blew the picture out of his hands. He moved quickly, grasping at the picture as he ran, snatching his hand into the air and moving further away from his dad. Further away from safety. Further into the clutches of who had been hiding, waiting for him. The picture landed on the wet ground, soaking up the rainfall from the night before. A pair of dirtied shoes filled Oliver's vision. Their frame was slight. Not like the man that his dad had shouted at earlier.

"Hey," the person said. Oliver thought he recognised him, but adults were adults, and most of them looked the same, especially dressed how he was with something over his face. He was crouched behind the back of a blue car. Oliver liked the colour blue, but he also liked the colour pink, but he didn't ever tell anyone because pink was for girls, and he might be called a sissy in school. But he liked pink. Flamingos were his favourite. The person snaked their hand and peeled the paper from the floor and held it up, it dripping onto the floor. "Did you draw this?" Their voice sounded like one of his teachers telling him he had done really good handwriting. He just got a pen at school and felt so grown up. He could write joined-up writing in the lines now. He was the last one in his class to get one, and now he felt like the king of the world. He didn't like that it smudged his hand, though. He was left-handed like his dad and had to sit at the end of the desk or his hand would bump into the kid next to him.

"Yeah," Oliver said quietly. Who was this person? "Why are you sitting by the side of a car?" The face covering creased into a smile.

"I like to play hide and seek. Do you?" Oliver felt that feeling in his stomach again, the same as when his dad got mad. He shrugged.

"Sometimes," he said. "I need to go back to my dad. Can I have my picture back?" The person regarded the drawing.

"I like it," he said. "Can I keep it?" Oliver felt uneasy. He shifted in his stance like the ground was slowly heating up, but he was nailed to the spot.

"Oliver!" He heard his dad's voice in the background. "Oliver? Where are you mate?" Oliver went to turn, but a hand grabbed his shoulder.

"Don't leave," he said. "You know it's rude to turn your back on a grown-up, don't you?"

"You're a stranger," Oliver snapped. The person shook their head.

"No," he said. "I know your dad. Jamie, right?" Oliver felt the confusion dissolve a little.

"Yeah," he said quietly. He turned and saw his dad returning to the store entrance. His mouth turned dry, and he hopped on his feet more fiercely.

"You remind me of someone," the person said. Their eyes seemed kind. They pulled the mask down. Their smile was big, like a clown. "I know someone just your age that you can draw with and play games with. Do you want to come and play?" Oliver toyed with the idea.

"What's their name?"

"Daniel." Oliver didn't know a Daniel. There was a kid in school called Daniel in Miss Johnson's class last year, but he used to have packed lunches that smelt really bad, wiped his boogers under his armpits, and ate them when they dried on the way home from school.

"I need to ask my dad," Oliver said. The figure looked out to the car park.

"Your dad won't mind. We know each other, remember? I will call him and tell him you're at my house playing with Daniel, watching movies, and eating popcorn. Oliver did like the sound of that. His dad had made him sad, and he didn't know if he would be able to watch the movie as promised, even if they had bought the stuff already. He didn't really feel like it anymore. But another kid? That sounded wicked cool. Oliver felt like he had ants in his pants.

"Okay," Oliver said. The man smiled.

"Brilliant," the man said. He took Oliver's arm. "We're going to have such a great time."

Chapter Twenty-Four

Jamie

The house was silent. The boarded-up front door eclipsed all light that could push through from the lazy morning sun. Jamie felt his heart in his throat. His son. His son was inside this dark shell. Consumed by it. Unable to get out. Breathing in the stale air, unable to call for help. The blood stains on Jamie's hands and clothing. A reminder of the promise he made, trying to collect the fragments before he was hand fed to the fires of hell.

In a deal with the devil, the devil always wins.

"Where should we look?" Jamie said.

"He said he keeps everything in his bedroom," Ryan said meekly. Jamie gulped dryly.

"Then you check up there," John said, his tone heavy. "I'll go through the rest of the house. You take Ryan with you." Ryan moved to Jamie's heel like a well-trained dog.

"Oliver?" Jamie shouted. "Oliver, Dad's here, mate. Can you hear me?" Not a sound from the house other than aching pipes settling with the cold. The stairs yearned under Jamie's feet as he ascended. Crying for him to turn back. Crying at what he will find. They reached the landing. All doors closed, the walls marred with fingerprints and grime. A small window allowed some small light to pass onto the landing. The carpet underneath their feet thin and blue. Floorboards pushing through. A blue slip of a search warrant on the windowsill. Detective Laura Warburton's name as authorising officer. They had been inside the house, and they didn't find him. Wouldn't they have brought a police dog? Then Jamie thought of the police dog he had maimed, the wound on his arm throbbing. He had caused this, and not only that, he was the reason his son was still missing. He felt guilt eat him alive.

The air was stale with stagnant cigarette smoke and rotting takeaways. Jamie's feet crunching atop of discarded beer cans. He stepped into the first room. A small bathroom. Clothes lay soaking and mould ridden in the bathtub. The tub marred with a scummy circle of grime. The basin of the toilet was broken away from the wall, and Jamie could hear the buzzing of flies pushing from beneath the stained porcelain lid. The stench was sharp in his nose, and he closed the door.

"Oliver?" Jamie whispered. Dead silence answered. In another room, they found a single bed where covers had been discarded onto the ground. The mattress didn't have a sheet and was stained more shades of brown than he could count. Other than the single mattress and the chipped walls and faded wallpaper that resembled the colour of pus gushing from an infecting wound, there was nothing else of note other than a small side table that was home to more discarded beer cans and bottles that had insects crawling around the tops of them and an overflowing ashtray.

Ryan called from the other room. Jamie moved into it. This room was a little more furnished, with boxes of clothes, an open suitcase with a passport, and bundles of money.

"Was he going somewhere?" Jamie whispered, eyeing the suitcases. He rummaged through them and found a plane ticket to Spain due to leave this morning.

"Why would he want to leave?" Ryan said. Jamie knew the answer. He was running.

"I'm going to look around more," Ryan said, slipping out of the room. Jamie hardly noticed him leave. He moved through the suitcase and found a stack of old photos. Some with Gary holding a baby. Some with him looking younger playing football. The brightness of the sun marring the edges of the photo and his childlike smile. Some with family. Some with friends. Then Jamie eyed one that made the world fall apart around him.

A picture of Jamie and his son at the park. Another of them through a shop window as they were picking out some snacks a few weeks back. And then one that brought tears of rage to his eyes. A picture of Oliver lying on the ground somewhere dark, his eyes vacantly staring back at the camera. He put his hand to his mouth, trying to keep the stifled cry from escaping his trembling lips.

"Jamie." The voice came from behind him like a whisper. He turned. It was John. "I've found something," he said. John took it out of his pocket. "It was taped under the coffee table in the living room." He unfolded it. Jamie knew exactly what it was. He didn't notice the blast of anguish that escaped his mouth that bounced around the room as John passed him the picture. Everything he had feared staring him straight to in face.

The drawing of Thanos and The Avengers.

Chapter Twenty- Five

Laura

The team marched through the police station, grabbing their kit and strapping their stab vests on. Jeremy grabbed his gas whilst Francis got his taser. They moved to the back door, updating the radio as they went.

"Where's Alice?" Jeremy asked as they moved towards the exit. "We should get her to come join us."

"We don't need Alice," Laura said fiercely, her name like vomit on her tongue. "We have enough with me, you, Catherine and Francis." Jeremy didn't ask any more questions. Laura was doing that *tone*, the one that said *ask another question, and I'll rip your balls off*. He liked his balls, so he didn't ask anything else.

They stepped out into the morning cold. Some of the cars had frozen over, resembling metallic igloos. Laura hissed a plume of cold air.

"Go and find me a car that isn't frozen over," she said to Jeremy and Francis. Catherine followed too. Laura went over the game plan in her head. They had the suspects. The motive. The means and ways of modus operandi. All she needed now was some wrists in handcuffs and a CPS lawyer with a set of nuts to remand the lot of them. She had a feeling, she didn't know why, but she thought that if she found them, they would find Oliver.

She felt a pang of woe in her chest like a weight of lead attached to her heart. She had been so unfocused. So preoccupied with her own shit, that she had let herself drop the ball. This wasn't a job stacking shelves where the worst that happened was a loaf of bread was labelled wrong. No. These were people's lives; if she didn't do her job right, people died. That changes today. When this is all done and dusted, she was going to get her shit well and truly together. She was going to take some time off and get her head straight. Now, it wasn't just her that would drown if she wasn't strong enough to swim.

"Laura." The voice caught her off guard. She turned and saw Alice standing by the corner of the building, tucked away. How long had she been standing there? The sight of her made Laura's skin curl off her bones. She could taste the bubbling of bile creeping up her throat. Her jaw tensed. Stomach churning like a cement mixer. Laura marched to her.

"You've got some fucking nerve."

"What?" Alice said. "Not the right brand of vodka?" Laura felt a surge of rage. She slammed Alice against the wall, her forearm against her neck.

"Fuck you," she spat. "I could have you fired." Alice choked a laugh.

"Out of the two of us," she spat, her face turning red. "You know damn well that it wouldn't be *me* who gets thrown into the frying pan. How long have you been drinking on the job?"

"That's none of your business," Laura snapped. "I should suspend you with immediate effect."

"You say that to everyone you assault in the car park?" Her lips curled into a grin. Laura came to her senses and peeled herself away. Alice crumpled to the ground, dusting herself off and coughing, rubbing her throat. "Detective Laura Warburton," she laughed. "Famous investigator. Solver of murders. Fixer of broken things." She was mocking her. Was this what it was to her? One big joke? "All unravelled by a DC whose pussy she couldn't resist." Laura felt the jaws of consequence closing around her. The game was up. Checkmate.

"What do you want?" Laura said, vulnerability lingering on her lips. Alice could smell it like a bloodhound sniffing out a scared rabbit.

"I want," she said, dragging the words out. "I want everything you have. I want respect. I want power and a title. I want to oversee the MIU." Laura barked a laugh.

"That's not going to happen," Laura bit. Alice smirked and then shrugged. She pulled something out of her pocket, and Laura had to fight to stop her bones from rattling. It was a pair of her underwear from her home.

Laura eyed the garment with disgust, like Alice was holding a diseased rodent.

"What are you doing with those?" Laura hissed. Alice fingered them.

"Well, when I tell the professional standards that you have abused your position to get me into bed, I need a little proof, don't I?" She rubbed her throat. "And I don't have to say it was consensual, either. You had been drinking to cope with the stress of work. Family emergency. Tragedy." If she had a tongue, it would be forked. Not all serpents crawl on their bellies. It had all been a ploy – The looks in the office. The touching of hands. Brushing past her body. The kindness. The ear to offload on. All a ploy. A manipulative ploy. "I tried to comfort you," she continued. "But you wanted more. I said no, but I was scared of your reputation. What you would do to me." She sneered wider, her eyes turning pale. "And here we are," she dangled the underwear in the soft wind. "Bye bye, DI." Laura felt the world cave in around her.

"You wouldn't…"

"You have until the end of the day to resign and hand me your position." Alice's words were like a bullet through Laura's soul.

"Alice," Laura said quickly, pressing her hands to her face. "You don't understand. You're a detective. You can't just become the leader of the MIU." She tried to reason. But reasoning didn't work with monsters.

"Then just resign. Fire Jeremy. Do something. You're a clever *girl*." Laura felt her throat sewing up.

"Alice, please…" Laura begged. "You have no idea what I have been through these last twelve months."

"Not my problem," Alice said, laughing. "People are suffering because of you. I'm going to put a stop to it."

"You're doing this out of some kind of altruism? Some grey morality? Blackmail?" Laura began to tremble. She felt hot. Her heart beating rapidly. "Just… I can't…" She tried to finish the sentence, but her throat closed shut." Laura's phone began to ring in her pocket. She took it out. It was Jeremy. Alice eyed the phone.

"You better answer that," Alice said. "You have until the end of the day to make your choice. Resign and keep your dignity and then rot in a booze-filled hole, or I'll tell everyone what you did to me." She began to move away. "Make your choice. Stop thinking about yourself for a change." With that, Alice slipped away, leaving Laura to crumble in the ensuing silence.

"Laura!" The voice called. It sounded so far away. The world spun around her. A hand grabbed her, and she barely registered it. Jeremy's face met her burning eyes. "Hey," he said. "We moving or what? I've got firearms to meet us at the address." Laura nodded slowly. "You okay?" he said, concern etched onto his face. Laura sniffled and wiped her eyes.

"Yeah," she lied. "I'm just a little tired. Stuff at home. Celine has been taken into the hospital."

"Oh shit," Jeremy said. "That's awful. Do you need to leave?" Did she need to leave? To return to her empty hollow home where she could drink herself stupid until the nightmares stopped festering into her thoughts? She shook her head.

"No," she said, forcing the tears back. "We have a job to do."

Chapter Twenty - Six

Jamie

Jamie marched out of the house like he was walking through a dream. He wasn't thinking. Wasn't feeling. The world blurring around him, his eye focused on the car with the man that took his son. He tore open the back door and grabbed Gary by the throat. Gary erupted in a frenzy of hands, teeth and feet. In a flash, he back elbowed Simon in the nose, exploding it in an eruption of blood and cartilage. He grabbed Jamie's dog bite and dug his fingers deep into the wound, separating the makeshift stitching. Blinding agony flooded through Jamie, and he recoiled back, his arm drenching in red. Gary was on his toes, hobbling, stumbling, falling down the street.

"Help!" He screamed loudly. "Someone help me!" Lights flickered on in the dormant houses. Faces peeping out from behind curtains. Gary got a little further down the street before Jamie was on top of him. He dragged Gary onto the floor, his blood filled with fury.

"You fucking murderer!" He screamed, his voice that of a man that had lost everything. Unbridled and unchained rage. His knuckles smashed against Gary's jaw, knocking his rancid crooked teeth onto the ground, where they rattled like stained runes. Gary didn't have time to react, his blood dousing Jamie like hot rain. Jamie gripped him by the back of his neck and drove his knee into his stomach, and Gary vacated the contents of his gut onto the ground. Jamie tossed him onto the floor like a rag doll and sank his boot into his chest, ribs cracking under his boot. Gary spurted blood from his broken mouth, trying to finger Jamie's clothing. Jamie shook his treacherous hands off like they were hungry leeches, before driving another kick to his chest.

Cries and calls for mercy erupted around him, from familiar and unknown voices. Jamie didn't listen, lost in his own rage. Nothing mattered to him anymore. Not getting caught. Not going to prison. Not even death itself. This man had taken the one thing that meant the world to him, the very being that signified his new life. He had taken it from right under his nose, so openly, in broad daylight, and had taken pleasure in doing it. The police had missed it. The useless fucks. They had missed the vital piece of evidence that would have helped him get his son. He crouched down, scooped Gary's bloodied shirt in his fist, and rained pain into his bloodied face.

"Where is he!" Tears pushed from Jamie's eyes. Tears he hadn't shed, wouldn't allow himself to shed, that were now flowing freely.

"I haven't…"

"Liar!" Jamie screamed with murderous rage. He brought his head to Gary's, the pulp of his bleeding nose matting around his face.

"He's had enough, Eric!" John screamed, grabbing his shoulder. "Get him in the car! You fucking idiot! Look around! All the damn street out!" Jamie shoved John away.

"I'll decide when he's had enough!" He screamed, reeling his fist back for another blow. "You brought us here! You knew that my son was here! Where have you taken him?"

"He told me to bring you here," Gary croaked, surrendering his hands to Jamie's face. His nails had been removed from his fingers, and his hand resembled a starfish that had had a night with a sadistic child and a razor blade. The confession stabbed Jamie's hatred.

"What do you mean?" He barked. "Who?"

"The guy's broken, Eric," John said. "His mind's all sorts of fucked up. He doesn't know what he's saying."

"Shut it!" Jamie barked. He returned his gaze to Gary. "Who told you? Tell me!"

"He told me to bring you here," Gary croaked, barely holding on. "That if I did, he would let me go." Jamie felt his mind begin to fracture. He released the mess of a man who crumpled like a sack of moaning meat onto the ground. Jamie erected himself, standing firm. In his eye were John and Ryan. Ryan looking away from the scene like a scared child. His father standing in front of him like a bear guarding its cubs.

"What's going on?" Jamie hissed. John looked at Gary, then at the drawing in Ryan's hands. He let out a small laugh.

"I always liked you…" John said.

"The fuck are you talking about?" Jamie croaked. "Where's my son!" He looked out into the street, almost hoping that his son would materialise from somewhere. "Oliver!" He screamed. "Oliver!" His voice cracking and straining. His eyes returned to John who stood motionless. Tears burned in Jamie's eyes. "Where's my son!" People came out of their doors and looked out of their windows. Some with their phones to their ears, yammering away quickly like they were trying to keep a dirty secret.

Times ticking, he thought. *The jaws of the law will be here soon.*

"Blood is thicker than water, my friend." John said, calmly. "I'm sorry." Jamie didn't hear Simon get out the car. Didn't hear the cosh slide from under his jacket sleeve into his hands and didn't feel the crack against the back of his skull, only the feeling of being dragged back to the car, his world spinning while Gary screamed for help.

Oliver cried for help as Jamie raced to him. The world around him a sheet of black. Oliver's face a twisted etch of terror, his mouth hanging in a long scream.

The slap of ice-cold water jolted Jamie awake. The hellish pounding in his head reminded him that he was very much alive, and pain was very much a real thing indeed. He tried to move his hands as his eyes craned open, him spitting and spluttering back to consciousness.

"He's awake." The voice sounded far away. He felt the icy water drip down his bare chest. His neck stiff. He tried to move his hands to wipe the water and dried blood residue away. They wouldn't move. He was tied to the chair, just like Gary had been. The raw burn of the duct tape gnawing into his flesh. His vision was blurred, looking around the dark room. "Jesus, Simon," the voice said. "How hard did you hit him?" A laugh followed. "Poor Eric looks like he's been through the mill and back." A fierce sting of a slap rung out across his face, the rip saw in his mind gnawing fiercer, like someone had supercharged the power and forgotten how to turn the thing off again. "Oh, we're losing him again. Wake up!" The voice snapped. Jamie's eyes cracked open. The world around him was blurry and moving, like looking through frosted glass into murky water.

"Where am I?" Jamie croaked, his throat painfully dry.

"Welcome to hell," John said, coming into focus.

"What's going on?" He whispered, confusion filling his brain. "Where's Gary?" John shrugged.

"Gary won't be an issue anymore." Jamie flexed his fingers. He felt numb, like his body wasn't his own.

"Why am I on the chair?" He knew exactly why he was on the chair, the pain in his mind not catching up to the flesh yet. "Where is my son..." John pursed his lips. He stood up and sparked up a cigarette from the pack in his pocket before pacing around the room.

"How far would you go to save one of your own, Eric?"

"I kept you out of prison," Jamie whispered. "For loyalty." John laughed.

"Loyalty," he pursed his lips. "You left me out to rot, Eric. By not turning me in, you made our associates ask questions so I couldn't work. We were on the verge of starving. You kept me out of any deal. Kept me out of any bargain. You knew that with you getting locked up and thrown in the big house, you would have a new life when you got out of there. You saved your own skin."

"You have it wrong," Jamie urged. "I have known you for a long time, John. My family, our families, have known each other for a long time. I did it out of loyalty, not spite."

"Bullshit!" John erupted, closing the gap between the two men, his face inches from Jamie's. "You know nothing about loyalty! You destroyed my living. My empire. All I had worked for just to save your own skin. And then when my fucking grandson died," his voice was raw. "My little Daniel, Simon's little Daniel, I couldn't even bury him properly. The cops froze everything I had. I had to borrow money, Jamie. Me! Borrowing fucking money to bury my own flesh and blood. Do you know what that does to a man? Makes him feel less than human. Makes him feel weak. The fact that I couldn't even put him in a decent hole in the ground. Not to mention the destruction of everything else I had worked my entire life to create. And that's all because of you."

The pieces began to fall into place. *Gary.*

"Why Gary?" Jamie whispered.

"What?"

"Why Gary? You were so adamant about him. *He's responsible.* That's what you said. Gary said he killed that boy. He wasn't talking about Oliver, was he?" John laughed.

"Still got something ticking in that head of yours, haven't you?" He prodded Jamie's bleeding cranium. "Gary was unfortunate collateral damage." He pulled up a chair and parked himself on it. "Simon loved taking Daniel fishing. Something they both loved. Every Sunday, he would take him to the pier, and they would hire a boat. Spend hours catching fish and talking until the sun went down. Never seen a man so devoted to his boy. Gary was in charge that day." His voice turned grave. "The boat sprung a leak. Daniel's life jacket was punctured. The boat went down, and Simon nearly drowned trying to rescue that boy. He screamed and screamed for help, but Gary had drank himself silly. My grandson died under that man's watch. The police did their thing, but couldn't prove Gary was responsible. Then he vanished. Never to be seen again. And then you brought him to our attention and told us where to find him. It was like fate." Jamie felt tears burning his eyes.

"But," he croaked. "Oliver?"

"He had nothing to do with it."

"Where is my son, John!" Jamie screamed, a bolt of anger rattling him. Everything they had done. It had been for nothing but for John to get his own revenge. "Cut me loose! Cut me fucking loose! I swear I will gut you and feed you your heart." John cracked a sinister smile.

"There we go," he said. "That's the Eric I knew. Ruthless. Heartless. A force of nature. Not this weak, puny, emasculated suburban happy family father that *Jamie Green* has become." He took a long drag of his smoke and blew a large plume of blue into Jamie's face, the smoke stinging his eyes and making him cough, his chest rattling like someone had filled it with marbles and burning like they were doused in acid. "Now, about your son," he said. "Well, that really was a tragedy. He was a sweet boy. Such a kind, sweet boy. Just like my grandson. Just like my own boys. Tell me Eric, how far would you go to save the ones you love? You would kill anyone who tried to harm them, wouldn't you?"

"Ryan loved spending time with Daniel," John continued. "Every day he would spend time with him. He took his death terribly. He always was a strange boy. I would come here and find him playing with rats trapped under the machinery that had slipped. Did you know a rat will chew through its own tail if it's trapped? Chew through its own tail, Eric. Think about that! Would you chew through your own arm to get out of that chair? Are we much better than rats? Are rats, in fact, the dominant species in this world? The lengths they are willing to go to in the name of self-preservation truly boggles the mind. First, it started with trying to free the rats. But then I would find him torturing them. Sticking pins into their eyes. Cutting off their feet and trying to make them eat them. I told him he shouldn't be doing that, but I wasn't firm enough. It got worse. I found him once in his room playing with a dead dog that he had dragged home from the road, cutting it open, and looking at the slippery parts inside. I made him get rid of it immediately, but his thirst for blood was suppressed too much."

"He would play with our grandson. Nothing sinister. I had told him never to hurt the children, and that seemed to placate him for a while. He didn't have any friends. Only his dead animals. But the boy made him feel normal. Kids don't judge, Eric. They just love." His voice began to break. Jamie listened in silent agony. A morbid curiosity came over him. He *had* to know the rest of the story.

Somethings you can't ever un-hear, as they gouge themselves into your psyche never to be forgotten, to manifest and bring you from the brink of sleep and leave you screaming through the night for the rest of your life.

"When the boy died, Simon stopped talking. Just stopped. Not a peep out of him. He came to work here, and he began to rebuild the legacy that you destroyed. And the hatred inside him. The hatred for Gary Murphy."

"What did you do to my son?" Jamie seethed, pulling at the binds, barely holding it together. "Tell me what you did!"

"It wasn't me," John said. "It was an accident. It wasn't supposed to be this way. But as these things are – God, Karma, nature, or the random acts of the universe, there is something to be said about the beauty, poetry and chaos of it all." Jamie went to speak, to scream and call him a liar, that he hopes he burns in hell with the cruellest of Satan's demons and devils with the utmost depravity and malice making him pay for what he had done after Jamie had finished feeding him his own stomach. And then Ryan walked through the door, his face etched with both wonder and horror holding the picture of Thanos that his son had drawn, and in that moment, Jamie knew everything.

Oliver

They pulled up to the scrap yard and Ryan jumped out of the driver's seat, moved to the back and unclipped Oliver. He took his small hand as he helped him out of the car and led him through the front entrance.

"Be careful of your step," he said to Oliver giddily, as he half walked/half carried him through the mess of the reception. The sound of drilling and sawing blasted through the back of the warehouse. Simon had been working nonstop the last few days to get some scrap ready to be sold overseas. Ryan liked to watch him work. The way the metal could bend when it was glowing the colour of tomato soup. Simon wasn't the same since the accident. The only time he heard him make a sound was in the night when he would scream himself awake. But since the vodka and sleeping pills, Ryan didn't hear him at all.

"Where are we?" Oliver said, mesmerised by the amount of broken metal and dirt lying around. It was like a young boys' playhouse. "It's so cool!"

"This is where I live!" Ryan said with childish wonder. "Let me show you my room. I have lots of cool things up there!" He peered his eye past the door frame and saw Simon working. Sparks flew in a showering arc onto the floor as he welded, cut and soldered.

Oliver reached the top of the dusty staircase a few steps behind Ryan. There were old coke bottles and cans of pop on the floor. There was no carpet, which reminded him of his mum's house. But he got to have a carpet in his room, which he was happy about. He wore his spiderman slippers when walking around the rest of the house because the gaps in the floorboards pinched and hurt his toes if he stepped onto them. He didn't have any brothers or sisters and he didn't like that very much. His mum and her boyfriend never wanted to play, and he wasn't allowed to play with anyone from school. His dad played with him a lot, but he didn't see him very often. So, the thought of playing with another kid in somewhere so cool with comics and video games and sweets was so exciting for him! He walked through the door followed by Ryan who closed it after him. He was going to draw a new picture for his dad.

A picture that he would never see.

The room was empty, other than a small stack of comics on the floor next to a small bed that had avengers bedding on. A few crudely drawn posters were stuck onto the walls, and a lamp was on that elicited a dull gloom around the room. In the corner of the room was a small television set with an old Xbox and a stack of games that still had the price tags on.

"Where's Daniel?" Oliver asked, perplexed.

"He'll be here soon buddy," Ryan said. "Just take a seat and relax and we can play some games. What do you like to play? I have Rayman, Spider Man, Sonic…"

"I like Sonic," Oliver croaked. Ryan smiled, his teeth showing behind his thin lips. His mouth curled at the corners like a crumpled piece of paper.

"Sonic it is." He fired up the machine which buzzed and hummed to life. Ryan began selecting through the options of the menu as the cheery computer game music came to life. Sonic the Hedgehog burst onto the screen, surrounded with bright shapes and dazzling lines and pixels. He handed Oliver the controller. They played a game and Oliver laughed as he beat Ryan. Ryan laughed sourly as the digital hedgehog pounced on Ryan's character with the words LOSER lit up in great red writing.

"I like that game!" Oliver laughed hysterically. "Let's play again!" Ryan turned the game off.

"I don't want to play that game anymore," he said, getting up from the bed and looking through the other games. "You're better than Daniel," he said bitterly. "I can always beat him."

"When is Daniel coming?"

"Soon," Ryan bit, pulling out a game of Crash Team Racing. "Have you played this one?" He showed Oliver the cover. He shook his head. Ryan placed the game into the console and put them on multiplayer. Oliver beat him again. Ryan could feel the rage building up inside his chest. "This game is stupid," he said. "You cheated."

"I didn't." Ryan's temper flared like throwing petrol on an open furnace.

"Don't fucking lie!" He snapped, his face red, his breaths deep. Oliver recoiled back, eyeing him with terror, the glistening of tears on his eyelids. Ryan receded in his rage. "I'm sorry," he said quickly, trying to soothe his new friend.

"I want to go home," Oliver croaked. Ryan shook his head quickly.

"No," he said. "Not yet! We have some more games to play. If you leave now, we can't have popcorn and watch movies when Daniel comes back. I can get some sweets and we can read some comics." Ryan dove off the bed and looked through some more games, furiously trying to find one he was good at and could beat Oliver. "What about this one?" It was a game of Call of Duty. Oliver swallowed dryly.

"I'm not allowed to play that one. My dad said it's too old for me."

"Well," Ryan said, seeing his opportunity to beat Oliver at a new game. "He isn't here, and I want to play it. If you don't, I'll tell your dad that you cheated at the other game."

"But I didn't."

"Just play."

"Where's Daniel? You told me he would be here, and I would be playing games with *him* not *you*." Ryan didn't answer. He was already putting the game in. The game loaded up and Ryan thrust the controller into Oliver's hands. "I don't want to play."

"Do it!" He screamed. Oliver's tears trickled down his cheeks, but he kept the cries tucked away behind his lips. They played the game. Oliver pretended to engage, and Ryan mowed him down repeatedly, screaming gleefully like a hyena with every kill. The game finished and Ryan turned to Oliver. "Wasn't that amazing!" He screamed. "I had so much fun!" Oliver nodded shallowly. "Let's play again!"

"I want to go home now, please. I want to see my dad. I don't want to play anymore." Ryan felt an uncontrollable rage build up inside him. He couldn't leave. Daniel never wanted to leave. Why wasn't Oliver having as much fun as he was?

"You won't get to see Daniel if you go," he said mockingly. "Just upset because you lost?" Oliver shook his head. "Good," Ryan said quickly. Oliver put the controller on the bed.

"I don't want to see Daniel anymore." Oliver's lip was trembling. "I want my dad."

"No! Stay and play!" Ryan screamed into Oliver's face. Oliver began to cry. Something inside Ryan snapped. He snatched Oliver's controller and slammed it against the screen of the television. Oliver bolted for the door screaming. His fingertips graced the handle. So close. An eyelash away from freedom before Ryan grabbed his foot. Oliver slipped. Ryan tried to grab him but missed. Oliver's skull cracked off the side of the wall. He crumpled onto the floor, deathly still. Ryan froze, staring at the little body in his room. Fear encased him. The room went bitterly cold. Eyes wide, he moved his trembling hands over him, terrified to touch him. "Oliver?" Ryan quivered. "Hey…" Ryan grabbed Oliver's coat and shook him. "Wake up. Wake up! I was only kidding. I'll take you home." He pinched his face and said his name again. Before Ryan knew it, he was screaming.

Ryan jumped to his feet, running his hands through his hair, pacing around the room. The weight of the world crashing down on him. "Oh no… oh no… no no no NO NO!" He threw the television onto the floor and drove his foot through the games console. He screamed bloody murder and fell onto his bed, hammer fisting the mattress. His eyes on the unmoving boy who lay on the ground, a swelling of red and black pooling into the carpet. He curled his arms around his feet and nestled onto the bed against the wall, taking out a cigarette from the side of the bed and lighting it up.

He wouldn't last in prison. He would be made fun of for being different, which is why his dad didn't let him go to school or meet with other guys his own age.

"You're just a little slow, Ryan," his dad would say to him. *"The other kids won't understand it. You won't fit in. They're too grown up for you. Too smart."* He could hear his dad's voice now in his mind's ear. Then another voice, much more menacing.

"Life imprisonment. The freak. Get him out of here!"

He stayed static in that silent room until the daylight died away. The sound of heavy footsteps coming up the stairs and leading into his room. The darkness broken by the spilling of the landing light as his father came through the door. Ryan doesn't remember how it happened. Who said what, what happened first, or anything else about the events of those few minutes, only that he knew his life would never be the same again.

Chapter Twenty – Seven

Jamie

His entire world crashed to the ground before him, like a mountain collapsing and falling into the deepest ocean, sending a terrible tsunami across the globe which rocked and fissured under the gigantic wave. As if the sky had been carved open, severed by the fiercest lightning man had ever witnessed, and devils and serpents were crawling out from the cracks in the earth to feast on the souls of men. His revelation. His rapture. His very own *End of Days* coming to life around him. Monsters were real. They didn't hide under your bed or lurk in the sewers at night to snatch wandering souls. No. They lived amongst men. Shopped at the same supermarkets. Held the same smiles. Prayed at the same churches. Monsters who breathed the same air and held the same warmth of flesh and blood as men. And as Jamie eyed Ryan, who did not return his gaze, he knew that he had been played like a fool's fiddle. This whole ordeal was a charade. A sordid pantomime of twists and turns. The execution of an innocent to hide the real predator that was under his nose this whole time in a malevolent, convoluted sense of revenge and righteousness.

Simon moved to Jamie with a knife in his hand, ready to carve him open and let his insides spill out onto the ground. Jamie eyed the blade. The light glinting off the serrated steel.

This was it, he thought. *This is where it all ends.* He thought of his life. Of Oliver. How he had failed him. How he hadn't protected him.

"Sorry it has to be this way," John said from the dark corners of the room. "But you know how it goes."

"Fuck you," Jamie bit. He stared Simon dead in the eye. "And you. Go fuck your mother." Simon cracked a small smile. He grabbed Jamie's shoulder. His eyes pits of emptiness. Jamie held his gaze. He wouldn't look away. Not for one second. Even as he began to pull out his insides and let them slop onto the floor like the off cuts from a butcher's meat slab. He would not look away until the life left him. He would be dismembered and buried. His destiny was fulfilled, and those responsible would scatter in the wind to the four corners of the earth, as he was laid to rot next to the carcass of his son whose eyes had been eaten away by maggots and rats who have made their home in his belly. Something caught Jamie's ear. John turned his head to the door, hearing the noise too.

"What's that sound?" John said, rising to his feet. Simon's hand relaxed, and that break in pressure is all Jamie needed. Jamie pulled his arm free of the duct tape in one swift movement, grabbing hold of Simon's collar and brought his face to his, sinking his teeth into his cheek until he felt his incisors meet. Simon shrieked and screamed, the mute awakened. Simon tore himself away and Jamie felt the flesh of his face dangle loose like tough taffy. The fat and muscle lingered on Jamie's mouth as he heaved himself away, waving the knife around and holding a hand to his bloodied face.

Jamie ripped his other hand free and spat the remnants of the fleshy morsel onto the ground, his mouth dripping with crimson. He raced towards Ryan who was cowering by the wall. The sound of Simon's screams booming around the room as he heaved himself onto his feet with one hand on the shelving which rattled the racks of torture toys.

John burst into action and met Jamie with a fist to the jaw. The blow rattled Jamie but didn't put him down, like a hunter firing at a stampeding elephant. Another fist slammed into his temple. Jamie wobbled and nearly lost his balance, catching himself on a chair which skidded under his momentum. Jamie picked up the chair and wrapped it around the front of John's torso, it exploding in a flurry of splinters and jagged edges.

"Murderer!" He screamed in hellish anguish. Jamie pulled a fragment of the destroyed chair away. A large pointed wooden stake in his hand. Jamie went at John again, aiming the tip of the spike at his jugular. John slipped backwards, batting him away in fluid movements. Jamie went in for another strike, the weapon veering for the Butcher's head. Again, John parried it away, the weapon splintering against this forearm, breaking off into smaller, sharper shards. John reeled his fist back and pounded Jamie to the jaw, chest and temple. The rage was knocked out of him as his vision splattered with white, like lightning flashes across a black night sky.

He fumbled, stumbling. John rushed him, going for the knockout shot. Four pounds of pressure to the jaw. That's all he needed, and it was lights out for Mr. Green. Jamie rallied, adrenalin in overdrive. He slipped out of the way just as John's arm buried into the concrete wall, a sickening array of pops and clicks which was followed by a loud and agonising scream.

Jamie took the opportunity. He stepped back, turning on his foot and brought his shin up hard into John's chest, bending him in two as he pulverised what little air he had in his aged, tar-filled lungs. John doubled over, clutching his stomach as bile and blood exploded from his mouth. Jamie went in for another blow when an explosion of brick and dust pelted his head. His ears ringing out. He turned and saw Simon holding the pistol. A Glock 9mm.

Jamie ducked out of the way as another flash erupted from the barrel and the snatch of the bullet rang in his ear. The warehouse lit up quickly in flashes of detonating lead as Simon pressed the trigger repeatedly. The ground and walls popped and exploded as Jamie ran for his life up the set of steel stairs, before diving for cover behind an overturned crate filled with engine parts and old tyres. The crate blasted and the tyres popped and hissed as bullets slammed into them in quick-fire succession. The gun clicked empty as Simon screamed into the air.

"Give me that!" John screamed. "Have you lost your fucking mind!?" He screamed. "The ballistics! The fucking ballistics Simon!" John snatched the gun from Simon's hands. Jamie got up and moved, racing deeper into the warehouse after Ryan.

"Fuck!" John screamed, racing to the metal railings and pulling out the box of ammunition.

The door of the warehouse burst open.

"Police! Stay where you are!"

John trained the gun onto her, and all hell broke loose.

Chapter Twenty – Eight

Laura

Laura and Jeremy pulled into the compound. They eyed the graveyard of scrap metal around them. A bathtub that was coated with grime and stagnant water was placed out in the open next to a large grid. She looked at the warehouse in front of them, and the stench of burning permeated the still air. The windows were black and coated in thick dust and grime. Memories of the warehouse. Of Craig. Of his house of horrors. She pushed them away. She could think about demons later. Right now, she had a set of handcuffs that were longing for a wrist to cuddle.

"We should wait for backup," Jeremy said. "We have ARV en route and a helicopter on its way. They should be here soon." Laura eyed the unmoving monolith. Its walls told a story of distress. Its insides that of secrecy and pain.

"Fuck that," she said, stepping out onto the gravel. Jeremy rushed out of the car to join her.

"Ma'am," he said hurriedly. "We should wait. We don't know what we'll be faced with." She turned and faced him fiercely.

"We know exactly what we're going to be faced with, Sergeant. Bad guys who don't want to get locked up.

Dangerous people that have a shopping list of debauchery and criminality. Like we always deal with." He went to respond, but she had already begun walking to the front door. She stopped, placing her ear to the wooden door. Jeremy moved to her, the gravel crunching under his feet.

"Laura," he said breathlessly. "We need to wait for backup!" She raised a hand, brushing his concern away. "This is dangerous," he said. "What's gotten into you? I want to catch these guys as much as you do, but we need to —"

"Will you shut the fuck up?" She hushed. Jeremy fell mute. Laura placed her ear to the door of the warehouse. Voices. Only two. Both male. Adults. The sound of gravel behind her. She turned and saw Francis and Catherine drive into the compound. They got out, both kitted up. Francis' stab vest chewed and bitten. Catherine's almost fresh out of the box.

"Where's the rest of us?" Francis said, touching his cuffs. Jeremy shook his head. Laura pulled her ear away.

"Okay," she said in a whisper. "I can hear two voices inside but there may be more of them. "Francis and Catherine, you go around the back and secure any back exits. Try not to be seen. Me and Jeremy will hold on here."

"Yes ma'am," Francis said. He and Catherine moved through the graveyard of forgotten metal, old washing machines and rusted car parts. Laura put her ear back to the door. She could hear the voices rising. Her heart rate began to pick up. She swallowed dryly. Was she going to do this? Was this going to be the end? You never know what you're walking into. This was her last rodeo anyway. Alice had her future in her hands. If she was going down, then she was going down swinging.

A loud crack erupted from inside, followed by a series of explosions and pops. Laura and Jeremy dove to the ground, bringing their hands to their heads. They heard bodies slamming against walls. Something fell over. Someone screamed loudly. Laura clambered to her feet, her hand wrapped around the door handle, her nerves holding steadily. Jeremy rushed to her and grabbed her shoulder.

"Don't you dare," he hissed. "Move away now. You're putting everyone at risk!" She scoffed.

"Sitting by and waiting is what caused all this," she bit. She eyed Jeremy's hand moving towards his handcuffs. "Touch me with those, and I'll break your damn fingers."

"You're out of line! I'll report you! You'll be finished after this!" She released the handle and grabbed Jeremy by the shirt, her teeth an inch from his.

"Do it," she hissed. "Join the queue. Join Alice. Join the rest of the world that wants to bring me down." Jeremy's eyes went wide, both flaring anger and total confusion.

"What're you talking about?" Another loud crack split the tension. The gunshot erupted through the compound.

Jeremy went to talk, to protest, to reach out and grab Laura, but she was already through the door, rushing head-first into anarchy.

Chapter Twenty - Nine

Jeremy

Jeremy rushed in after Laura. He pressed the emergency button on his radio, screaming for all units to attend the address immediately. The crack of a bullet snapped past his head and dislodged brick from the wall in an explosion of dust and shards. He fell to the ground, looking around him. Laura was locked in a battle with another. Simon. The one from the body camera. The one who killed his colleagues. Another man standing there. John, pointing the barrel of a Glock at Laura and the tussling bearded man.

Something awakened in Jeremy. A deep rage that bubbled and spilled over. He was back on his feet before realising, racing to John. He charged into him as another shot went off, it blasting the racking next to a chair that had torn duct tape on the arms and more blood stains than he knew possible. It brought it back to him. The room. Craig. Strapped to the chair. The sticky red pool of blood he had been laid in. Jeremy frenzied, wrestling with the John, forcing Jeremy onto his back where John straddled him. Laura screamed as Simon grabbed a fistful of her hair and dragged her head back, before throwing her onto the hard ground.

A hand wrapped around Jeremy's throat and began to squeeze. He scrambled for his throat, unable to break free. Life leaving him, his throat being forced shut by murderous fingers. Jeremy's panicked eyes found Laura's. The Simon drove a boot into Laura's stomach and her lungs and ribs were shattered in a burst of expelled air.

Jeremy remembered his training. Like instinct, he reared up and grabbed the back of this assailant's head, bringing it into his chest. Then, he swung his leg out and placed it onto the ground, and bridged his back in a high ark, using the momentum to throw his attacker off him. The death grip around his windpipe unlatched, and Jeremy gasped air. He got to his feet. Simon lining up for another destructive kick. Jeremy dove to him, slamming into the racking of utensils. Hooks and tools and blades fell from the racking and rattled onto the ground like metallic rain. Jeremy saw Laura getting to her feet, with John racing up the stairwell into the depths of the building. He could see it in her eyes. Determination. Desperation. Self-annihilation.

"Do no pursue!" Jeremy screamed, but Laura was already going after him, face bloodied and clambering up the stairs. Jeremy went to stop her, but felt a rough hand grab his shoulder. He span to Simon, his face a myriad of gore with soulless eyes.

"You can come quietly," Jeremy said, moving for his cuffs. He felt like he was trapped in a room with a starving dog. This man only knew pain, and pain is what he wanted. Jeremy unracked his baton, eight ounces of bone breaking steel. Simon gave a crooked sneer. He stepped back to the racking and Jeremy watched as he pulled the instrument off. There, nestled in his hand was a blood-stained hatchet. Jeremy swallowed dryly. Simon's lips moved, and a growl escaped his throat.

"Worm."

Simon drove forward in an overhead swoop, the head of the axe inches from Jeremy's head. He slipped out of the way just as Simon brought the weapon back around to carve his stomach open. Simon brought the hatchet down to Jeremy's face. Jeremy raised his baton, the hatchet carving and sliding off the instrument in a blaze of sparks. Simon raised his leg and slammed his boot into Jeremy's chest. He stumbled backward, his back meeting the wall. Simon moved again, the hatchet down by his side, his knuckles wrapped tightly around the handle. Jeremy unclipped his gas and doused Simon to the face. Simon recoiled, grabbing his eyes and screamed into the air. He swung the hatchet widely, blinded and face on fire. He screamed incoherent syllables. Jeremy drove the steel tip of his baton across Simon's thigh. Simon dropped to one knee. Jeremy went for another hit, but Simon rushed him, the baton burying into his muscular frame. His hand propelled outwards, grabbing the baton and snatching it from Jeremy's hand before throwing it across the room where it rattled onto the ground.

Fear flooded Jeremy's bloodstream. Simon peeled his eyes open, flared and red. He shoved Jeremy against the wall, the back of his head bouncing off the brickwork. Simon grabbed his shirt and buried his forehead into Jeremy's nose. A blinding pain rattled through his bones. Simon snaked his leg around Jeremy's and his body met the floor. Through the blurring of pain, Jeremy saw Simon standing over him, the head of the hatchet ready to drop like a guillotine blade.

Chapter Thirty

Jamie

Jamie raced through the warehouse after Ryan, feet slamming against the decrepit floor filled with rat traps and old food boxes. Ryan vanished through a small door which swung back at Jamie. He burst through like a cannonball fired at a wall of glass, hot on Ryan's tail. Ryan moved for a window that was half open. He dove for it like trying to escape a burning building. Jamie dug down further, driving deep from the balls of his feet. His rage propelled him faster, his arms outstretched, fingers like the talons of a hawk ready to ensnare a fleeing rodent.

Jamie wrapped his hands around Ryan's collar as he clung to the window frame, trying to quickly haul himself out. Jamie grabbed him and pulled him backwards. Ryan screamed, like the devil himself was trying to drag him into the pits of hell. His fingers turned white as they clung to the dirtied window frame before slowly peeling away, and Jamie threw him back onto the ground where he landed with a hard thud, the wind knocking out of his stomach like it had been kissed by a speeding baseball bat.

"Where is my boy!" Jamie screamed with murderous vitriol. A hatred most men will never know. A hatred that only those in the deepest of contempt for their fellow man, who are lost in the deepest and darkest abyss of depravity. Only those knew this rage. It was beyond words. It was a black void that hungered for vengeance, flesh, and bone. Jamie sank his knuckles into Ryan's jaw so hard his eyes seemed to bounce around his head like a pinball machine played by a child with a mouth filled with a hundred gummy worms. "Where is he?!" Jamie wrapped Ryan's top inside his knuckles and slammed the back of his head against the hard ground.

"I didn't mean to hurt him," Ryan coughed, blood running from his trembling lips. His words fell on deaf ears. Jamie pounded him again to the nose which popped in a visceral ooze of thick blood and gristle.

Jamie felt the bullet hit him before he heard it. The wind blown out of him and the force of the shot thrusting him to the ground. No pain, only heat. Just heat and a feeling of dread wrapping his body. The stench of gunpowder emanated from his shoulder. The ringing of the shot in his ears. He touched the side of his head and found a river of crimson pouring onto his fingers, the ringing in his bloodied ear deafening. At the foot of the room, John stood with the smoking gun in his hand. He rushed over to Ryan and pulled him to his feet, training the gun on Jamie.

"Sorry it had to be like this Eric," John shouted, hauling Ryan to his feet who wobbled like he was trying to ice skate for the first time. "But I won't let my boy go down for this. He's just a kid. I'll set the world on fire before he goes to prison, and I don't care who gets burned in the process." Jamie writhed on the ground and began to crawl to his feet. John pushed him back to the ground with his foot. "Stay down!" John screamed. Jamie turned onto his back and saw the barrel of annihilation pointing to his head. He raised a bloodied hand.

"Why?" He croaked. "I trusted you."

"You fucked me, Eric," John said. "You ratted on the crew. You put me out of business. Our employers thought I had something to do with it. If it didn't end like this, I would have killed you myself eventually. My boy. Your boy. The opportunity presented itself to get even. Ryan is special!" He screamed. "He's just a kid himself, in his head. Jesus. When Daniel died, our family was broken. Ryan saw your boy as a reminder. It was an accident. When I found your boy lying on the floor. My son facing life in prison, I did what any father would do. I protected my child. You needed someone to blame. Gary Murphy was the perfect scapegoat. You think it's him, you don't suspect my boy. It all goes away."

"I'm going to kill the both of you," Jamie hissed.

"You figure?" John mocked. "Because where I'm standing, looks like I hold the aces." The door opened behind the three men. Laura eyed John standing over Jamie, the gun in his hand.

"Drop it," Laura said. John let out a long breath. He began to turn slowly.

"Stop moving," Laura barked. She licked her dry lips. "I have a gun." John laughed, eyeing her like a puppy baring its teeth.

"Oh, I have been desperate to meet you." He turned to face her. His eyes were grey. Two spheres of cold. What she saw was a man. Flesh, blood and bone. But behind those eyes, she saw nothing. She had seen the look before in the face of Ron. Nothing behind the eyes. A façade. Fake. Hollow and soulless. He wasn't a human. He was a monster. Laura stepped back, giving some distance between him. Ryan was clinging to his father. John smiled at the sight of her. "Where's your gun?" He laughed. Laura felt the world fall from beneath her. "You think you're going to bring me down?" He spoke calmly, like he was talking to a taxi driver about the weather. Not a bead of sweat graced his brow. Laura felt like the room was filling with water and sharks were going to be thrown into the party. He could *smell* her fear, and he loved it.

"We have armed response making this location," she said. "In a couple of minutes this building will be surrounded with blue lights. There's nowhere to run. The game is up." She reached her hand out. "Now put the gun down. Let's not make this any worse." John eyed her with venom.

"How long have you been a police officer for?" He smiled.

"Twelve years," she said. "I'm detective inspector Laura Warburton of the Major Investigation Unit." He searched his mind, his tongue thumbing the inside of his mouth.

"Spare the introductions, sweetheart. I've heard of you. Those murders you solved? Grisly stuff." He snorted like a pig. "Well done for finding me. Shame you won't be able to tell anyone about it."

"Look," Laura said, trying to stop her voice from trembling, eyes flitting to Jamie lying on the ground, the floor beneath him filling with blood. "This has gone on long enough. I want you to listen to me. You're going to put the gun down, and we're going to talk."

"We're talking now, and I'm not doing anything you tell me."

"Put the gun down."

"Make me." Laura pointed to Ryan that was dithering and crying into his father's chest.

"That your son?" She said. John's smile fell into scorn.

"What of it?"

"Think about him. If you do this, then he will go down too. This whole thing, it's gone on too long now. Please," she took a step forward. "Let's put the gun down, and we can work through all of this. Maybe we can come to an agreement." John looked like he was toying with the idea.

Something moving behind those hateful eyes. They fell onto Laura, and her blood ran cold.

"I know what kind of *agreement* you pigs come up with. Let me guess – ten years in a cat B prison with the chance of getting out on license after five?" He spat onto the ground. "Fuck you. Whore. Do you think you will get out of here alive young lady? I've eaten cops three times the size of you." He smiled. "Watch this." In a flash, John thrust Ryan into her. Both of them falling to the ground. Ryan screamed and wailed as she fought him off her, getting to her feet. Heart hammering. Breath ragged in her chest. Her breath stopped as she saw John above her, the gun inches from her face. "It's been a pleasure meeting you, Miss Warburton," he said, and pulled the trigger.

Chapter Thirty - One

Laura

They say your whole life flashes before your eyes the moment before you die. Laura saw her childhood. Her parents. Their car crash. The rain that pelted the window as the police car pulled up to take her to her grandmothers. The cries and wails through the night from the house. Her old lovers. Her first gay experience with Sophie Ashton in the music room of sixth form in detention for calling her teacher Mr Daniels fat. She saw the cheers of onlookers as she and her intake graduated from initial training. Turning up to her first violent domestic where she was punched in the face as she wrestled a six foot four boxer to the ground and slapped him in cuffs while his beaten girlfriend tried to stop her. She saw Ron walk into the police station for the first time, and sit next to her at the office. She saw the black sea that consumed him. She saw the curve of Celine's breasts as she removed her shirt for the first time. She saw herself holding the wine bottle in the middle of the night, trying to get a few more drops out before Celine got home. She saw the faces of dead women as Craig stood over her with the knife in his hand. She saw Alice smile as she promised to ruin her life.

She saw it all in the barrel of John's weapon. She saw Jamie's fist collide with his jaw, and the blast of gas erupt from the barrel, as the slug tear into her thigh and she crumpled to the ground, a scream blasting from her burning lungs. Ryan cowering in the corner, his hands smothering his ears.

Jamie fell onto him, throwing everything he had. His fists, his pain, his wrath and agony into every shot. Like a flurry of hammers, Jamie drove his knuckles into John's body. John fired the gun. Another explosion of chaos. Jamie didn't let up, giving every last bit of what he had. John let off another round, and then another. A window smashed. Brick removed from walls. John slammed the handle of the pistol into Jamie's frame and brought up his knee and jammed it into Jamie's stomach. The air expelled from Jamie's lungs like stomping on a whoopie cushion, a loud grunt escaping his mouth. He stumbled back, gasping for air. John got to his feet, Jamie ready for round two.

Then he felt the blood. Slowly at first, like touching drywall and finding a spot of damp. But then it came quicker. He looked down at his stomach and saw his clothes sodden with red. The air left him. His skin turned waxy, as he fell backwards onto the ground with a hard slam. John stood over him, training the weapon on his old friend.

"Tell your son I said I'm sorry." For that moment, as brief as the hiss of a candle after being extinguished, Jamie saw a flicker of something in John's eyes. A whisper of emotion. A hush of humanity in his eyes. Jamie coughed up thick clumps of blood, his mouth tasting like he was chewing iron. He closed his eyes and thought of his son. How he had failed him. How he had left him to fend for himself for those crucial few seconds. How he had forsaken him as a child. The voice of Claire in his mind.

Find our son, or die trying.

He had done just that.

The gun went off. The sharp scent of gunpowder filled the air.

But Jamie continued to breathe. He creaked his eyes open. John stood over him. His stomach gushing with blood. His face pasty and pale. Another officer stood in the doorway clad in body armour, a smoking rifle in his hand. John turned slowly, a rasping sound escaping his throat. John went to raise the weapon, but the officer fired another round into him. John snapped back sharply. The officer marched forward, emptying another round into him, and another, until John was blasted through the window and fell out of view in a song of hellfire and sirens.

Chapter Thirty – Two

Gary

Gary awoke to the smell of petrol forcing its way down his throat. The fierce bite of the cold numbed him, but the pain of his broken body threaded through. He tried to move, but he felt the stab of metal shards and piping under his body. The clouded sky could be seen through the gaps between the cars and scrap metal. His eye sticking together from coagulated blood. His other eye was swollen completely shut. He was broken in every way imaginable, and yet death had not claimed him. Fear gripped him. Something innate. Sheer terror. He began to moan at first, and then began to scream. He heard the shuffling of weight somewhere in the shadows.

"Who's there?" He croaked. More shuffling came. Endless moments stretched out into endless time.

Then a small voice filtered through.

"I'm cold."

Chapter Thirty -Three

Laura

Laura watched as the firearms unit marched into the room, scanning the corners with their rifles, throwing open doors and moving through. The sound of the helicopter above, its propellers eliciting a loud rumbling. Jeremy stumbled through the doorway. His shirt bloodied. Face the colour of blended summer fruits.

"Hey boss," he said.

"Thanks for joining us," she said with a weak smile. The ARV officers dragged Ryan to his feet. Francis and Catherine moved into the room. Francis moved to Laura and began working on stopping the bleeding in her leg. She felt the grip of the cold nestle into her bones. Catherine ran to Jamie who was laying silently, his eyes open. His skin was cold, like touching a wax dummy.

"He's breathing!" Catherine cried. The ARV moved to him quickly like an army of beetles. They grabbed hold of Jamie and began working on him, stuffing his wounds with a powder that turned into a foam and stopped the blood loss. Paramedics moved in and dragged Jamie, attaching him to an oxygen mask, tearing open his shirt and fixing the stem of blood that was gushing from his stomach. Their faces were etched with determination to get him out of here alive, but their eyes said otherwise.

Outside, the dog patrols had appeared, and they were snuffing and moving around the mountains of scrap metal. They found the burnt-out van along with scraps of clothing. CSI officers moved to the van and began setting up tents, covering themselves with thin plastic white clothing to preserve the scene and picking up scraps of charred clothing and placing it into evidence bags.

Laura got checked over in the back of an ambulance. The wound in her leg wasn't as bad as it had first seemed. It had more maimed, than wounded her. She would have a nice scar and may need to walk on a crutch for the next month, but she'd live. Laura eyed the CSI officers. She thought of Celine holed up in a hospital bed, pretending to be ill and she felt her stomach churn. She had loved her, but she had also been part of the problem. She wasn't *ready* for love. For intimacy and that is what drove her back to the bottle, causing her to leave a trail of destruction in her wake. She thought of Alice, and the predicament she was in. And just like the heavens had heard her, she felt a buzzing in her pocket. She took out her phone, fingering the screen with bloodied fingers which left swollen imprints of the smooth glass. It was a text from Alice.

'*Times ticking.*'

The thought of what she was being forced to do made her feel sick to her stomach, and she was expecting the rising anxiety to manifest into an expelling of bile onto the ground littered with rusted bolts and screws. But she didn't. She kept it together, and she felt the tide of her life turning. She knew what she had to do.

Gary moved through the darkness and felt the hand of the small boy. He was cold. Shivering. He squinted, making out his shape.

"Come over here, lad," he said, moving him into the light that broke through the metal casing around them. Oliver fumbled forward, his body in pain, him wincing as he moved. He saw the lad's face in the gloom of daylight. His stomach plummeted. "I know you," he said. The wounds on his body burned to life again like tearing the scab free. It was the boy. The boy from the car park. The boy he had been tortured over.

"I'm cold," Oliver said. Oliver stared at Gary, his body a silhouette in the dark. A dark thought entered Gary's mind. This child. He was the catalyst of everything that had happened to him. He was the reason why he was bloodied. He should bloody him too. Right here in the blackness. He should force feed him the discarded drill bits and dead rats that carpeted the mud beneath their feet. He could be cruel. Oh, so cruel to this child as revenge for what had happened. But instead, Gary Murphy wrapped his arm around Oliver and pulled him into him. He nestled his head against his thick blonde hair.

"There, there lad," he whispered. "I'll get you out of here."

Laura sat at the back doors of the ambulance. Catherine appeared with a mug of coffee.

"We need to stop meeting like this," Catherine laughed. Laura took the cup.

"We do." They drank.

"You're a badass, you know that?" Catherine said grinning. "Running in there with no backup. Chasing someone down with a gun? Jeremy said you lied to them and told him you were packing." Laura shrugged.

"Yeah. Don't ever do that. I'm going to get my ass chewed about all this when I get back." She stared into the coffee cup. "But sometimes you just have to bullshit your way through." She reached for her pocket and took out her cigarettes. She offered Catherine one. Catherine eyed the pack.

"I don't smoke." Laura scoffed to the wind.

"Liar," she said. "I've seen you sneaking one around the back of the nick when you think no one is looking." Catherine toyed with the discovery, then took one out of the back and Laura lit it up. They watched the law run in and out of the building, carrying supplies, items and taking photos. Dogs were let loose inside the building, searching for anything that might be amiss.

"You think the boy is in there?" Catherine said vacantly, like speaking to the wind. Laura pondered the thought then shook her head.

"No. Whoever took him, wherever he is. He won't be here. I don't think Gary Murphy was ever involved in the abduction, which leads us back to square one." They sat in silence for a moment. Jamie was carried out on a gurney, paramedics running alongside him with blood packets and saline solution, and was placed in the back of an ambulance. The medic established early on that he had a broken jaw, a couple of broken ribs and horrific blood loss. He should be dead already, yet Jamie still fought on, pulling at the IV drips and tearing the oxygen mask from his face, fighting until his last breath. The paramedics slammed the back doors of the ambulance shut, eclipsing Jamie's screaming. "Come on," she said, looking at the sky. "We're losing daylight. Still need to find this boy. Tell some uniform to ride with Jamie." With that, Laura stood up and walked to the car. Catherine liaised with a group of officers, and they moved to the ambulance where Jamie was, before joining Laura to the squad car.

Gary kicked and pushed at the metal casing around them while Oliver searched for a way out. He saw the cop in the distance through the metal.

"Hey!" He shouted into the air, his fingers wrapping around the pipes and rusted metal. "Hey!" He called as loudly as he could. Oliver moved to him and joined in the screaming. He watched officers move to their cars and fire up the engines.

"What're they doing?" Oliver said, on the verge of tears.

"They can't hear us…" Gary whispered with a lacing of terror. He moved down into the hole. The wall of steel surrounding them blocked by a forklift truck that stood at the entrance. He had to find a way out. He had to get to the police before they left. Gary began throwing himself at the metal, bouncing back into the pile, his arm seething with pain. He watched the cops begin to drive away. He ran at the walls harder and heard something come loose.

Catherine fired up the engine.

"You know," Laura said. "Gary Murphy. Where did he end up?"

"Concrete shoes at the bottom of a river, ma'am?" Catherine said morbidly. They watched the rest of the units packing up for the day and moving back to their vehicles. They had what they needed for now. Laura let the morbid comment linger. She shrugged.

"Suppose we'll find out." She turned on the heating, the painkillers the paramedics gave her numbing the pain in her leg.

"How is the leg?"

"Agony. But they gave me some good pain killers. Take me the hospital please. I suppose I should get a proper examination." She laughed.

"Hey," Catherine said. "You mind if I grab another cigarette? My boyfriend doesn't know I smoke. Don't really want him to find out." Laura searched for the pack.

"Oh, shit," Laura said frustratingly. "Left them on the back of the ambulance." Catherine nodded then stepped outside. Another message vibrated through on her phone. It was Alice again.

'Don't test me.'

Laura put the phone in her pocket. She heard the sound of barking, then voices calling out from the distance. Something was happening. She stepped out of the car and looked where cops were running too. Standing by the side of a large container that was rusted and filled with old car parts, Gary Murphy stood drenched in dried blood and looked like a man who had been through more than any human being should ever need to bear. But that wasn't who she was looking at. In his arms, a small blonde boy.

Chapter Thirty – Four
Jamie

Jamie felt hands pinning him to the gurney, and the fight vanished from him. His body falling limp, he slipped under the sea of unconsciousness. He saw him there. His boy. Calling for him. Standing there with his arms outstretched. His son. His flesh and blood. Calling for his help.

But something was different. Oliver screamed for him, but it was coming from *elsewhere*. Jamie fought the abyss of blackness that consumed him. Fighting, clawing, dragging himself out of the depths. His eyes snapped open, forcing himself back from the precipice of oblivion, something guiding him back from the void. His senses alert. The dampness in the air. The roar of the overhead helicopter. Boots dredging through the filth and murk under their feet. Dogs barking. Sirens in the distance mixing through the wind. And then, like an angel's song breaking through a carrion's cry.

The voice of his boy.

Jamie jostled and fought with the restraints of the gurney. The paramedics moving to him again, grabbing him, forcing him down. Jamie knew no fear then. Nothing on this earth could stop him. He ripped his arm free from the ties that bound him. All his regret. All his rage. Ripping through. He ripped off the second binding and erected like a revenant from the brink of death. The kicked and pulled, throwing officers and medics away with the force of a mighty beast. His son. His son's voice. He could hear him. Hear him calling to him.

"Dad! Dad!"

"I'm coming Oliver!" He screamed. He got loose, his feet shaking under his weight, and forced his way out of the moving ambulance. Jamie stumbled out into the cold, the sharp gravel meeting his face. The impact expunging the dead air in his lungs. With what little strength he had left, he hauled himself up on the bonnet of a rusted car. His legs shaking under him, face the colour of snow, blood pouring out of him, drenching his shaking body.

In the distance, he saw him. Carried in the arms of the man he had tortured. His face awash with terror, screaming for his father, his saviour in a world of monsters. Each small step was agony. Jamie's lips turning a hypothermic blue. The gunshot wound in his stomach had torn back open, and the shrapnel lodged in his hip and thigh were grinding against the bone and dancing on the nerves. Still, he moved with the determination of a father that had come from the precipice of the abyss and was moving towards the morning sunlight.

Officers rushed to him, but he batted their hands off like they were hot coals. His son metres away. The blood pouring from him. The hand of death closing in. Oliver's eyes met him, and the terror in his face evaporated.

"Dad!" Oliver tore himself free, diving to the ground and pumping his legs fiercely, racing with all he had to his father. Jamie drove forward with what little strength he had left, stretching out his arms. Jamie's legs went from underneath him, his knees burying into the ground.

Oliver's arms found him, holding him up from collapsing into the ground. Their eyes meeting, and bright smiles lit up along their faces. They cried, screaming into each other as Jamie wrapped his hands around him, holding his small body in his weak arms. Breathing in him, holding so tight he feared should he let up, the world will snatch him from him. Jamie ran his bloodied hands along Oliver's tear drenched face.

"I'm here, mate," Jamie cried, kissing his cheek. "I'm here."

"I thought I wouldn't see you again," Oliver cried into his ear. "I thought you had left me."

"I'll never leave you, son. I love you. So very much." He held him tightly, kissing his head over and over. The pain mixed with the relief. The joy with the hatred. The guilt with the love. If he had to do it all again, if he had to watch the world burn to save his kin from the fire, then he would. In a second. In a heartbeat. The echo of love. It transcends all pain and all fallibility. He saw officers moving to them slowly. Their voices stretching. The bright sun above him blurring and fading away. He stared into his son's eyes one last time, and reached out his hand to touch Oliver's face.

His hand never made it. The world fell away as he crashed to the ground in a heap. The smile faded from his face.

Laura watched from afar. Paramedics hauled Jamie back to the ambulance and sped away on blues. Oliver was taken to the back of a police car, his face etched in pain.

"How are you doing?" Francis said, approaching her. Laura forced the lump in her throat away.

"Never better," she cracked a tight smile, watching officers move around with their heads in their hands. Some crying. Some pushed their emotions down until later. Gary was taken to the back of another ambulance. Laura watched it all with an absence. Just observing. No thought. No feeling. Just being in the middle of a storm and that's it.

"I have something I need you to do," she said eyeing Francis. His face went like pudding.

"Anything you need ma'am." Laura opened up her phone and saw the text from Alice.

"I'm going to be going away for a little while. Clear my head. I need you to take primacy over this investigation." Francis's eyes lit up.

"You serious?" He said, trying to not sound too excited, but Laura could hear it in his voice. He was thrilled at the chance to prove himself.

"Deadly serious," she said calmly, the wind blowing through her hair. "Go speak to the boy and go and question the suspect in custody. Speak to the witness too. Gary. Everyone. With the look of him, I'm sure he has more than enough information that he wants to share with you about the whole thing." Francis took out his notepad and began writing down some notes, action points. He paused and looked upon the scene. The wind blowing along his face. "It's awful," he said, his voice turning meek.

"It's the job we do," Laura said. "We stand between the public and the monsters Francis. The thin blue line." They stood silent for a moment, before he tapped his pen on his notepad, ready to get to work. He went to move away but he stopped in his step and turned back.

"You going to be okay?" He asked. Laura smiled and nodded shallowly. She didn't say anything else. Just stared at him until he left her alone. The truth was, she didn't know. She didn't know if anything would ever be okay again. But she knew what she needed to do. And for once, she was going to face her problems instead of trying to run from them. Laura called Catherine over who was speaking to officers. Catherine moved to her. "I need you to drive me somewhere," she said. "There's something I have to do."

Chapter Thirty - Five

Alice

Alice sat in her one-bedroom apartment near the centre of Wigtown on her leather sofa that had parts of the fabric missing, resembling a cow with chunks missing from its hide. It was nine in the evening. She had heard about what had happened. About the police raid, and that those responsible for the crimes they had been investigating had been brought into custody. But Alice wasn't excited about that. No. She sat on her own in the dim light of her living room lamp with an untouched pizza for another reason. She looked at her dirty home with stained walls and missing wallpaper. The sound of police car sirens filtered through the air over the local news station that played quietly from her television.

Alice was tense, looking at her phone every thirty seconds. Ready to hit SEND on the email exposing everything that had happened with her soon-to-be ex-detective inspector. She had arranged it carefully in a folder – Times, dates, photos, maps of her movement when she had her GPS tracking on. Even an audio recording that was on in her pocket when Laura took her to bed. She was ready to blow Laura's life apart. Looking around the dishevelled living room she was sat in, she knew she would pay up. She needed the money. She needed the opportunity.

Laura was treacherous. A predator. Someone that should not be put in a position of privilege or rank and respect in the Wigtown Constabulary. She was the real villain in all of this. A face with a fake smile and nothing behind the eyes. How many days had she been drunk on the job? How many investigations had gone to rat shit or nearly fallen through due to her ineptitude and inebriation? Even her own girlfriend Celine was in the hospital as a result of Laura's disregard for anyone other than herself. She was the problem, and Alice was the solution. Hell, she should send the email anyway. She would be hailed as a hero. But that wasn't enough for her. Laura needed to pay for what she had done.

Laura had given in to her feelings and clouded mind, which Alice was counting on. A suggestive comment here, a touch of the hand there, and bingo, she had her right where she wanted. Once Laura arrived at Alice's home and she showed her all the evidence she had against her, then there was nothing stopping her from getting a better life. Laura was just the start. The first domino to fall. Then, she could put her moves on Jeremy. He was married. He wouldn't want anything to be exposed. He would resign at her wishes. Then the MIU would be under her control. Then, she could look higher up the ladder. Who else had dirty secrets they didn't want to be exposed? Who could she smile to at the right times? There was nothing that she couldn't do. People were flawed and will do anything to not let those flaws be laid out for the world to see and mar their white armour of altruism and vigour. Alice's phone buzzed. She checked the text.

LAURA W

Outside.

A smile crept along Alice's lips. The curtains of her face parted ever so slightly to reveal the malevolence of her soul. Alice moved to the intercom and pressed the door release button. She heard the security door open and then slam shut. The sound of footsteps. One set, coming up the stairs. She had come alone. This was really happening, and Alice was already imagining the home she was going to buy with her new sergeant's salary. The footsteps stopped behind the door and Alice waited for the knock. A stretched silence.

"Are you going to open the door?" Laura said nonchalantly. Alice looked through the spy hole. It was only her standing there. Perfect. Alice opened the door and Laura strode in without missing a beat, like she was a Gestapo soldier hunting for enemies of the state. Alice checked the stairway. Just the two of them. She wondered if she should have brushed her teeth before Laura got here, or at least put on some nice underwear.

Alice shut the door and followed Laura into the living room where she was standing and watching the news cycle flicker. A helicopter over the warehouse and police tape stretched around it. The faces of the three men, Simon, John and Ryan, flashing up for the world to see. They had left Jamie and Oliver out of the news. She was thankful for that.

"Can I get you a drink?" Alice said, with the same tone as if she was speaking to a five-year-old that was about to be thrown into a tank filled with sharks. Laura turned on a dime and eyed her like a poisonous snake.

"I'm going to resign." The words knocked Alice off her balance. No warm-up. No foreplay. Just straight in for the climax. She ran her fingers through her hair.

"Do you want to talk about it first?" Alice said. Laura shook her head.

"No. I need to leave this unit in more capable hands. You are right. Despite being a privileged and entitled little cunt, you're right. I'm not in the right frame of mind to lead."

"Well, I'm glad I could help," Alice said with a slight snigger. She moved to the centre of the room and picked up her phone from the counter. "I have the email ready to send to Professional Standards. You know what I want, and if you don't do as I want and exactly how I want it, they will get the full file. Your pension. Your reputation. Your career. It will be all over with the click of a button." Alice leaned forward to Laura. "Do I make myself clear? Ex – DI Warburton?" Laura felt her skin crawl like lice had burrowed under her skin and were digging into her bone marrow.

"We're clear."

"We're clear, 'Detective Sergeant' Alice Hudson," she corrected. Laura shook her head.

"Not quite." Alice's face wrapped with confusion.

"Excuse me?"

"You mind if I sit down?" Laura said, moving to the couch. "My leg hurts like a bitch. Just a flesh wound, they said. But Jesus."

"What do you mean? Not quite? You think I'm bluffing?" Laura shook her head.

"Not at all," Laura said. "Please, send the email. I won't stop you."

"I will!" Alice said, holding her phone. "I'll send it and then your career is over." Laura scoffed.

"I'm afraid you're too late Alice," she said. "Professional Standards know everything." Alice felt a wave of heat flush through her.

"You're lying." Laura blurted a laugh.

"I am many things Alice, but a liar isn't one of them."

"I'll send the email," Alice said.

"I hope you do, and you should. I deserve whatever happens to me. But you won't be getting promoted. You won't get anything for what you have done. Well, maybe one thing." Footsteps began marching up the stairs. Alice turned her head to the sound.

"What's that?" Alice said, feeling the walls close in around her. Her mouth becoming dry. Laura eyed the front door.

"Prison." With the death of the word, Alice raced to the front door which burst open as officers moved in. They took hold of her and dragged her to the ground, forcing her hands behind her back and fixed them in handcuffs. Alice lay on the floor in a state of shock, her breathing rapid. Catherine emerged from the sea of bodies and Alice was hauled to her feet, her hair sticking to her face.

"DC Alice Hudson," Catherine said. "You are under arrest on suspicion of blackmail." Catherine began to caution Alice and read her rights. Alice didn't hear her, her voice sounding miles away like an echo through a distant cannon. Her eyes fixed on Laura who sat motionless with her arms crossed over.

Laura didn't know how Alice would react when she was locked up. She imagined she would protest, scream or fight back. The weight of the law crushing her under its boot. But instead, Alice cried. A low sob that was barely audible. Laura had seen it before with others who abuse their position or get locked up for drunk driving and when stood at the custody desk, the sea of sharks that spiral in their mind begin to snap at the thin chords that hold their careers and life suspended above the great precipice that are about to come crashing down on them.

When the police had left, Catherine moved to Laura on the chewed-up sofa and was staring at the repeat of the news on the television.

"You did the right thing, boss," Catherine said quietly. Laura figured she had, although it didn't feel like it. Self-immolation wasn't always honourable, but it was often needed to get the job done and to right your own wrongs. A self-crucifixion to stop the world from tearing you apart. This way, you controlled the way you went out.

"Thanks," Laura said, watching the TV vacantly. A moment of silence went by.

"Boss?" Catherine said.

"I'm not an inspector anymore, Catherine," Laura said, trying to keep the tears from breaking through the stinging in her eyes. They shared a silence. Catherine trying to find the words.

"Laura," Catherine said softly. Laura turned her eyes to meet hers. Her face was awash with pain. Laura knew she didn't want to do this, but she had asked for her specifically. Catherine both hated and respected her for that. "You need to come with me now," she said. Laura stood and moved with Catherine out of the building, as Laura slipped into her car, and they moved into the night.

Chapter Thirty – Six

Laura

Laura was driven back to the police station and was led upstairs into the office of the superintendent. He was an older man, his face an inch from the computer. Catherine went to knock, but he spotted her and waved them both in. Laura followed like a sad puppy that was going to be scalded by its master.

Bill, Laura thought, his name crashing through the brain fog as she stepped into the office. *His name is Bill Bennet.*

Bill Bennet was firm, yet kind with Laura. They hadn't had many dealings since he took over from Dutton. He was near the end of his career. He was a recluse in his office, but he knew everyone by name. Bill looked up from his computer. They exchanged pleasantries, before addressing the report in his email inbox Laura had sent en route to Alice.

"Alcoholism is not a crime, Miss Warburton," he spoke with such clarity and formality. He commanded respect, like when someone stops talking, you wait for them to continue. "However I cannot condone such things in my police station."

"I understand, sir," she said robotically. She knew that this was just a formality. She would be cleaning out her locker in a few minutes, struck from the police database like she never existed. Her legacy. Her triumphs and her wins all gone and scattered into the wind. But at least she had the bottle. The bottle never judged her and was always there when she needed it to keep the nightmares away.

"You have caused great upset," Bennett continued. "You are highly regarded as being one of the best. I have looked at your stats and this most recent case you have been involved in. You have managed to uncover and disseminate a criminal organised gang as well as protect a vulnerable child."

"Thank you, sir," she said once more robotically. She was waiting for the *but*. But it never came.

"It is with great sadness to see you go. And if this information would have been brought to my attention prior to your resignation for the very same reasons, then our conversation would have gone very differently."

Differently? What is he saying?

"Through your hard work and frankly, awful trauma that you have undergone these past few months, I wish to put you on a period of conditional unpaid leave for the time being."

You have got to be shitting me…

"I beg your pardon?" Laura said aghast. Bill Bennet furrowed his brow. His white eyebrows were bushy like two arctic fox tails curled towards the rims of his glasses.

"Does my statement confuse you?" He asked. "I do not intend to accept the resignation of such a fantastic officer. Nor do I intend to throw you to the kerb side." He stood up and moved to the window and gazed out at the dying sunlight and the lights of Wigtown. "You have been through a hell of an ordeal. That is clear. And your failings incredulous, selfish and harmful to both you and the constabulary you represent, cannot be dismissed. However, I am aware that through your hard work and compassion to victims, you have been able to have funds injected into the poorest parts of this town, and you have been able to help and support those crippled with substance abuse and addiction. As a result, I feel that you should at least be offered the chance to redeem yourself. To get clean, as it were, and to return to work when you have shown that you are in a better and more stable frame of mind." Laura nearly fell from her chair.

"Thank you, sir," she said, with more emotion breaking through the numb that was melting away by the second.

"I bet you're wondering why I am not dismissing you," Bill said, still staring out of the window.

"It did cross my mind, Sir," she said. Bill turned and moved back to his chair. He took off his glasses and cleaned them. Less of an act of repair, but more as a way of articulating his discomfort with what was going to come out of his mouth next. He eyed them both, then put the glasses back on.

"I once had a problem with alcohol myself," Bill said. "My wife passed away and I didn't know how to cope. I lost jobs. Friendships and family relationships that are still not fully mended to this day." He spoke with the tone of a man that has lived his life with deep sorrow. "However. I got help. Pulled my socks up high and got myself better. I've been twenty-two years sober since. Which is why I wish to afford you with the chance of redemption." He leaned forward and took Laura's hand into his. His hands were soft and warm, and she no longer saw him as her superior, but as another human being with love in his heart that wished to help those he came into contact with. The true meaning of a police officer. Not statistics. Arrests. Prosecutions. But helping those that can be helped, if and when they need it. "I have arranged a meeting with a rehabilitation charity, one that was set up by the money you had injected into the town following the demise of Craig Sinick and that awful string of crimes he committed. I wish for you to undertake it, as well as some therapy to let out your darkest demons. When you are feeling better, I want you to come back to us." He smiled a warm grin. "How does that sound?" Laura didn't know what to say. She wanted to scream for joy. Wanted to crawl into a hole at the bareness of her failings. Her trauma wanted to break free from the locked box it was held in and tear the face off of everyone in the room with teeth and claws. But instead, she felt the tears that hadn't been able to come, finally break through. It was like the rain over a desert that was desperately needed, and when that rain came, it didn't know how to stop.

Chapter Thirty - Seven

Laura

Pain is something that all men feel. Trauma too. Be it PTSD, CPTSD, or in other acute forms. Pain and trauma are sides of the same coin. One cuts and scars. The other wounds and maims for the rest of your life. It can manifest in a multitude of ways. Sometimes people try to block out the pain in their heart through sex, drugs, alcohol and even food. Sometimes exercise is the self-harm for the body. Other times, it's fights and dangerous activities. But in every case, the reason is the same: A person's mind and heart have been broken, and the body wishes the sufferer to feel that pain for it to heal. One must feel their pain, no matter how much it hurts. The body finds a way and keeps score of its scars and wounds, be it in the flesh or in the mind. Often, it's both.

In the months that followed, Simon Heywood was to recover from his injuries and was to be imprisoned in a psyche ward for the remainder of his life. Ryan Heywood was interviewed by Francis, and he confessed to everything. Francis will later say that it was like interviewing a child who had had his favourite toy taken from him, and he pled with the CPS to not pass a ruling of diminished responsibility or infantile mindset. After much toing and froing with the courts and an independent psychiatrist, Ryan Heywood was sentenced to life in prison for the abduction and wounding of Oliver, joint enterprise for the murder of the two officers, perverting the cause of justice, torture and his part in the criminal enterprise.

John Heywood was cremated the month following the incident once the autopsy had been completed. Nobody attended his funeral. His death was not mentioned in the news. His toxic flame was snuffed out once and for all.

Jamie Green died on the operating table around midnight. His body was visited in the hospital by a tall man in a suit, who left a copy of War and Peace on his bedside chair, before slipping out of the building before anyone noticed his presence.

As for Oliver. He was returned back to his mother who cried for nearly a full twenty-four hours at his return. Those around her would see them as happy tears. But secretly, in her heart, she cried for the loss of Jamie, and how he had done what she had asked. Find their son, or die trying. He had given his life to correct his wrong doings. She both hated and loved him. Something she will struggle with for the rest of her life.

A knock will come on the door in the next few weeks. Claire would answer and a tall man in a suit would be standing there. He would pass her a brown envelope and leave without saying a word and get into an unmarked black car which had no registration plate, and inside there would be a sizeable cheque and a set of house keys with directions. The keys to a better life, on the condition that she cut off all hangers-on and bloodsuckers from her existence, and by the time the sun rose in the sky, she would never be seen at that loveless home again.

Gary Murphy was released from the hospital and went on to write about his ordeal. He sold a few copies of his book and then vanished into the wind. That's self-publishing for you.

Laura Warburton left the office that day with her heart torn open, and the spilling of all the pain releasing into the cold air like devils made of black smoke that vanished into the ether around her. She took a detour on the way home and stopped at the hospital. Celine was asleep when she visited her by the bed. Laura felt immense remorse for her but knew that they could never be together. She left her a note at her bedside.

I'm going away for a while to clear my head. I'm sorry.
Don't call.
L x

Back at home, Laura set down her things and poured every sniff of alcohol out of her home. She took a shower so hot that she could almost feel her skin peeling away from her bones. Then, she threw out all the junk food in her fridge and cupboards and she cleaned the house from top to bottom. She booked into a rehab clinic for the next morning and packed her belongings and arranged a place for Bagpipe to stay. She went online and signed up for the gym, ordered journals, self-help books and even a meditation guide to be delivered to her new address at the centre.

Laura Warburton was a broken woman, and it took her to face herself in the mirror to realise that in this world, you have only yourself to blame for the good, the bad and the ugly. She wrote down everything that had happened between her and Ron, Craig, Sheree, her childhood and everything in between, scribbling away late into the night. When done, she closed the journal and placed it by her bedside and nestled into the fresh sheets, eager to start a new life upon waking. As she closed her eyes, she felt that the crushing foot of life that had been pressing into her chest for so long was finally being lifted, and Laura Warburton fell into a deep sleep that for the first time in as long as she could remember, wasn't plagued by nightmares.

What is next in store for Laura and the MIU?
Read book three 'Deadly Silence,' now by heading to
Amazon / Jay Darkmoore / Deadly Silence

If you enjoyed this title, please leave a review. Reviews are how indie authors make a name for themselves and are able to keep releasing content for you hungry readers to eat up.

Thank you for taking the time and spending it reading my work. I thoroughly hoped you enjoyed it.

Support me by scanning here for a free eBook bundle, exclusive news and updates and much, much more.

Jay Darkmoore is a UK-based author with a background in crime and investigation. He is a huge fan of all things dark - exploring the macabre, demonic and darker aspects of the human psyche.

Jay likes putting his characters in terrible situations and then turning out all the lights. To date, he has self-published novels of horror, crime and dark fantasy dystopia. His inspirations are Stephen King, Keith C Blackmore and Nick Cutter.

When not at his desk, Jay spends his free time making YouTube videos to help writers in their craft, promoting other books he has enjoyed, as well as hitting the gym and taking wild cold plunges with ducks.

He is a single parent to his son Joe who is his biggest fan.

Printed in Dunstable, United Kingdom